Praise for FO

★ "[A] deeply satisfying tale that will leave readers hungry for the final volume."
—*Publishers Weekly*, starred review

★ "Anderson seamlessly weaves her fictitious characters into history in a cohesive, well-researched narrative about the Revolutionary War that still focuses foremost on developing characters and their interpersonal relationships."
—*The Horn Book*, starred review

"Anderson's detailed story creates a cinematic sense of history while raising crucial questions about racism, the ethics of war, and the hypocrisies that underlie our country's founding definitions of freedom."
—*Booklist*

"It is difficult to imagine there will ever be historical fiction about this time in America that is more nuanced or respectful of time and place. . . . Anderson's *Forge* is a terrific return not only to the colonial era but to historical accuracy."
—*The New York Times Book Review*

Praise for CHAINS

NEW YORK TIMES BESTSELLER
NATIONAL BOOK AWARD FINALIST
WINNER OF THE SCOTT O'DELL AWARD FOR HISTORICAL FICTION

★ "Readers will care deeply about Isabel. . . ."
—*Kirkus Reviews*, starred review

★ "Startlingly provocative . . . nuanced and evenhanded . . . a fast-moving, emotionally involving plot."
—*Publishers Weekly*, starred review

★ "Anderson explores elemental themes of power, freedom, and the sources of human strength in this searing, fascinating story."
—*Booklist*, starred review

"Engrossing . . . a heart-racing story."
—*Bulletin of the Center for Children's Books*

"Knocks on the conscience of a nation."
—*Christian Science Monitor*

FORGE

ALSO BY
Laurie Halse Anderson

Chains

Fever 1793

Independent Dames:
What You Never Knew About the Women and Girls of the American Revolution

Thank You, Sarah:
The Woman Who Saved Thanksgiving

Laurie Halse Anderson

FORGE

SEEDS OF AMERICA

ATHENEUM BOOKS FOR YOUNG READERS
NEW YORK • LONDON • TORONTO • SYDNEY • NEW DELHI

ATHENEUM BOOKS FOR YOUNG READERS
An imprint of Simon & Schuster Children's Publishing Division
1230 Avenue of the Americas, New York, New York 10020

Also available in an Atheneum Books for Young Readers hardcover edition
Book design by Lizzy Bromley
Map copyright © 2010 by Drew Willis
The text for this book is set in Regula.
Manufactured in the United States of America
0421 OFF
First Atheneum Books for Young Readers paperback edition April 2012
12 14 16 18 20 19 17 15 13
The Library of Congress has cataloged the hardcover edition as follows:
Anderson, Laurie Halse.
Forge / Laurie Halse Anderson. – 1st ed.
p. cm. – (Seeds of America)
Sequel to: Chains.
Summary: Separated from his friend Isabel after their daring escape from slavery, fifteen-year-old Curzon serves as a free man in the Continental Army at Valley Forge until he and Isabel are thrown together again, as slaves once more.
ISBN 978-1-4169-6144-4 (hc)
1. Pennsylvania–History–Revolution, 1775-1783–Juvenile fiction.
[1. Pennsylvania–History–Revolution, 1775-1783–Fiction. 2. Valley Forge (Pa.)–History–18th century–Fiction. 3. Soldiers–Fiction. 4. African Americans–Fiction. 5. Freedmen–Fiction. 6. Slavery–Fiction. 7. United States–History–Revolution, 1775-1783–Fiction. 8. New York–History–Revolution, 1775-1783–Fiction.] I. Title.
PZ7.A54385For 2010
[Fic]–dc22
2010015971
ISBN 978-1-4169-6145-1 (pbk)
ISBN 978-1-4424-4308-2 (eBook)

When

ABIGAIL ADAMS

was mourning the deaths of her parents,
she quoted a popular paraphrase of a Psalm
in her letters to her husband, JOHN:

"The sweet remembrance of the just
Shall flourish when they sleep in Dust."

And thus,
this book is dedicated to the memory of my mother,

JOYCE HOLCOMB HALSE,

and my father-in-law,

WILLIAM ROBERT LARRABEE SR.

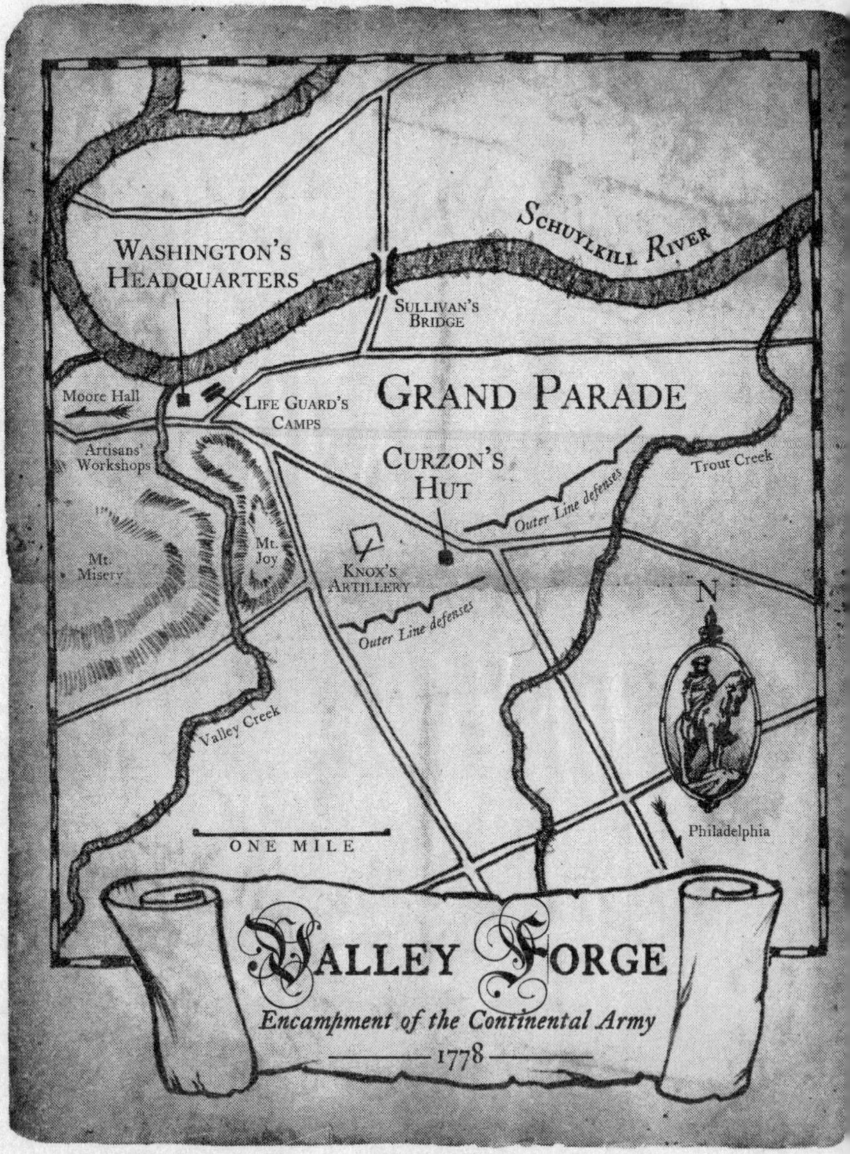

Schuylkill River
Washington's Headquarters
Sullivan's Bridge
Grand Parade
Moore Hall
Life Guard's Camps
Artisans' Workshops
Curzon's Hut
Trout Creek
Outer Line defenses
Mt. Joy
Mt. Misery
Knox's Artillery
Outer Line defenses
N
Valley Creek
Philadelphia
One Mile
Valley Forge
Encampment of the Continental Army
1778

Part 1

PRELUDE

Sunday, January 19, 1777

WE HAVE IT IN OUR POWER TO BEGIN THE WORLD OVER AGAIN. . . . THE BIRTH-DAY OF A NEW WORLD IS AT HAND.
–THOMAS PAINE, *COMMON SENSE*

"CAN YOU WALK?" SOMEONE ASKED ME.

I blinked against the bright light and squinted.

I was sitting in a rowboat half pulled onto a snowy riverbank. The cold was a beast gnawing at my fingers and toes. I closed my eyes and struggled to think past the ice cluttering my head.

This is a fantastical dream created by my fever. In truth, I am still a prisoner of the war in the Bridewell.

I sniffed. The air here was cold but clean, without the stink of jailed men and death.

No matter. 'Tis still a dream.

I drifted back toward sleep.

"Curzon!" Someone twisted my ear. "I beg you!"

I flinched.

"Open your eyes!" the voice commanded. "We must hurry away from here!"

I blinked again. Before me sat a girl, her right cheek scarred by a branding iron, her eyes swollen with fatigue.

'Twas Isabel, who was my friend.

I blinked for the third time and took a deep breath. Isabel's hands lay in her lap, bleeding from torn blisters. The handles of both oars were bloodstained where she had gripped them.

Like a flint hitting steel, a memory sparked, then flared.

Isabel had freed me from the Bridewell Prison. She'd rowed a boat, this ancient boat, all night long. Rowed us away from Manhattan, the British army, and those who owned us.

The memory exploded.

We are free!

I stood, legs quivering, head pounding, heart leaping. "You did it! How? Don't matter. Country, you did it!"

She shook her head violently and pulled me back down to my seat, a shaky finger on her lips to quiet me. "Hush!"

"But it's wondrous," I said, voice low. "Is it not?"

"Yes," she whispered. "No." The wind swirled a veil of snow between us. "Perhaps."

"Do you know of a safe house hereabouts?" I asked. "The name of folks who would help us?"

"We have to help ourselves." She looked over her shoulder at the field beyond the riverbank. "We have a handful of silver coins, some meat, and a map. I forged a pass too, but the river ruined it." She wrung out the water from the bottom of her skirt. "We have to walk to Charleston."

"Charleston? Why?"

"That's where Ruth is."

I knew then that her mind had been addled by the exertions of our escape. Isabel's little sister had been sold away to the islands. The child was likely dead, but I could not say this to Isabel. Not right then.

The river gurgled and tugged, trying to pull the boat back

into the current. I clutched at the sides of the unsteady craft and shivered. Isabel had brought us this far. Now it was up to me.

But how?

We were escaped slaves, half froze and exhausted. We needed to warm ourselves, sleep, and eat. But above all, we had to stay hidden. The business of returning or selling runaways was profitable for both redcoats and rebels.

I tallied our advantages: A few coins. Food enough for a few meals. Disadvantages: No horse. No gun. No one to trust.

A large piece of ice floated down the river as the second truth crackled in me.

This freedom could kill us.

CHAPTER I

Tuesday, October 7, 1777

"Begin the game."
—General Horatio Gates's order to start the Second Battle of Saratoga

THE MEMORY OF OUR ESCAPE STILL tormented me nine months later.

It did not matter that I'd found us shelter and work in Jersey or that I'd kept us safe. Isabel was ungrateful, peevish, and vexatious. We argued about going after Ruth, then we fought about it, and finally, in May, she ran away from me, taking all of our money.

I twisted my ear so hard, it was near torn from my head.

No thoughts of Isabel, I reminded myself. *Find that blasted road.*

I'd been looking for the back road to Albany since dawn on account of my former boss, Trumbull, was a cabbagehead and a cheat. The Patriot army had hired him and his two wagons (one of them driven by myself) to help move supplies up to the mountains near Saratoga. Thousands of British soldiers waited there, preparing to swoop down the Hudson, cut off New England from the other states, and end the rebellion.

Trumbull cared not for beating the British or freeing

the country from the King. He cared only for the sound of coins clinking together. With my own eyes, I saw him steal gunpowder and rum and salt from the barrels we hauled. He'd filch anything he could sell for his own profit.

'Twas not his thieving from the army that bothered me. 'Twas his thieving from me. I'd been working for him for three months and had no coin to show for it. He charged me for the loan of a ragged blanket and for anything else he could think of so he never had to hand over my wages.

The night before, I'd finally stood up to him and demanded my money. He fired me.

Of course, I robbed him. You would have done the very same.

I stole an assortment of spoons and four shoe buckles from his trunk after he fell asleep muddy in drink and snoring loud as a blasting bellows. I put my treasures in the leather bag that held Isabel's collection of seeds and her blue ribbon (both left behind in her haste to flee from my noxious self). The leather bag went into my empty haversack, which I slipped over my shoulder as I crawled out of Trumbull's tent.

I had walked for hours in the dark, quite certain that I'd stumble upon the road within moments. The rising sun burned through the fog but did not illuminate any road for me, not even a path well worn by deer or porcupines.

I climbed up a long hill, stopping at the top to retie the twine that held my shoes together. (Should have stolen Trumbull's boots, too.) I turned in a full circle. Most of the forest had leafed yellow, with a few trees bold-cloaked in scarlet or orange. No road. Had I been in my natural environment—the cobbled streets of Boston or New York—I could have easily found my way by asking a cartman or an oyster seller.

Not so in this forest.

I headed down into a deep ravine, swatting at the hornets that buzzed round my hat. The ravine might lead to the river, and a river was as good as a road, only wetter. Because I was the master of my own mind, I did not allow myself to believe that I might be lost. Nor did I worry about prowling redcoats or rebel soldiers eager to shoot. But the wolves haunted me. They'd dug up the graves of the fellows killed in last month's battle at Freeman's Farm and eaten the bodies. They'd eat a living man, too. A skinny lad like myself wouldn't last a minute if they attacked.

I picked my way through the brush at the bottom of the ravine, keeping my eyes on the ground for any sight of paw prints.

Crrr-ack.

I stopped.

Gunfire?

Not possible. I was almost certain that I was well south of the dangerous bit of ground that lay between the two armies.

Crrr-ack.

Heavy boots crashed through the forest. Voices shouted.

Crrr-ack BOOM!

An angry hornet hissed past my ear and smacked into the tree trunk behind me with a low *thuuump*.

I froze. That was no hornet. 'Twas a musketball that near tore off my head.

The voices grew louder. There was no time to run. I dropped to the ground and hid myself behind a log.

A British redcoat appeared out of a tangle of underbrush a dozen paces ahead of me and scrambled up the far side of the ravine. Three more British soldiers followed close on his heels, hands on their tall hats to keep them from flying off, canteens and cartridge boxes bouncing hard against their backsides.

There was a flash and another *Crrr-ack BOOM*.

A dozen rebel soldiers appeared, half in hunting shirts, the rest looking like they just stepped away from their plows. Smoke still poured from the barrel of the gun held by a red-haired fellow with an officer's black ribbon pinned to his hat.

There was a loud shuffling above. A line of redcoats took their position at the edge of the ravine and aimed down at the rebels.

"Present!" the British officer screamed to his men.

"Present!" yelled the American officer. His men brought the butts of their muskets up to their shoulders and sighted down the long barrels, ready to shoot and kill.

I pressed my face into the earth, unable to plan a course of escape. My mind would not be mastered and thought only of the wretched, lying, foul, silly girl who was the cause of everything.

I thought of Isabel and I missed her.

"FIRE!"

CHAPTER II

Tuesday, October 7, 1777

I HEARD BULLETS WHISTLE AND BELIEVE ME,
THERE IS SOMETHING CHARMING IN THE SOUND.
—LETTER FROM THE TWENTY-TWO-YEAR-OLD GEORGE
WASHINGTON DESCRIBING HIS FIRST TASTE OF BATTLE

THE MUSKETS ON BOTH SIDES FIRED; lightning flew from their barrels. The ravine darkened with gunpowder smoke and the curses of soldiers.

I moved my toes in my sorry shoes, my fingers in the mud. I was still one shaking piece of Curzon. I peered at the two lines of soldiers. None were bleeding. Not a one had been hit.

"Half cock your firelocks," a redcoat called, ordering the men to begin loading for the next shot.

The rebels would not give them the time they needed. "Advance!" bellowed the American officer. He charged across the bottom of the ravine and his men followed, all pulling hunting knives or hatchets from their belts. In two heartbeats they were halfway up the slope.

"Fall back!" the British yelled. "To the redoubt!"

They turned on their heels and ran, only a few steps ahead of the screaming rebels.

After they disappeared, I counted two score, and then

two score more, without moving. Gunfire crackled in the distance, then faded. I forced myself to stay hidden and listen for the sound of cannon fire.

The British and Americans had been skirmishing for weeks since September's battle ended in a draw. The Americans were desperate to push the British back into Canada before the winter hit. Some fellows said there would be one last battle and that it would be signaled by the firing of the cannons. The two armies would fight until blood soaked the ground.

I listened. Geese honked high overhead. The wind shook the trees, sending leaves twirling to the ground. There was another crackle of faraway muskets, but no cannon. The great battle had not begun.

I stood, brushed the leaves and dirt from my hat, and set it on my head. I was well and truly lost. The only way out was to retrace my steps, past the shadows and the wolves. Just as I prepared to set out the way I came, I heard the sound of more boots crashing toward me.

I hid behind the log again.

"I said halt," shouted a voice.

A short British soldier stumbled into the ravine, chased by a gap-toothed rebel boy near my age, white-skinned, uncommonly tall, and armed with an ancient musket.

"Stop there!" the boy yelled.

The redcoat glanced behind him, caught his foot on a half-buried root, and fell hard. His musket flew from his hand, but he quickly crawled to it.

"You are my prisoner, sir," the boy declared in a shaky voice. "Lay down your musket."

The redcoat had no intention of becoming a prisoner. He pulled out a gunpowder cartridge, ripped it open with his teeth, and poured powder into his firing pan. His hands were shaking so violently that most of the powder fell to the ground. He pulled out a second cartridge and poured with care. When the pan was primed, he shut it and poured the rest of the powder down the barrel.

"Stop!" The boy brought his musket up to fire. "I swear I'll shoot." He wiped his right hand on his breeches, then cocked the firelock and slipped his finger into the trigger guard.

The redcoat fumbled in his shot bag for a lead musketball.

The boy squeezed the trigger. His flint hit the empty firing pan with a dull *click*. The musket did not fire. He'd forgotten to prime his pan.

The redcoat pulled out his ramrod.

The boy grabbed the cork out of his powder horn.

My palms were sweating, my eyes going back and forth trying to figger who would win the race to load and shoot. A year earlier I'd been a Patriot soldier, enlisted as a substitute for the man who owned me. When the British attacked us at Fort Washington, I spent the entire day loading muskets for other fellows to shoot with. I could prepare a musket for firing in my sleep.

The redcoat rammed the musketball the length of the barrel.

The boy fumbled his powder horn. It dropped to the leaves.

The redcoat pulled out his ramrod and threw it aside. He raised the barrel without a word.

The gap-toothed boy was about to be slaughtered.

I had to help.

My fingers curled around a muddy rock. The boy filled his firing pan and shut it. The redcoat cocked his firelock and reached for the trigger. I rose up from my hiding place and threw the rock hard as I could. It hit the redcoat square in the shoulder and threw off his aim just as he squeezed his trigger.

The redcoat stared in disbelief at the hole he'd shot in the dirt.

Then the boy fired his gun. This time the flint sparked the powder in the pan, which set off the powder in the barrel that exploded the bullet across the ravine and into the body of his enemy.

The British soldier fell backward–screaming, screaming, screaming–his hands clutched at his belly. He'd been gut-shot. The musketball had ripped his middle right open. He rolled back and forth–screaming, screaming–as the blood welled up, covering his hands, rushing out of him to flood the fallen leaves and the dirt. His boots twitched, his entire form shook, shuddered, and then he choked, for the blood filled his throat, and his red-washed fingers clawed at his neck. Broken leaves flew into the air from the violence of his thrashing, and the gore and blood kept pouring from the black hole in his belly and from his mouth–surely enough blood for ten men, a sight horrid enough to make God Himself weep–and suddenly, his boots stopped running and his form stilled and then . . .

. . . Death caught him.

CHAPTER III

Tuesday, October 7, 1777

Saw sev'ral Dead & naked men lying dead in ye woods close by, or Even where ye battle was fought.
—Journal of Private Ezra Tilden after the Second Battle of Saratoga

THE REBEL BOY DROPPED HIS MUSKET, bent over with a mighty groan, and puked. My belly went sour too, but I choked back the bile. I'd seen dead men before.

I rose up from my hiding place with caution. The birds had gone quiet. My footsteps snapped twigs. I was sure every wolf in the forest could hear me, smell me.

The boy puked his last, coughed and spit, then sat on the ground, his skin as pale as the dead man's. He did not look in my direction as I walked toward him.

"Do you have any water?" I asked.

He stared at the crumpled form of the redcoat.

I removed his canteen from his shoulder, uncorked it, and placed it in his hand. "Drink."

He looked up at me then, blue eyes red from the crying. He had a shadow of whiskers growing under his nose, but I did not think he'd begun to shave yet.

I held the canteen to his mouth. "If you don't drink, the shock will burn through you till you're as dead as he is."

He nodded like a small child and sipped.

"Again," I urged.

He took a second swig, a longer one, then wiped his mouth and his eyes on his dirty sleeve. "Are you certain he's–"

"Yes." I drank from his canteen, for the shock was burning through me, too.

Out of the stillness came the ripping noise of a large volley of musket fire. The boy blinked, roused by the sound. He scrambled to his feet.

"We must join them," he said urgently. "Oh, dear God, make haste!"

"Was that your patrol?"

"Not a patrol," he said. "The entire army is marching. Uncle says if we win today, it could end the war." He looked at my hands, then at the ground near my feet. "Where's your gun?"

"I don't–"

I paused. If he thought me a soldier, then a soldier I would pretend to be. The truth was dangerous.

"My barrel cracked," I lied.

The rolling thunder of cannon fire shook the earth.

"Take his," the boy said.

"What?"

"Take his gun." He pointed at the dead redcoat, sprawled atop his musket. "He won't mind."

"But how?" There was very little of the man that was not soaked in his blood.

"I'll lift him." He walked to the body and took a deep, shaky breath.

"You gonna puke again?" I asked as I followed him.

"Don't have time." He bent down, grabbed the redcoat's jacket at the shoulders, and turned his head to the side, eyes squeezed shut. "Ready?"

"No," I said. "But go ahead."

He lifted.

I pulled out the musket and stood, horrified by the sticky blood that covered the wooden stock and my hands. My belly revolted and I gave a hard puke. I did not drop the musket.

The rebel boy grunted with effort and rolled the body so that it was facedown. The sight of the dead man's arm flopping to the leaves gave me a chill. My belly heaved again and I bent over, coughing and spewing foulness.

"Uncle says it gets easier after you see a lot of bodies," the boy said.

"Your uncle is wrong."

The sound of firing guns was coming in regular waves now; an ocean of lead and gunpowder crashing toward the ravine.

"Quick." The boy's eyes were sharper now; his senses had overcome the shock. "There should be powder and shot in his knapsack."

'Twas easier to go along with his version of who I was until we parted.

"Do you have enough powder?" I asked.

"Aye." He shifted from one foot to the next, watching the brush as if expecting the entire British army to suddenly appear.

"Then run. I'll be close behind you," I lied.

He reached out and punched my arm hard, the way one friend does to another. "I thank you for saving my life."

I nodded back, startled into a rare speechlessness.

He gave an awkward bow, then broke into a run toward the ravine. "Grab your powder! Make haste!"

CHAPTER IV

Tuesday, October 7, 1777

BUT WHEN I SAW LIBERTY POLES AND THE PEOPLE ALL ENGAGED FOR THE SUPPORT OF FREEDOM, I COULD NOT BUT LIKE AND BE PLEASED WITH SUCH THING. . . . THESE CONSIDERATIONS INDUCED ME TO ENLIST INTO THE AMERICAN ARMY, WHERE I SERVED FAITHFULLY ABOUT TEN MONTHS, WHEN MY MASTER FOUND AND TOOK ME HOME.
—PENSION APPLICATION OF JEHU GRANT, A RHODE ISLAND SLAVE WHO ESCAPED TO FIGHT FOR THE PATRIOTS

I WAITED UNTIL HE WAS OUT OF SIGHT before kicking off the tattered remains of my shoes and pulling off the dead man's boots. I had to pause after the first one, for my belly threatened again. I scolded it; the battle was too close for me to be soft. I'd take what this fellow no longer needed, then flee.

The boots fit perfectly, which I took to be a good omen. My luck was finally changing.

I removed the rolled blanket that was tied to the flap of the redcoat's knapsack; more good luck, for I was in dire need of a blanket. If he had food, I'd be rich beyond measure. I unbuckled the straps and opened the flap. His reserve ammunition was on the top. I filled my jacket pockets with gunpowder cartridges and musketballs.

I should have run then, but I was greedy and very hungry.

I dug out tools for cleaning and oiling the musket—those would be most helpful—a clean pair of stockings, and a white linen shirt, as well as a tin box containing flints and dried moss, a drinking cup, and two pencils along with papers covered in writing and three maps, all wrapped in oilcloth. No food.

A close-by cannon roared.

Hurry!

I quick grabbed the ramrod from the leaves, fetched my haversack, and filled it with everything I'd removed so far, then pulled out the last items from the knapsack: a hinged wooden box as big as my hand and a square of black cloth wrapped around a miniature painting of a pale woman with solemn eyes. She wore a pink flower in her hair.

His wife. That gave me pause. Did they have children? How long before the news reached them that their father was dead?

I did not have time to ponder his family.

The box was chipped on two corners and cracked in the middle. I slid open the brass latch.

A compass.

An expensive compass, finely crafted, with a brightly colored compass rose painted under the needle to show the path to thirty-two directions. My former master, Bellingham, had owned several sailing ships before the war. The tables in the library were often covered by maps and charts when his captains called. Once, a compass such as this had been used to keep the papers from flying on the sharp breeze that came from the harbor. Bellingham had been amused by my curiosity and showed me how the device worked. I considered it a magical thing, for I was still a child then.

This compass, however, had no magic or usefulness. The glass was broken and the needle bent.

I glanced at the body. Redcoat soldiers were not commonly equipped with compasses. This fellow was likely a surveyor or an engineer.

He died because I threw a rock.

I shook my head. *No, that gap-toothed boy lives because I threw a rock.*

Hundreds of voices were shouting beyond the ravine. Drums sounded their battle call.

I stood with the compass and spun around in a slow circle. The needle tried to wobble on its thin post but was too broken to show me the way. I had to reason out my situation. The battle had to be north of me, for the British camp was north of the American. South was the direction I needed. South meant the path to Albany, maybe riches, maybe work and a home with a roof and friends and a girl who likes flowers.

No. That's a lie.

A good thief can lie to everyone else, but never to himself.

There was nothing waiting for me in Albany. Nothing waiting anywhere. The shape of my life had altered when Bellingham enlisted me. It changed again when I escaped the prison. It shattered when Isabel left.

I turned the compass in my hand, trying to wish the needle into showing me the way out. It mocked me, refusing to budge. I had no heading.

A cold wind carried the scent of gunpowder smoke down the ravine, and a strange wildness overcame me, as if a compass needle buried inside of me swung violently. I put the compass on the ground and picked up the bloody musket, ready to smash its wooden butt into the glass and finish the job of destroying it.

But, no.

I could sell it, maybe earn enough to feed me for a few weeks. I slung the strap of the musket over my head and stored the compass in my haversack along with the redcoat's stockings and shirt. I wrapped the black cloth around the portrait and returned it to the dead man's knapsack.

As I lifted my haversack, I winced from the pain in my arm where the boy struck me. He was stronger than he knew. I rubbed the sore spot.

Was this really the battle that would win the war, like he said?

The aimless needle inside me spun and spun again. My heart beat to the sounds of the approaching drums. I liked the smell of gunpowder. I was not afraid to fight. My hands liked the feel of holding a musket again. And to my surprise, I felt bad about lying to that gap-toothed boy.

I headed into battle.

CHAPTER V

Tuesday, October 7, 1777

BUT WE WHO HAD SOMETHING MORE AT STAKE THAN FIGHTING FOR SIX PENCE PER DAY KEPT OUR GROUND TIL NIGHT.
—JOURNAL OF NEW HAMPSHIRE MAJOR
HENRY DEARBORN

GUNPOWDER SMOKE COVERED THE field like a heavy fog, turning men into ghostly smudges. The fire erupting from musket barrels looked like exploding lanterns, and then there was more smoke. Unseen cannons blasted without cease, shaking the ground and splintering the air with unholy roars. The commands of officers were matched by the screams of the wounded and panicked whinnying of terrified horses, and underneath all of the layers of sound, the drums pounded like the heartbeat of a tremendous beast.

I did not see the gap-toothed boy in the confusion of sounds and smoke. I looked behind me at the woods. Would anyone notice if I ran for them?

Isabel's voice cropped up in my head and whispered, *Coward.*

I yanked my ear savagely.

"Forward," screamed a ragged voice. A blue-coated officer on a bay horse rode through the pack of men, standing tall in his saddle and pointing ahead with his sword. "Now, boys, now!"

He galloped away like a demon.

The fellows in front of me started to run, and those to my left and right did as well. The man behind me shoved and cursed at me, and so I ran. I could not see what we were running toward until it was almost too late.

The British were dug in above us on a small hill.

An officer in a hunting shirt and deerskin leggings pointed at me and a handful of others and waved us to a rail fence. That would offer some cover.

A redcoat screamed, "FIRE!"

We all threw ourselves to the ground and covered our heads as the British volley ripped above us. I thought sure I'd piss myself with fear.

Our officer hollered at us to make ready. The soldiers around me all prepared their weapons. I did the same, though it was hard trying to stay flat to the ground and load a musket at the same time.

The redcoats rained hot fire down on us—grapeshot and musketballs and a cannon that tore through the air like a comet.

Our officer stood and yelled, "FIRE!"

We leapt up, pulled our triggers, then fell to the ground to load again.

The British shot faster than we did. They had arranged themselves in two lines, so that as the front line shot, the men in the back loaded. As the back line shot, the front line knelt and loaded. The bright flash and the explosions of firing guns were quick followed by the *thud, thud, thud* of musketballs hitting the dirt and fence rails around us.

Far to our left was a wooded area where two rebels were

stationed behind every tree. There was brisk fire between the woods and hilltop, so fierce that the air itself seemed to burn. I thought I saw the troops down the right side of the line push forward, but the smoke was so thick, I could not be sure.

A second wave of Patriots came up behind us, and we were able to keep up a strong attack. The British guns slowed and the cannons stopped. There were fewer figures atop the hill.

"Follow them!" Our officer leapt over the fence, his hatchet in his hand.

We charged up the hill, past fallen redcoats and dead Hessians dressed in green, past the horses used by the British to pull the cannons, shot dead in their traces. We ran to another stand of trees, and the British guns again fired; they'd dug in around an abandoned barn.

I found me a sturdy oak with a trunk broad enough to hide behind and pulled out another gunpowder cartridge. When I ripped it open with my teeth, grains of gunpowder spilled on my tongue. The bitter tang tasted like the smell of the smoke that hung in the air.

I poured in the gunpowder, rammed home the bullet, primed the lock, and peered around my tree. The British were just within range of a musket such as mine, but the smoke made it hard to see anything. I shot, loaded and shot, loaded and shot, never knowing if I'd hit anyone. The soldiers around me worked as I did, some daring to stand in the open whilst loading. One fellow was shot through the leg as he reached for his powder horn. He screamed so loud, I could not hear the commands of our officer. The fellow behind the next tree threw an acorn at my head to get my attention; he was out of powder. I tossed him two cartridges and prayed the battle would soon end.

Company drummers *rat-a-tat-tatted*, telling the troops which way to move. I dimly remembered the commands from the battle in Brooklyn. Smoke thickened. Confusion choked both sides of the field. Discipline fell away as men did not wait for commands from the officers. Each man loaded and fired to the tune in his own head.

The wounded screamed.

Time slowed and Death rode hard. The sun began to set, but then it hung in the sky without moving. I had four cartridges left. *Three.*

Two . . .

And then our officer waved his arms and called out something, and the fellows closest to him stopped firing and waved their arms too.

I shook my head to clear the ringing from my ears.

Either I've gone deaf or . . . No.

The cannons had stopped.

Was it over?

A horse galloped through the wall of smoke. "We flanked them!" the rider called. "They've abandoned the field and are running!"

"Huzzah!" The American roars shook the trees. "Huzzah! Huzzah! Huzzah!"

CHAPTER VI

Tuesday, October 7–Wednesday, October 8, 1777

THE COURAGE AND OBSTINACY WITH WHICH THE AMERICANS FOUGHT WERE THE ASTONISHMENT OF EVERYONE, AND WE NOW BECOME FULLY CONVINCED THEY ARE NOT THAT CONTEMPTIBLE ENEMY WE HAD HITHERTO IMAGINED THEM.
—BRITISH ENSIGN THOMAS ANBUREY AFTER THE BATTLES OF SARATOGA

THE CELEBRATION DID NOT LAST LONG. Companies were sent to chase after the retreating British. More men were sent to guard the river in case the enemy tried to float past the encampment and attack us from the rear. The officers ordered the cannons back and bellowed for carts and water to be brought to the field.

The fellow at the next tree handed me a canteen. "Just take a little," he cautioned. "The wounded need it more than we do." He walked over to a fellow who sat clutching the bleeding gash on his arm and helped the man drink.

I could not move.

"Find yer strength, boy," the fellow yelled at me. "They need yer help."

I followed his example, kneeling beside a lad in a fine

brown coat who lay curled on his side. I helped him to sit up and gave him water.

"Can you walk?" I asked.

He shook his head and lay back down on the ground, as if I'd woken him from a nap. I could not figger if he had an injury to his body or if he'd lost his wits. Or both. I moved along to the next thirsty fellow.

When the water was gone, I made my way out of the woods to where a large group had gathered. An officer directed me to help carry the wounded back to camp on hastily made litters, which were no more than a blanket secured between two poles.

I was partnered with a mud-spattered militiaman whose pale face was creased with lines of melancholy. Our burden was a boy with powder burns and a bayonet wound through the meat of his thigh. He moaned as we lifted him onto the litter, then fell into a blessed swoon. We laid our muskets on either side of his form, grasped the poles of the litter, and lifted it.

Camp lay two long miles away, mostly uphill. We passed Patriot dead, including a woman who was killed running ammunition to the field; she still gripped gunpowder cartridges in her cold hands. Living women moved around her, some tending to the wounded, others stripping the bodies of our enemies. One of them found a man she must have loved. She sank to her knees and howled, a bone-chilling noise far worse than wolves.

I wished someone would make her stop.

My hands and arms quickly tired, then burned from carrying the unconscious soldier. I welcomed the pain, for it blotted the battle from my mind.

At last we reached the hospital tents. Lanterns stood on

wobbly benches so that the surgeons could better see as they dug out grapeshot and musketballs from groaning men and boys. Screams came from the tent that stood farthest from the others.

"Amputations," said the sad-faced man. "Turrible business, that."

We delivered the boy to a surgeon in a bloody apron, guzzled a cup of water, picked up the litter, and went back to the battlefield.

The fat, pumpkin-colored moon rose, turning bloodstains into shadows. All of the colors of shirts and jackets and uniforms paled to the same shade of gray.

We could not find the officer who first ordered us to carry the wounded. My partner would have wandered the field all night, but I stopped a fellow carrying a horse's saddle and inquired.

"The wounded are all up t'camp, but ye can dig graves if you want." His words came Irish-wrapped, which forced me to listen close.

"We show'd 'em, din't we?" he continued. "Killt two a' them for every one of us. Chased 'em from the field, the damn'd cowards." He walked off still talking to himself, without waiting for any reply from me. My partner dropped his poles and followed the man.

I carried the litter back to the camp, for it seemed a sin to waste the blanket. After I set it in front of a hospital tent, I dragged my bones up the last hill, following shadowy, silent men. Candles were set on upturned logs, lanterns hung from chains off tree branches, and campfires burned bright. I slid into a line for grub. A fellow with a flour-stained shirt handed me bread and a charred piece of meat, then a round-bellied woman filled my stolen cup with water.

I ate by a fire and shook with chills. When my food was gone, I picked at the bits of meat and grains of gunpowder that were stuck between my teeth. Stray bits of talk drifted through my battle-muzzy head. One of Morgan's rangers shot a redcoat brigadier general with a rifle whilst perched in a tree. We'd killed more than two score redcoat officers and hundreds of their men, with hundreds more captured and held as prisoners. A thick-skulled fellow had a bullet stuck fast in his head and lived. Another took grapeshot in his mouth and lost his tongue and most of his teeth.

The stories wound on and on. . . .

My head bobbed forward, startling me awake just before I crashed into the dirt.

The fire-talk was quiet. Most fellows must have crawled off to their tents or brush huts. Some slept on the damp ground like it was a feather bed. I pulled the dead man's blanket out of my haversack, spread it over my legs, moved the sack so it would pillow my head, and laid my musket next to me. I reached for my hat.

It was not on my head. I sat up straight and searched, but it was not in my haversack, not tucked into my shirt.

I rolled back the day's events in my mind. I'd worn the hat while searching for the road, had clutched it to my chest whilst hiding from the skirmishing patrols. I was sure I had it when I opened the compass box and when I ran to join in the battle. I must have lost it in the confusion after that.

You might find it dishonorable, but my eyes watered thinking that I'd lost that hat. You'd understand if I shed tears for the fathers and husbands and brothers and sons who died that day. And the woman killed carrying gunpowder into battle. You'd say that only a fool would cry over the loss of a raggedy felt hat.

But that had been my father's hat, a castoff from young Master Bellingham. I'd worn it on my head since the day the redcoats shot Father on Breed's Hill.

Now I'd lost it.

I lay down under the pumpkin moon, shamed and heartsore. The tears would not stop. I covered my face with the blanket lest anyone take notice of me.

CHAPTER VII

Wednesday, October 8, 1777

I TRUST WE HAVE CONVINCD THE
BRITISH BUTCHERS THAT THE COWARDLY YANKEES
CAN & WHEN THEIR IS A CALL FOR IT, WILL, FIGHT.
—JOURNAL OF NEW HAMPSHIRE MAJOR
HENRY DEARBORN

THE CAMP AWOKE BEFORE DAWN—carts rattling, cook pots clanging, axes biting into wood, bold conversating voices, and the drummer boys at their task, announcing the day.

I stood and brushed the dirt from my breeches, then wrapped my blanket around my shoulders, shivering. My head was particularly cold.

A group of Oneida and Stockbridge warriors, the best scouts in the army, strode by, followed by a pack of lean riflemen in hunting shirts, likely from Virginia. I rolled my blanket and packed my sack and tried to listen in on every voice around me. General Gates had already ordered several companies out of camp to harass the British. Yesterday's victory meant nothing until all the redcoats surrendered and became our prisoners.

The thought startled me. *Our prisoners.* When had the affairs of this army again become mine?

My stomach growled, reminding me of larger concerns. I'd been fed the night before in the befuddlement that followed the battle. I'd be spotted as a scoundrel seeking a free meal in the light of day. I walked, pondering my predicament and keeping a watchful eye out for Trumbull.

The encampment was a huge, rusticated city of tents and brush huts for the thousands who had come to fight the British. Most of the soldiers were white-skinned militiamen who had enlisted with their neighbors and kin. This made it hard for a stranger like me to blend in at dinnertime without being questioned. But every regiment of the Continental army had a goodly number of black and molatto soldiers. I had a fair chance of passing myself off as a Continental, at least long enough to get something to eat.

I'd conversated with Agrippa, a friendly chap in Paterson's brigade, a few days earlier. He resembled me close enough to be a cousin, which amused us both. But I dared not seek him out. The Massachusetts regiments were positioned dangerously close to the wagon drivers' camp. The thought of being so close to Trumbull made the hair on the back of my neck prickle, as if lightning were about to strike.

I'd try my luck with the Connecticut troops. They had the most black soldiers of all of the states in camp, plus some Narragansetts. If Fortune was smiling, I'd find a company cook there in need of spectacles and eat until I was ready to burst.

I made my way through the camp, following the nose-trails carved by the smells of roasting meat, fresh bread, and bubbling stews. The first cook I approached was not as nearsighted as he seemed and sent me off with a wicked scolding. The second one did the same, and the third threatened me with his knife when my hand brushed accidentally against a bowl of apples on his table.

I dragged myself down row after row of tents and cook fires, feeling ever more out of sorts and famished. By a washing tent I spied a young white girl with long straw-colored braids carrying a baby on her hip. She paused to talk with a woman, likely their mother, who was scrubbing bloody bandages in a tub. The girl then took two pieces of bread from a trencher on the table, gave one to the babe, and walked away from the tent, bouncing up and down and singing softly.

The bread was smeared with apple butter. I wanted it.

Stealing from children is wrong, I thought. *Worse than wrong.*

But the notion planted itself in my head and grew deep roots. I would wait until the girl drew farther away from the tent, run past and snatch the bread out of her hands, and dash away. She would not go hungry; there was more bread on the table.

The mother squeezed brown water from the bandages and hung them on a line strung between two trees. The bump of her skirt showed another child was on the way, and my thievish thoughts shamed me. I resolved to pay for my meal. I would drop one of Trumbull's spoons in the road as I grabbed the bread from her daughter. It would be a frontier sort of purchase, not stealing.

"Ho there! Master Stone Thrower!"

The voice was loud, but I paid it little heed, worrying that if any gun-toting soldiers saw me take the bread but did not notice my payment, they might well cause problems. Mayhaps it would be safer to trade with the washerwoman direct.

"I say, you there!" that voice called again.

I was on the verge of giving the woman a cheery halloo when someone plucked at my sleeve.

"Master Thrower of the Stones," said the gap-toothed rebel boy from the ravine. "I was beginning to think you were dead."

His homespun shirt was torn at the right elbow and his face was still dirty from gunpowder and smoke, but he appeared to be in one piece, body and soul.

"Not dead yet," I said. "But I will be soon if I don't eat."

He reached into his sack. "Can't let that happen." He handed me an enormous red apple.

I grabbed it and took a bite. "Hank yoo," I said, juice running down my chin.

"My name is Eben," he said, removing his hat and nodding politely. "Ebenezer Woodruff of the Sixteenth Massachusetts, in your debt and at your service."

The heavenly taste of apple made it impossible to lie. I wiped my face on my sleeve. "My name is Curzon."

Eben barely noticed. "I told my uncle what you did for me yesterday, what you did for the whole family, because Woodruffs, we set quite a store by family, and my uncle said, 'You go out there and find that lad. We need to thank him proper and make sure he's come to no harm.'"

I took a second large bite and chewed, uncertain about what I ought say.

"Are you headed out on duty?" he asked.

Two more quick bites and a swallow. The taste compelled me to further honesty. "I'm not a soldier."

"What are you, then?"

"I'm on my own and looking for work."

His face brightened. "You could enlist. We lost a few fellows yesterday. Captain needs replacements."

I shook my head. "I served once. That was enough."

"The war's almost over," he said. "Wouldn't be for long."

I ate the core and shook my head.

"I can't change your mind?" he asked.

"Wolves couldn't change my mind."

Eben sighed. "More's the pity. Come along for a meal, at least. Uncle will be mad if I let you walk away hungry."

"You can get me more food?"

He punched my shoulder so hard, my fingers went numb. "Eating is the best part of soldiering!"

CHAPTER VIII

Wednesday, October 8, 1777

As the General is informed, that Numbers of Free Negroes are desirous of inlisting, he gives leave to the recruiting Officers to entertain them, and promises to lay the matter before the Congress, who he doubts not will approve of it.
—General Orders of George Washington

THE SIXTEENTH MASSACHUSETTS Regiment was camped on ground that sloped toward the Hudson. I resolved to keep a keen lookout for Trumbull and flee as soon as my belly was full.

Eben jabbered a flood of stories about his uncle and his uncle's wife, and all manner of cousins on both sides of his family, and thinking about cousins made him tell a story about his favorite plow horse. The boy could talk the bark off a tree; he didn't even pause to draw breath.

Just as I began to wonder if his wits had been rattled in the battle, he stopped in front of a dirty tent that sagged with damp.

"Best to store your kit in here," he said. "We've had some pilfering by the cook fires. Can't trust no one, it seems."

I hesitated. If I did cross paths with Trumbull, it would be safer to have my stolen treasure here and not on my person. But if I had to flee, how would I get back here to claim what was mine?

"The cook made biscuits for the chicken stew," Eben said. "Are you fond of biscuits?"

My belly voted louder than my wits. I dropped the haversack and followed him.

Ebenezer Woodruff was an honest rebel. The biscuits were sand-dry, but they were entirely free of worms and dirt. The chicken stew tasted strongly of fish. I et two bowls and begged for a third. When the cook saw how hungry I was, he rummaged in his trunk and drew out a salty hunk of cheese that he cut in two pieces, then he refilled our cups with cider.

"Does your cook always feed you so much?" I asked as we walked away.

"I get extra on account of he lost a game of cards to my uncle last week."

"I must ask your uncle to teach me how to play."

"He won't. Says card-playing is a sin."

"But he plays?"

"Uncle is allowed to be a sinner, I'm not. Look!" He grabbed my arm and pointed somewhere at the crowd of folk who swarmed around us. "There he is. Uncle!" he shouted.

"Shhh," I warned.

He ignored me. "Uncle Caleb!" he hollered, waving his hat in the air. "I found him, sir! His name is Curzon!"

"Don't shout." I felt like every man in the army was staring at us.

"He didn't hear me." Eben replaced his hat on his head. "We'll chase him down."

From within the crowd came a familiar roar of rage. My bowels twisted.

"Come on," Eben urged me.

"I need a privy," I lied, looking for the source of the Trumbull-like noise. "I'll meet you at your tent."

Eben grinned. "Don't get lost!"

I turned to run in the opposite direction just as Trumbull spotted me.

"Found you, you thieving rogue!" he bellowed.

I leapt over a cook fire, stumbled on a rock, fell to the ground, and scuttled on all fours like a crab past a collection of soldiers cleaning their muskets.

"Get him," yelled Trumbull. "Stop that boy!"

A few fellows gave me chase and caught me easily. Trumbull approached, snorting and steaming. He drew so close that I could smell his rotting teeth.

"Where are they?" he demanded.

"Where are what, sir?" I asked, trying to appear innocent.

"You know what I'm after," Trumbull growled.

"I don't know what you're talking about, sir," I said.

He smacked the side of my head with his fist. "My bloody spoons, whelp!"

The blow staggered me and a few fellows cheered. Trumbull drew back his fist again, and I raised my arms to protect myself.

"Sir!"

"The sergeant!" someone warned.

All the soldiers fell silent and stood ramrod straight as a tall man strode toward us with Eben close on his heels. They had the same large ears, high brows, and long, freckled noses. Eben had not mentioned his uncle was a steel-eyed sergeant. The man glared at me, and I stood straighter too.

"What cause have you to beat this boy?" the sergeant asked my former boss.

"He stole from me," Trumbull said. "Four shoe buckles and a handful of spoons. 'Tis no concern of the army."

"Is this true?" the sergeant asked.

"No, sir," I said. "Absolutely not."

"He can't breathe without lying." Trumbull grabbed my arm tight. "I'll take care of the matter. We'll not bother you any longer."

"He's a soldier," Eben blurted. "You can't take him."

"You're a soldier?" the sergeant asked me.

"He wants to enlist, sir," Eben said quickly. "I told you what he did yesterday. He's exactly the kind of fellow we need. In fact, him and me were just on our way to your tent to sign the enlistment papers."

We were?

The sergeant looked me over. "Where's your kit? Your gun?"

"I know where it is," Eben said.

"Bring it to my tent," his uncle answered. "You two"—he pointed at Trumbull and me—"come this way."

The sergeant's tent stood with the other officers' in a grove of birch trees with golden leaves. Before I could figger a plan of escape, Eben arrived, grinning like a lackbrain and carrying my haversack and musket. He hailed his uncle, who was setting a piece of paper, a quill, and a bottle of ink on an upturned log.

"This is his." Eben handed the musket to his uncle and set my sack on the ground.

The sergeant examined the flintlock. "You took this from the redcoat who shot at Ebenezer?" he asked me.

"Yessir," I answered.

"He could have stolen it from one of our boys," Trumbull said.

The sergeant leaned the musket against the log and picked up the haversack. "And this is yours too?"

That broken compass was not a good omen, I decided. It was a curse.

"I believe so, sir. Many haversacks look alike."

He untied the knotted rope and spilled the contents of the sack onto the ground. "Shirt, stockings, blanket, musket tools, knife," he listed, setting each item apart from the others. "Drinking cup. Tinderbox." He shook out the sack to prove it was empty. "I see no spoons, Mister Trumbull."

Nor did I. Not only were the spoons and buckles missing, but so was the compass and Isabel's little bag of seeds. I'd been robbed!

Trumbull frowned. "He must have sold them yesterday. Search his person and you'll find the money."

"He was occupied yesterday," said the sergeant. "Fighting the British."

"Another lie," said Trumbull.

"This boy saved my nephew, sir," the sergeant said sharply.

Trumbull spat in the dirt. "Don't believe it."

"Hand upon the Bible, I swear," Eben said, "I'd be dead if it weren't for him."

"We are beholden to you for that," the sergeant said as he bowed to me.

He bowed. At the waist.

To me.

Gentlemen bowed out of courtesy. Out of respect. I'd seen thousands upon thousands of bows whilst serving Judge Bellingham and later his son. They bowed when greeting each other. Upon taking their leave. They bowed to ladies and to their elders. They did not bow to slaves or thieves or ditch scoundrels.

But Sergeant Woodruff bowed to me and I was all of those things.

I returned his bow slowly, and more deeply, to show I understood the honor he paid me. "Sir."

"I claim possession of that weapon," brayed Trumbull. "To pay for what the whelp stole from me."

The sergeant leveled his gaze at Trumbull. "A soldier needs that musket more than you."

"He'll not enlist," Trumbull said. "It's a ruse."

"Care to wager on that?" The sergeant uncorked his ink pot and dipped his quill. "What's your name, lad?"

I had the unpleasant sensation that I was about to jump from a fry pan into the fire.

CHAPTER IX

Wednesday, October 8, 1777

I WENT DOWN . . . TO THE OFFICERS TO OFFER MY SERVICES . . . THEY QUESTIONED ME A LITTLE AND FINALLY SAID THAT I MIGHT STAY . . . IF I THOUGHT THAT I COULD DO THE DUTY OF A SOLDIER.
—JOURNAL OF DANIEL GRANGER, WHO ENLISTED IN THE CONTINENTAL ARMY AT AGE THIRTEEN

"AH . . . ," I STAMMERED. "UM . . ."

Caution was called for. I needed a name with no connection to me or my father or the family that had owned us.

"His name is Curzon," Eben said.

"Likely another lie," Trumbull said. "He's got all sorts of dark blood running in him; could be injun as well as negar. He'll slit your throats as you sleep."

I took a deep breath and fought the desire to beat in Trumbull's skull with my musket. I'd grown used to his insults—they were, in part, why I felt no remorse at stealing from him—but to hear him call me such foul names in front of Eben and his uncle was hard to bear.

That's his aim, I realized. Cause me to lose my temper and attack him, then he'd win.

In that moment I resolved to be a soldier again.

I took a second deep breath and spoke calm and refined,

the way I'd learned whilst serving at Judge Bellingham's table in Boston. "My name is Curzon Smith, sir."

"You are free to enlist, not run away from a master or indenture?"

"I am my own master, sir."

Trumbull wagged his finger at the sergeant. "You'll rue this day if you enlist him. He's nothing but a bag of trouble."

The sergeant pressed his lips together and drew a slow breath. "If you do not leave this moment, sir, I shall summon the guard."

Trumbull spat on the ground, turned on his heel, and stalked off, shouting to himself like a madman. I sorely wanted to stick out my tongue and make a rude noise, but it would not have been a soldierly gesture.

"What a foul-smelling, son-of-the-devil!" Eben said.

"No cursing, Ebenezer. Now, then." The sergeant again picked up the pen. "How old are you, Curzon Smith?"

"Near sixteen," I said, which was not entirely a lie, for I would turn sixteen the next October, which was only eleven months and some weeks hence.

He scratched on the enlistment paper with his quill. "Your regular pay will be twenty shillings a month. You will be provided with two shirts, two pair of breeches, a cap, and two pair of shoes when the state's shipment arrives. If you don't want the clothes, I am authorized to pay you a cash bonus of twenty dollars, which you will receive from the paymaster at the end of the month."

"What about the land, Uncle?" asked Eben.

"Some say that every soldier will receive a hundred acres at war's end," the older Woodruff said. "I don't know how much truth there is to the notion." He dipped his quill again. "Do you want to enlist for three years or for the rest of the war?"

"Three years!" Eben exclaimed. "Only a fool would sign up for that."

I weighed the choice. A ship would have to carry the news that we'd beat Burgoyne to the King across the ocean, then another ship would have to sail back, bringing the British offer of peace. War would likely end by February or early March, if the seas were rough. The British wouldn't fight after winter set in; the armies would hole up in encampments and wait for spring. That meant I'd have a place to sleep and food to eat for months, along with new clothes and pay.

"I would like to enlist for the rest of the war, sir."

The sergeant scratched out a few more words. "Can you write your name?"

"No, sir."

He handed the quill to me and pointed at the bottom of the paper. "Make your mark there."

I made my *X* with a bold hand.

"There now." The sergeant took back his quill. "Private Curzon Smith, you are a soldier in the Sixteenth Massachusetts Regiment, Second Brigade of the Fourth Division, of the Northern Continental Army of the United States of America. We keep our powder dry and our eyes open."

"Yessir."

What with meeting the others in the company and listening to the sergeant's rules, it was near supper by the time Eben and I were out of the earshot of others. We'd been ordered to go to the ammunition tent and roll gunpowder cartridges. I had more important business first.

I stepped off the path and motioned for Eben to follow me a few steps into the shelter of the trees.

"Where is it?" I asked.

"This?" He pulled my small leather bag from his haversack, but he did not offer it to me.

"Why did you hide it?" I asked.

"That Trumbull is what Aunt Patience calls a dirty character," he said. "But these are his spoons, aren't they? And the compass, too?"

I shook my head. "That belonged to the redcoat you shot, same as these boots."

"'Tain't right to steal, you know."

"I only took what Trumbull owed me," I said. "He hasn't paid me any wages."

Eben grunted. "So this wasn't really stealing."

"Not at all."

He handed me the bag. "I figgered it would be something like that. But don't let Uncle see the spoons. He can be peculiar when the mood strikes him."

"I'll remember that. Thank you."

We made our way back to the path. "You going to farm after the war?" Eben asked.

"Zounds, no!" I vowed. "I'm city born and bred."

"Why do you have seeds in your bag, then? And that lady's ribbon; who did that come from? Is she pretty? Is she waiting for you to come home from the war?"

I kicked at a rock on the path. "You are overly fond of asking questions, Ebenezer Woodruff."

"I know." He grinned. "Aunt Patience says it's one of my worst sins."

Before

Isabel wore the ribbon around her wrist.

She collected the seeds and kept them in a small bag made of waxed sailcloth. The seeds came from her home in Rhode Island, the garden behind the house she worked in New York, and a New Jersey field near last winter's army encampment.

We'd stayed near that camp and found work. Isabel repaired soldiers' clothes for a seamstress. I was hired on by a cussmouth blacksmith who paid me poorly to keep his forge burning.

We had started out as friends, Isabel and me, but grew to be more like brother and sister—mocking, arguing, and occasionally tormenting each other. I teased her about being a country bumpkin. She called me "Curse-on" because it irritated me and tried to get me to explain the meaning behind my name, which I refused to do, because of my father's advice. I did not like her to walk alone in the dark. She did not like me telling her what to do.

Everything changed one day in April when I told a funny story about the blacksmith that made her laugh. The sound of it and the sight of her smile caused my heart to gallop and my throat to close up so that I could not speak. I suddenly realized that I did not want her to regard me as a brother anymore.

Of course, I did not tell her that.

CHAPTER X

Wednesday, October 8–Friday, October 17, 1777

THIS DAY THE GREAT MR. BURGOYNE WITH HIS WHOLE ARMY SURRENDERED THEMSELVES AS PRISONERS OF WAR . . . THE GREATEST CONQUEST EVER KNOWN.
–JOURNAL OF NEW HAMPSHIRE MAJOR HENRY DEARBORN

IN THOSE FIRST DAYS I DID NOT REGRET enlisting. The army fed me regular. I had a blanket, boots, and a musket. Sleeping with five fellows in a small tent was a bit of a challenge on account of the snores and farts, but at least I was warm enough.

Most of the wagering around the campfire centered on how long the war would last. Eben thought we'd be free of duty by November. Others said Christmas. One fellow in our tent, a fusspot old tailor with watery eyes named Silvenus, said we'd be in service for years. He was not well liked.

Uncle Sergeant (I thought of him in that manner, tho' I was careful never to address him so) teamed me with Eben and posted us to the river guard to keep watch for any British boats. We saw snapping turtles, hawks, the paw prints of a large bear, and countless leaves swirl to the ground. The only redcoats we saw were deserters, approaching with their hands in the air.

The British were trapped and hungry. They had no supplies. They could not survive the march north to Canada. To the east lay the New Hampshire Grants, bristling with Patriots. To the west stretched wilderness and certain death. Our army waited in the south, ready to finish the job started on the battlefield.

More than a week after the battle General Burgoyne finally agreed to surrender. Messengers rode back and forth between the two camps (always with a white flag flying so's nobody would shoot at them), and arrangements were made so that the American army could accept all of Burgoyne's soldiers as prisoners.

Our days guarding the river ended. I bet the turtles were grateful.

The officers ordered all Continentals and militiamen to line both sides of the road for the official surrender. The day was cool and damp, with dark clouds to the north that Eben said were heavy with snow. He liked to pretend he knew all about the weather, so I figgered we were in for a stretch of sunshine.

While we waited, I piled stones next to my boots. I had a handful of acorns in my right pocket too. Eben asked vexing questions about my weapons, but I didn't answer. Eventually, he gave up and dove into a story about his mother's uncle's cow that gave birth to a calf with two heads. One was the head of a goat, the other a cat; a terrible omen, he said, that foretold the fire that burned the old man's barn and the fox that killed all his chickens.

I rolled my right boot back and forth over a stone that was as round as a wicket ball.

Near a year earlier I'd been with the American troops who were captured by the British at Fort Washington. They marched all two thousand of us down the Greenwich Road into New York City, where a crowd of lobsterbacks and Tories threw eggs and rotted garbage at us, screaming curses, foul names, and insults.

We had no firewood in the prison. No glass in the windows. They fed us spoiled meat and moldy biscuits, when they remembered to feed us at all. Within weeks, hundreds had died of the cold and pestilent fevers. If Isabel hadn't stolen me out of there, I'd be long dead too. (I gave my ear a hard tug to force all memories of Isabel into retreat.)

As the British marched by in defeat, I aimed to pay them back for their treatment of me. Pity that I'd not thought to bring a bucket of horse dung.

Distant drums began to beat. Our regimental drummers picked up the call and rattled their instruments like approaching thunder.

"Here they come!" someone hollered.

Our fifers burst into song, playing "Yankee Doodle" to insult our enemy. We all stood straight, muskets at our sides, forming a Patriot gauntlet stretching as far as the eye could see.

The lobsterbacks came first, their regimental flags fluttering weakly. Their arms swung freely, for they had surrendered their guns before this forced parade. Many of the arms were bandaged, the famous red coats torn in their flight through the wilderness. Their breeches were more mud-stain than white. Nearly every man had lost buttons from his coat.

I stuck my hand in my pocket and gripped a fat acorn. I would not throw the first one, for that would bring too much attention to myself. But as soon as the throwing started, I'd join in the fray with pleasure.

The British passed us, row by row by row. On the whole, they were shorter than we were, and mostly man-aged. Their uniforms, though dirty, made them look to be the proper army. They moved as one body with thousands of arms and legs.

We looked like what we were: an army of farmers and poor craftsmen. Some rebels were white-haired grandsires. We had boys younger than me with no hint of whiskers or manhood upon them. Our fellows of middle years came from New England, New Jersey, New York, Virginia, and Pennsylvania; fishermen, farmers, cobblers, preachers, schoolteachers, woodsmen, and every other job under the sun. We conversated and joked mostly in English, but some spoke in languages from over the ocean, and others in the speech of these mountains, for Oneida, Stockbridge, Tuscarora, and Narragansett warriors stood with us.

We wore all manner of shirts, waistcoats, breeches, and shoes, tho' some were barefooted. Looking down our lines, I saw every possible color of hair and eye (tho' some were missing an eye and others were bald-headed), as well as all colors of skin, from the darkest black of men born in Africa to the snow-white pallor of the Scotsmen, and all shades in betwixt the two. The appearance of our army recalled the variations of the trees and leaves in the forest behind us. Each soldier stood tall, each soul afire with pride.

But no one threw a thing. They didn't shout insults or mock our captives. Even Eben's mouth was closed.

"Why is no one jeering?" I whispered. "We should shame them."

"Uncle said we must give them honor," he said quietly. "This is the first time a British army has surrendered, ever."

I tightened my fist of acorns. They had not honored us in the prisons of New York. Was not the point of war to beat the enemy? To make them feel the pain of losing?

The drums and fifes ceased. Our ranks stood silent as walls of granite. The enemy continued to march, their boots shuffling along the dirt road. After the British came the Hessians, Germans who fought on the British side for money. Most of them wore green uniforms, some blue. All were filthy, but their curled mustachios were combed neat. After the Hessians came their women and a few children, and a handful of soldiers leading the animals that had become German pets: raccoons, fawns, and two bear cubs.

We stood for hours, all that afternoon, as our six thousand prisoners paraded between our lines in defeat. I did not understand why, but I chose the course of honor. I stood, shoulder to shoulder with the other Patriots, in a powerful silence.

When all the prisoners had marched down to the clearing where they would be guarded until they were escorted to Boston, I took myself down to the river. The turtles were all hiding, so I threw my weapons at the last of the sun on the water.

CHAPTER XI

Saturday, October 18–Saturday, November 15, 1777

WE MARCHD BEFOR DAY FROM THESE WOODS & TRAVELED ALL DAY IN THE STORME & THE WORST TRAVELING I EVER SAW—THE RHODES WAS MOSTLY CLAY WHICH WAS LIKE MORTER—WE TRAVELD TO A SMALL TOWN.
—1777 DIARY OF SERGEANT JOHN SMITH,
FIRST RHODE ISLAND REGIMENT

THE NEXT DAY WE QUICK-MARCHED forty miles south to Albany. Rather, my company marched and arrived dog-tired from the pace. On account of my worldly experience driving oxcarts for Trumbull, I drove the company's supply wagon. Earned myself a few splinters in my backside, but kept my boots dry and my spirits high.

The officers ordered us to build barricades and more barricades in our new camp. We had captured Burgoyne's men, but the main body of the British army, some thirty thousand soldiers, lay one hundred fifty miles away in the city of New York, a hornet's nest ready to explode. After the first week's work, the skies opened and we near drowned in cold and ceaseless rain. A burly lad named Greenlaw claimed he saw Noah sailing up the Hudson in his ark filled with animals. We had a heated argument in our tent about which would be a more lethal foe: twenty redcoats or two oliphants from an ark.

Rain, snow, hail, sleet; no matter what fell from the sky, we shoveled mud and hefted timbers and rocks. At day's end we looked like muddy ghouls rising up from the grave.

We made sport, of course. The mud formed itself nicely into balls that needed to be flung at the targets we set up—bits of planking shaped with an axe to resemble the tall hats worn by the lobsterbacks. Eben was determined to best me. He would need more practice than Albany could give him. Other fellows joined our competition a few times, which then turned into a great muddy battle. We armed ourselves with clods of dirt and hollered and hooted, reliving the Battle of Saratoga, only no one ever wanted to play the role of the British, so all was chaos.

The washerwomen ended our warfare. They marched to the captain and said they would quit if forced to clean the clothes of boys and men who had ruined their breeches and shirts in play.

Washerwomen were sour-headed and cheerless.

I finally sold my stolen bits of silver and pewter, along with the dead redcoat's papers and pencils, to a toothless man in a dark tavern. He cheated me on the price, but I had no choice, for our regiment had still not been paid. I bought a new red felt hat, a heavy blue jacket, and a dull knife. The few shillings that remained I spent on a bottle of ginger syrup and vinegar of squills that an herb-lady swore would preserve me from any putrid fevers.

I shared the remedy with the fellows in our tent: Eben; thick-necked Luke Greenlaw, who was an apprentice joiner with scarred hands; Hugh Faulkner, a stoop-shouldered son of a fisherman who liked to draw; the gloomy tailor, Silvenus; and Peter Brown, a farm boy said to be the fastest runner in the brigade. They had started out formal and cautious with me (excepting Ebenezer), for they had never lived side by side with anyone whose skin was not white. One night the cook served us beans and more beans for dinner. Instead of sleeping, we farted all night long, which caused us to choke, sputter, complain loudly, and laugh so hard, our sides were still sore two days later. After that, we were more like friends.

Uncle Sergeant commanded two score of privates—four tents' worth of us. The tent closest to us was home to a yellow-haired fellow whose enlistment ended before I ever learned his name; the Janack twins, who looked so much alike, it befuddled me when they stood next to each other; and two boisterous fellows, Aaron and Henry Barry, who were distant kin to Eben, but not, he said, from the good side of the family.

The last lad was John Burns. His rude manner declared him my enemy the first time he clapped eyes on me. Burns had white skin that turned red when he was angry (a frequent condition), dirt-colored hair that never stayed tied back in a queue, and small eyes like a badger's that were forever seeking a way to avoid work. He spat at my feet whenever I walked by. He accused me of stealing my new hat. He said the crudest kinds of things about my parents and grandparents, and he convinced the Barry brothers to join him in his foulness.

My father told me many times that a lot of white people have twisted hearts. "It prevents them from seeing the world properly," he'd say, "and turns them into tools of the

Devil." Father would have advised me to let God sort out the evil inside John Burns.

I couldn't wait that long. If I did not stand up to him, he would make my life a misery.

Our lieutenant had ordered that privates rotate the work of gathering firewood. Burns ducked his duty the first time it came round. The second time, the fire had near gone out and the fellows started up a hullabaloo.

"I told you, I can't," Burns moaned. "My arm is still poorly." He pointed at Eben. "Make the blunderhead fetch it."

Eben took his share of teasing on account of his trusting nature and tendency to talk, but he hated being called a blunderhead.

"Eben took his turn at dawn," I said loudly. "Get off your plaguey backside and do your duty."

A few fellows chuckled. Burns tossed a pebble into the dying flames and waited for silence.

"My arm hurts," he finally said. "Fetch the wood for me, you dirty negar."

I was on my feet and headed for him before anyone could grab hold of me. Burns stood up and stepped backward until he was flanked by Aaron and Henry.

"It's not just my arm," Burns sneered. "My feet are terrible cold. Give me your boots too."

"Leave off," called Greenlaw.

I calculated. Greenlaw might take my side in a fight, but then again, he might choose to stay out of it. I could probably beat Burns. He was a bit bigger than me, but I was faster and smarter. I would suffer mightily if all three of them joined in, but I had to make my stand now or forever be their target.

"You want these boots?" I asked. "Ten shillings and

they're yours. Ten shillings more and I won't piss in them first."

Burns stepped forward but did not raise his arm. He was afraid to fight, like most twisted-heart bullies. I would take him down hard and fast, before his friends hurt me too bad. If I succeeded, he'd trouble me no more.

"What is this foolishness?" The sergeant stepped between us.

Blast. Eben had gone running for help again. Had to cure him of that.

"Smith?" the sergeant asked. "Explain yourself."

"He ordered me to tend the fire, sir," I said. "I took my turn last night. Then he demanded I give him my boots."

The sergeant raised his hand to stop me from continuing. "What say you?" he asked Burns. "What right have you to take his boots or to force him to do your duty?"

"He doesn't belong here," Burns said with heat. "He has a ring in his ear like a sailor, but he doesn't talk like one. He is so cloaked in falsehood, I am certain he's a runaway slave, sir!"

The words were a blow to my gut. When my former master enlisted me in New York, he had promised me freedom for serving in the army. I had served that year and was thus free, but I had no papers to prove it, which could make trouble for me with some folk.

"He's not, you clodpate!" Eben argued.

"How do you know?" Burns asked. "Because he said he was free? Of course he did. They're worse than the Irish when it comes to lying. Where are his papers?"

A few voices in the shadows murmured agreement. My enemy was gaining strength. I had to attack.

"Private Burns makes a good argument, sir." I forced

an agreeable mask on my face. "Allow me to borrow it. He claims he was a tinsmith before the war, but he can't be much over eighteen. I wager he's still indentured to his master; could have another two or three years till his time is up. He's the runaway, sir, unless he has papers proving different."

"Enough!" The sergeant pulled off his cap, ran his hand over his pate, and set the cap back in place. "None of you are free men because you are in the army, and I do have papers that prove that. Now stop jabbering at each other and fetch the blasted wood. All of you!"

That night was the start of John Burns's open campaign against me. He became the best bootlicker ever was, waiting close to the sergeant's elbow for the chance to be of service or to whisper poisonous notions about me, or Greenlaw, or the other fellows who were not in his favor. Half the time the sergeant did not listen, but half the time he did.

When we marched south out of Albany, the muckworm named Burns was driving the supply wagon. I marched in the last line of our company and had to be quick-footed to avoid the droppings left by the horses.

CHAPTER XII

Sunday, November 16–Sunday, December 7, 1777

IT WOULD BE USELESS FOR US TO DENOUNCE
THE SERVITUDE TO WHICH THE PARLIAMENT OF GREAT
BRITAIN WISHES TO REDUCE US, WHILE WE CONTINUE
TO KEEP OUR FELLOW CREATURES IN SLAVERY JUST
BECAUSE THEIR COLOR IS DIFFERENT FROM OURS.
—SIGNER OF THE DECLARATION OF INDEPENDENCE
DR. BENJAMIN RUSH, WHO PURCHASED WILLIAM GRUBBER
IN 1776 AND DID NOT FREE HIM UNTIL 1794

OUR PATH TOOK US TO KINGSTON, THE new capital city of the state of New York. Rather, what was left of Kingston after the British burned it. We joined the companies cleaning out the ruin of the barracks building, dragging out half-burnt timbers and shoveling broken bits of furniture, walls, and ceilings.

I tried to keep my distance from John Burns. The sergeant assigned us to different work parties, which helped, but Burns was intent on spreading his mischief. False stories about my past surfaced, and fewer fellows cared to talk to me or sit near me when we stopped work for a mug of spruce beer and bread. Eben stayed a true friend, and a few others, but the poison from John Burns's twisted heart was spreading.

The company added a new soldier in Kingston, one Benjamin Edwards, who hardly looked old enough to be a drummer boy, tho' he swore to be fifteen. He was a bookish lad with a face much pitted from the smallpox, and he knew many stories from ancient times that he delighted in telling around the fire. John Burns disliked Edwards instantly. I could not figure why. Edwards was every bit as white as Burns, and he was polite and funny, if you took the time to listen to him. But Burns found something offensive about the new lad and teased him without mercy. I made a point of extending friendship to Edwards.

Sleep came hard in Kingston. I'd often crawl out of the tent and watch the stars pass overhead. One night the northern lights blazed a brilliant blue and ferocious green, the colors of my compass card, with the stars pointing arrows in all directions across the sky.

On our third Sunday there, we were preached at by a minister who blamed the ruin of the city on our sinful souls. That did not sit well with us, but we had to listen to the whole sermon. If we'd walked out, the captain could have ordered a flogging. After church we'd been given a half day free. Most of the fellows went off to search for treasure in the rubble of the ruined houses. Anything worthwhile had been sifted out long before we arrived, so I convinced Eben we should stay by the fire and dry out our damp blankets and coats.

Sergeant Woodruff found us there and handed Eben a folded paper. "This came from New Jersey for the captain," he ordered. "He's dining at the Hardenburgh house, out the toll road."

I looked at Eben and he looked at me, and that gap-toothed grin cracked open, 'cause we had the same thought. Colonel Hardenburgh was said to be the richest man in the county. There was sure to be plenty of leftover grub from his dinner table. We were sick to death of boiled beans and pork fat.

"Can Curzon go with me?" Eben asked.

The sergeant hesitated.

"Am I required here, sir?" I asked.

"No, the day is your own." He pulled off his cap and rubbed his head. "Colonel Hardenburgh heads up the militia here; Dutch folks mostly. They're different from us in Massachusetts, understand?"

"Yessir," we said.

"Strange bunch of bumpkins," the sergeant warned, putting his cap on again. "Let Eben do the talking. Do you grasp my meaning, Smith?"

No. He was talking in riddles.

"Of course, sir," I said.

Colonel Hardenburgh's house was big enough for four families, with two proper barns behind it and carefully tended fields stretching in every direction. The militia had pitched their tents around the house. A couple dozen of them stood about smoking pipes and enjoying the sun. A few held wooden plates with the remains of their Sunday dinner.

"Do you think we're too late for the grub?" I asked.

"Maybe there's a friendly lass in the kitchen who can help us," Eben answered. "I'll find the captain and meet you in the back."

He went to the door whilst I wove my way through the

crowd. The talk was a mix of English and Dutch. What I could understand was all war news; more British ships were crossing the ocean, more Hessians being hired to kill us. One man claimed the Spanish were about to invade us from Florida.

I hurried on.

The food had been served behind the house near the kitchen door, where a long board rested across three barrels. Crumbs and broken bits of corn bread littered one end of the board; the rest was covered with dirty trenchers and bowls. An empty soup pot stood on the ground. But there—on the seat of a chair—sat three fat slices of apple pie waiting for the right lad to come along.

The kitchen door opened. A short, round-cheeked black woman came down the steps, her hair covered with a dark blue cloth, her sleeves rolled up and apron greasy from serving. She was not old enough to be my mother, but older than a sister would be. She smiled warmly at me and said something in the Dutch to a person still in the kitchen. The door opened again, and out came the tallest man I'd ever seen, carrying two kettles of steaming water. He set one on the board and poured the second into the empty soup pot. Then he kissed the woman on her forehead, and I knew he must be her husband.

I nodded politely. "Good day."

The woman chuckled. *"Wat wil je, jij blaag?"*

"Pardon me?"

"Je wilt taart, of niet? Je meester voedt je niet erg goed als ik zo naar je kijk."

"I'm sorry, but I don't understand, ma'am."

"She has no English," the tall man said. "I do. I am Baumfree. *Min vrouw*, she is Bett. You?"

"I am Curzon," I said. "Pleased to meet you, sir, and your lady." I bowed.

"Het is me een genoegen je te ontmoeten."

That sounded friendly enough. "May I . . . can I . . . ?" I pointed to the pie and made a motion showing I wanted to eat it.

The woman shook her head and spoke quickly.

"For sojurs," the man translated. "No you. No me. No Bett."

I struggled to figger his meaning.

"Sojurs," he repeated.

"I am a soldier." I patted my chest. "Me. Soldier." I played at aiming a musket and firing it. "Pachooo!"

"You?" The man frowned. "Sojur?"

A barrel-bellied old white man with a well-coiffed wig, a red silk waistcoat, and a lace neck cloth stepped carefully down the steps, leaning on his cane and wincing. When he saw me, he spoke loud and fast Dutch to Baumfree. The tall man shook his head and answered in a soft voice. Bett watched the exchange, her face wary.

The old fellow pointed his cane at me. "My man here says you're pretending to be a soldier." His English was clear but spiced with a Dutch flavor. "Tell your master it's up to him to feed you, not me!"

And then I knew. Colonel Hardenburgh owned Baumfree and he owned Bett. He thought me a slave too, for my skin was as dark as theirs.

Eben came around the corner, whistling.

"Any luck?" he asked me.

"Your boy claims he's a soldier," Hardenburgh said. "Take him away from here."

"Sir?" Eben asked.

Hardenburgh's face flushed. "I won't have him stirring up my negars." He turned his back to us and spat out angry Dutch at Baumfree and Bett.

Baumfree tried to get in a word, an explanation, mayhaps, but the colonel cut him off.

"With respect, sir, you are in error," Eben tried again.

"Hush." I grabbed Eben's elbow. "We have to go."

"No." He shook me off. "I'll explain and then we'll get that pie. We deserve it after the miles we walked."

"A pox on the pie," I said.

The colonel's face grew redder and redder as he yelled. Bett glanced at me quickly, then plunged the dirty plates into the kettle of water. Baumfree stood still as a tree, but his clenched jaw gave him away. He was thinking of how to revenge himself on Hardenburgh. For each thought of revenge, he'd have another of fear, for if he lashed out, his master could make him and Bett suffer.

So he could do nothing.

Neither could I, which shamed me and kindled my rage in the same breath. I turned on my heel and stalked away.

"Hey!" Eben called. "Ho there! Wait!"

I fought through the crowd of militia, bumping into as many men as I could without begging pardon, hoping to goad some lout into fighting me so that I could hit and hit and draw blood to silence the thunder in my head.

They just stepped to the side and continued conversating, pipe smoking, laughing.

At the road I broke into a slow run. Eben didn't catch up to me for more than a mile, when I stopped at the crossroads.

"What was all that about?" He bent over, hands on his knees, and panted like an overworked ox. "The captain told me flat out we could have pie, and there you go insulting the colonel and knocking through the militia like they're the enemy. Have your wits cracked?"

"Leave me alone." I walked away.

The fool followed me. "Were you rude to the colonel's cook? Uncle says womenfolk need polite and proper handling, all of them. A man who treats a lady low–"

"I don't want to talk about this," I said harshly.

He walked so close, his clumsy feet near stepped on mine. "That old colonel looked ready to give you what-for. You better not have any of his spoons in your boots. I covered for you once, but I can't do it again. Uncle Caleb has been prickly of late and he'll think I had a hand in your thievery, and–"

"Don't you ever shut up?" I wheeled around to face him in the middle of the road. "I was not flirting with the cook. That plaguey lump of a colonel assumed I was a slave and chased me off the way he'd chase off a dog."

Eben stopped walking and frowned. "Why didn't you just explain–"

"Don't be stupid. He's not the type to listen to black people. That dastard thinks I am no better than his goat."

"Surely that was not his intention."

"Of course it was his intention. It's why Burns is after me, why your plaguey uncle gives me the worst duties. Half the fellows in our company don't think I belong there."

"I do." Eben shuffled his boot back and forth over a wheel rut in the road.

The hurt in his eyes stopped me. He had been kind to me, in his jabber-mouthed way. But how deep did his kindness go? How much could I trust him?

"Let me ask you something. We're fighting for freedom,

right?" I picked my words carefully. "So why is that man allowed to own Baumfree and Bett?"

"Well," he said slowly, "we're fighting for our freedom. Not theirs." He crossed his arms, uncrossed them, put his hands on his belt and crossed his arms again. "Nobody in my family owns slaves, you know."

"That is not the point. Do you think only white people can be free?"

"Of course not. There are plenty of free blacks, like you and those other fellows in Saratoga and Albany. We had a family two villages over from mine, they were all free black people."

"But the colonel's slaves are not allowed to be free."

He frowned. "They can't be free, Curzon. They're slaves. Their master decides for them."

"What if they ran away?"

"Then they'd be breaking the law."

"Bad laws deserve to be broken."

"Don't talk like that!" He kicked a rock deep into the field. "You want to get in trouble? Laws have to be followed or else you go to the jail."

"What if a king made bad laws; laws so unnatural that a country broke them by declaring its freedom?"

He threw his arms in the air. "Now you are spouting nonsense. Two slaves running away from their rightful master is not the same as America wanting to be free of England. Not the same at all."

"How is it then that the British offer freedom to escaped slaves, but the Patriots don't?"

"How am I supposed to know that?"

The wind had come up whilst we argued. Before Eben could say anything else, it blew the hat from his head. He chased it down the road and returned gripping it tightly.

I almost told him then; told him that I and my parents and my grandparents had all been born into bondage, that my great-grandparents had been kidnapped from their homes and forced into slavery while his great-grandparents decided which crops to plant and what to name their new cow. I wanted to tell him to convince him how wrongheaded he was.

"If you were that tall fellow back there," I asked, "wouldn't you want to be free to live your own life?"

"I don't like talking about this," he said. "But since you ask, no. If I were that fellow, I'd be happy for the food and clothes and good care my master gave me. I would know that God wanted me to be in bondage and I would not question His will."

The wind blew down the narrow strip of dirt between us, sending dust into the air and giving me the answer I needed.

"You're not my friend," I said.

CHAPTER XIII

Monday, December 8–Sunday, December 21, 1777

LIBERTY IS EQUALLY AS PRECIOUS TO A BLACK MAN,
AS IT IS TO A WHITE ONE, AND BONDAGE EQUALLY AS
INTOLERABLE TO THE ONE AS IT IS TO THE OTHER. . . .
AN AFRICAN, OR A NEGRO MAY JUSTLY CHALLENGE,
AND HAS AN UNDENIABLE RIGHT TO HIS LIBERTY:
CONSEQUENTLY, THE PRACTISE OF SLAVE-KEEPING,
WHICH SO MUCH ABOUNDS IN THIS LAND IS ILLICT.
–ESSAY WRITTEN BY AFRICAN AMERICAN LEMUEL HAYNES,
VETERAN OF THE BATTLE OF LEXINGTON

EBEN STOPPED SPEAKING TO ME AFTER that. I welcomed the silence.

John Burns saw the coldness between us and befriended Eben, pouring out hollow compliments and listening with false attention to stories of Aunt Patience and two-headed calves.

It mattered not to me. I worked. Slept. Ate. Cleaned my gun. Worked. Slept. Ate. Cleaned my gun.

The other fellows fell into a pattern of card-playing and dice after supper. Greenlaw invited me to join in, but my peevish mood was not suitable for games. I sat close to the light of the fire and tried to carve a bird from a piece of pine. Good thing Isabel wasn't around to see it; she would have mocked me endlessly on account of my carving looked more like a beaked pig than a bird.

It was harder than ever to soldier my thoughts about her. My mind would run off without leave and I'd find myself wondering if she had a warm place for the winter. Mayhaps she had made it to Charleston after all and wouldn't have to worry about the snow.

I jabbed the point of my knife into the meat of my thumb to remind myself that idle speculation about the girl who hated me was foolish.

We were soon ordered to move south again, marching and then marching some more, ten or fifteen miles a day. Sergeant showed us on a map that our path was as straight as a musket barrel. That map was useless. It did not show the mountains we had to climb, nor the treacherous mud that stopped the wagons, nor the empty miles of fields and trees we passed, ever nervous that British or Loyalists waited to ambush us at the next curve of the road. We passed three score of tidy villages flanked with farms and filled with generous folk who let us sleep in their barns and fed us as best they could. Do you think any of those villages were marked on that map? Sergeant said no, they weren't.

Seemed to me that mapmaking was a profession for addlepates.

We paused at a small camp in Jersey so the captains could confer with other captains about the state of the war and gossip about General Washington. Despite the near-freezing air, I stripped off my shirt and stockings and washed them with lye soap and hot water in the hopes of drowning all of the vermin that had begun to live in them. My clothes were still damp when we were ordered to march again, this time west into Pennsylvania. For all the talk of battles and gunfire, soldiering was mostly about blistered feet and itchy clothes.

We were on our way to join the main body of the army outside Philadelphia. The British had chased the Congress out of that city whilst we were busy in Saratoga and had settled in there for the winter. Our army was camped a short distance away, where it would stay until spring, for gentlemen did not like to fight in cold weather. We thought this was a foolhardy notion. We wanted to beat the British, take back Philadelphia, and end the war. Brown, the fast-running lad, had developed a wicked cough from sleeping in damp fields. He said such rude things about our lazy, lily-livered generals that Greenlaw cuffed him on the head.

The morn of our departure I saw a crow fall from the sky. Eben saw it too and shot me a worried glance, for it was an omen of disaster. I opened my haversack and pulled out my small tin box, which held the last of the salt from my rations. I pinched it in my fingers and threw it over my left shoulder to ward off the bad luck.

"Should have gone over the right shoulder," Eben said.

I did not answer him.

We stopped at Newtown in Pennsylvania and took on a wagon filled with heavy barrels of salted beef bought for the army. The roads were little more than rivers of mud, and the wagons got stuck over and over again, making us late by several days.

We arrived at the Gulph, the spot of the winter encampment, as the rain turned into falling bits of ice. There was no army to be seen, just a vast field of mud around a small stone house.

Captain Stanwell ordered the Eighth Company to take

their muskets and stand guard, then he went into the house with his sergeants. Our company stood upwind of the wagons, for the barrels had begun to stink. We blew on our hands, rubbed our arms, and stomped our feet to keep warm. Bits of ice bounced from the brims of our hats.

"They brung us to the wrong place," said Silvenus. "We're gonna march all winter and then the British will shoot us dead."

Brown coughed and muttered in agreement.

"No," Greenlaw said firmly. "Look at the boot prints in the mud, the remains of fire pits." He pointed behind us. "You can even see where the tent pegs were driven in the ground. They were here."

"They ain't here now," Burns snarled.

"Here comes the sergeant," said one of the Janacks.

Captain Stanwell and his officers walked out of the house as the falling ice turned to thick flakes of snow. The captain mounted his horse and started down the road that led west as companies scrambled to follow him.

Sergeant Woodruff hurried toward us, leapt into the wagon, and picked up the reins.

"What did you learn, Uncle?" Eben asked. "Where are we going?"

"The army moved to a new camp. If we make haste, we might reach it by nightfall." He turned up his collar. "Captain says it's in a more secure location. Let's hope he's right."

"Where is it, sir?" I asked.

"Valley Forge."

Part II

CHAPTER XIV

Sunday, December 21, 1777

WHAT THEN IS TO BECOME OF THE ARMY THIS WINTER?
—GEORGE WASHINGTON, WRITING FROM VALLEY FORGE
TO CONTINENTAL CONGRESS PRESIDENT HENRY LAURENS

I WHISTLED AS WE TRUDGED ALONG the muddy road.

Yes, I was hungry, footsore, tired, and cold. But it mattered not, for we were a few hours away from the winter encampment.

"How can you be in such good humor?" Greenlaw asked.

Eben, walking a few paces ahead alongside his distant cousins and Burns, glanced back, but he quickly turned around when I stared at him. We had been avoiding each other since Kingston.

"I was in Morristown last winter," I said. (This was truth.) "With the army." (A half-truth.) "We had a grand time." (Falsehood.)

"Did you have parties?" Benjamin Edwards asked. "With ladies who liked to dance and drink punch?"

This caused much hooting and laughter and shoving of poor Edwards's form. He protested loudly until we stopped.

"No dancing or punch, but we had regular rations," I said once we were again under way. "And there was plenty of firewood. And a commissary with fresh clothes and blankets." (All true, tho' Isabel and I partook of none of it as we had no proper ties to the army.)

Everyone groaned with pleasure at the notion. Our blankets had been worn bare since Saratoga and our clothes had not fared better. I wore the shirt I stole off the redcoat; my own shirt had been reduced to the rags that I wore around my hands and neck. Eben's only shirt had barely survived the washerwomen of Albany. Luke Greenlaw hadn't worn stockings for weeks and his coat was worn through at both elbows. Both of the Janack twins wrapped scarves over their heads on cold mornings, for their hats had been stolen one night in an Albany tavern. The shoes of old man Silvenus were made more of dirt than leather. He felt it necessary to remind us of this every day.

We were a filthy pack of tatterdemalions.

Greenlaw picked a bug crawling along his sleeve. "I can't figure how the officers are going to fill our hours. Won't be any fighting. General Washington might as well send us home till spring. We could come back after Easter, thrash the British, and return home in time to plant the corn."

"Ha!" exclaimed Silvenus. "His Excellency is no fool. He'll keep us busy a'marching and a'drilling because if we left for home, he might never see us again."

"The fellows at Morristown kept busy," I said. "They made musketballs, repaired guns, rolled cartridges; they had more to do than hours to do it in."

"What was your role?" asked Greenlaw. "Adviser to General Washington on the proper method of stone throwing?"

I waited for the laughter to die down. I had, in fact, once served General Washington a dinner of steak and kidney pie at my master's house in New York. But they would never believe that.

"I worked with a blacksmith," I said, which was both true and believable. "Warmest job in the entire camp. I'll wager you right now I'll get to do it again. Blacksmiths don't want clumsy oafs helping them in the forge. They need skilled chaps like me."

I stumbled upon a new thought and near tripped over a rut in the road. In Morristown some of the officers had hired privates to be their manservants for the winter. I was well suited to the task, and it would be less work and more comfort than working the bellows and breathing charcoal fumes at a blacksmith's. Once I got my bearings in Valley Forge, I'd make inquiries.

"I have no use for poxy blacksmiths or generals' advisers," grumbled Silvenus. "I need a cobbler before my shoes lie down and die."

"I'd be content with a cook," Greenlaw said.

The sun was in the west by the time we made our way up the winding road to the encampment. We passed by a first, then a second set of guards and were directed to a road that branched away from the river. All of us had fallen quiet. The sunset burned red, a coal buried deep in ash.

Darkness fell a mile later. We passed campfires ringed by tired-looking fellows warming their hands, tents pitched like sagging ghosts behind them. There was little talk. No laughter. On the far side of a muddy field stood a collection of large marquee tents fashioned for high-ranking officers, with room for proper furniture like beds and tables and chairs. Shadows moved inside them.

We removed our muskets, tents, and cook kettles from the wagon, then watched as the sergeant drove it into the darkness, taking with him Burns and Eben to help with the unloading of the beef barrels. He'd told us to wait whilst the captain reported to the general's staff.

The first stars shone overhead.

"Thought you said there'd be food," Greenlaw groused at me.

"The sergeant will bring back our rations," I said, still pretending to be an authority on winter encampments.

We fell quiet enough to hear the voices in the officers' tents, as well as loud voices in the distance. Then Sergeant Woodruff and another Massachusetts officer ran past us without a word, straight to the tent that the captain had entered.

"That don't bode well," muttered Silvenus.

Shadows in the tent rushed to and fro like puppets on a stage, and then there came all manner of shouting and foul explosions of language.

"What are they carrying on about?" Silvenus asked.

The sergeants burst out of the tent, putting an end to our palaver.

"Follow me," spat Sergeant Woodruff. "Not a word."

We tripped our way across a flat field in the darkness until we neared campfires bright enough to show a long line of cannons. The air smelled of burning wood, but not of roasting meat or bread. The fellows round their fires were uncommonly quiet.

Sergeant Woodruff halted. "Gather round," he said low.

We formed a circle around him. Eben and Burns had caught up with us but stood a few paces away.

"The blasted meat is spoilt," the sergeant said. "Every bite of it."

A few fellows groaned.

Sergeant Woodruff dropped his voice to a whisper. "The brine didn't have enough salt in it. Likely a British trick; they've been paying merchants to sell us spoiled goods, according to the officers. Some flour is due to arrive from Reading in the morning. That will tide us over."

Greenlaw could not keep quiet. "We haven't eaten all day, sir!"

The sergeant raised his hands in warning. "Most of the soldiers here haven't eaten for two days."

"I smelled food by the officers' tents," Greenlaw protested. "Surely they should share it."

The sergeant pointed at him. "That is the last word out of you on that subject, Private Greenlaw. Officers get fed first and best; that's the way of the army, and you shall not question it."

Greenlaw breathed hard but bit back his reply.

"Most of the Sixteenth Massachusetts will be sent to forage tomorrow. Our company has been attached to Fourth New Hampshire. We'll camp with them in the morning. Tonight you'll pitch your tents near those"—he pointed toward the shadows beyond the firelight—"with the artillery."

"Uncle," Eben asked softly, "wouldn't it be better to find the New Hampshire barracks tonight?"

"There are no barracks." The sergeant rubbed the back of his neck. "Not yet. His Excellency General Washington has ordered the army to manufacture a city of logs. Each squad is building themselves a cabin. Only he calls them 'huts,' the way they do in Virginia."

"Where do we sleep until the hut is finished?" Silvenus asked.

"In your tents," the sergeant answered bluntly. "Which you will now pitch."

"This is madness," Burns muttered.

Much as I loathed him, I agreed.

We fumbled with stiff fingers to put up the tents in the dark, but it was impossible. At last we laid the canvas on the ground and laid ourselves upon it. I was forced to sleep at the edge, with one side next to Eben and the other exposed to the night air. I wiggled until my back no longer touched his, then pulled up my collar, pulled down my hat, and tried to warm myself with thoughts of blazing bonfires and buckets of hot tea. Brown coughed without cease until Silvenus cursed at him. After that, he coughed with his face buried in his arms. Above his cough, I heard owls, the wind, and a chant echoing from campfire to campfire: "No meat!"

Thousands of hungry soldiers took up the cry. "No meat! No meat! No meat! No meat!"

CHAPTER XV

Monday, December 22, 1777

THREE DAYS SUCCESSIVELY, WE HAVE BEEN DESTITUTE OF BREAD. TWO DAYS WE HAVE BEEN INTIRELY WITHOUT MEAT. . . . THE MEN MUST BE SUPPLIED, OR THEY CANNOT BE COMMANDED.
—RHODE ISLAND GENERAL JAMES VARNUM'S REPORT TO GEORGE WASHINGTON IN THE EARLY DAYS OF VALLEY FORGE

WE WOKE TO THE SOUND OF CRASHING drums, the brigade's drummer boys pounding out the reveille five paces from where we lay.

"Get up! Rise! Rise!" shouted officers far and near.

We were all dusted with frost like loaves of bread sprinkled with flour. One by one, we sat up and struggled to our feet. Greenlaw and Faulkner stumbled off in search of privy holes. Peter Brown rolled to the middle of the damp canvas, curled on his side, and coughed without cease.

Eben sat rubbing his hands together. "I'm a brick of ice."

"Your mouth isn't froze shut," Silvenus said.

I walked briskly to and fro, slapping my hands against my arms to warm my blood. Eben said nothing to me, but he followed my example.

After more officer shouts and drum calls, we marched

to the large, muddy field we'd crossed the night before, aswarm now with thousands of ill-dressed soldiers, even more drummer boys, a few fife players, and officers trying to turn the maelstrom into something orderly.

"This is called the Grand Parade," explained Sergeant Woodruff.

'Twas neither grand nor a parade, but I kept that notion to myself.

The sergeant looked down our line. "Where's Brown?"

"He didn't get up," called Faulkner.

The sergeant sighed and pointed to the Janack twins. "Go back. If he's that poorly, take him to the hospital tent."

"What if he's dead?" asked one.

"He is not permitted to be dead!" snapped the sergeant. "The rest of you, shut yer gawps and stand proper."

I'd never stood roll in such a large and bedraggled company. Ancient blankets were wrapped round the shoulders of a lucky few. Many more stood in torn shirts with neither waistcoat nor greatcoat to keep out the cold. The sight of soldiers standing barefooted in the snow gave me a right shock. My own toes, warm and dry in my British boots, curled in horror. I blew on my stiff fingers and stuck them in my armpits to warm them up. How many days could a fellow go shoeless in the snow before the cold killed his toes and the doctors had to cut them off?

Sergeant Woodruff took our company's report—fourteen present, two present but unable to appear at roll, and four sick—to a lieutenant. He returned holding a cloth bag close to his chest. I studied it hard. A small side of bacon might fit in a bag such as that. A collection of biscuits would too, or bread, or cheese. Eggs. No, not eggs. They'd be long broken, or served to the highest-ranking officers. But it might contain oats. Or dried beans or peas. Mayhaps gingercake.

My belly rumbled.

After collecting the regiments' reports, an officer in a blue coat delivered a long paper to the officer of the day, who stood at the front of us all. He glanced at it, then shouted out orders from General Washington. Any soldier who fired his musket without permission would suffer twenty lashes on his back immediately. Major General Sullivan was going to build a bridge over the river. Each hut would soon be issued one pail for carrying water from the creek.

Finally, he nodded to the drummer standing to his left. The boy beat his sticks crisply as a woman wearing a muddy skirt, a man's greatcoat, and oversized shoes was led to the front. The way she held her head high reminded me of Isabel.

The officer shouted that this washerwoman from Virginia was being drummed out of the camp for stealing food. No one in the camp was allowed to help the woman, and if she was seen in the camp again, she would be arrested. She started shouting so loud, we could not hear the fellow's last words. The washerwoman was led away, screeching like a scalded cat, by two tall fellows carrying muskets.

"But it's wintertime," Eben protested as we walked off the field. "'Tain't right! Where will she go?"

"Hush, boy," scolded his uncle. "The general has to keep discipline. It's none of our concern. Besides"–he hefted the cloth bag–"it's time for grub."

CHAPTER XVI

Monday, December 22, 1777

"WHAT HAVE YOU FOR YOUR DINNER, BOYS?"
"NOTHING BUT FIRE CAKE AND WATER, SIR."
". . . WHAT IS YOUR SUPPER, LADS?"
"FIRE CAKE AND WATER, SIR."
–DIARY OF DR. ALBIGENCE WALDO,
SURGEON, FIRST CONNECTICUT REGIMENT,
VALLEY FORGE

THE CLOTH BAG HELD ONLY COARSE-ground flour.

"A pox on all the generals in the world," swore Silvenus after the sergeant left us. "We've got to make firecake."

"What's that?" asked Eben.

Silvenus swore violently. I cannot tell you the words he used out of respect for your tender ears.

"You two"–he pointed at Aaron and Henry–"fetch us water from that creek yonder. The rest of you build the fire higher and then find me rocks the size of your hand or bigger. I'll borrow a cook pot from somewhere."

We were all dazed with hunger and lack of sleep and did as he demanded without question. Once the rocks were gathered, Silvenus picked out the flattest and made us rinse them in the creek before he set them right on the coals of the fire.

With all of the elements in place, the cooking began.

Silvenus slowly poured our flour into the pot of muddy water, stopping every now and then to stir the concoction with a bayonet blade until it was thick as stonemason's mortar. Then Greenlaw, who had the longest arms of us all, wrapped his hand in some rags to shield it from the heat and spread the dough onto the stones with the blade. We crouched around the fire, wordless. The dough hissed and sputtered. One of the rocks exploded, sending a piece of firecake into the heart of the flames.

Fellows from the artillery units gathered behind us.

"We had firecake three times yesterday," one said. "Best eat when they're hot enough to burn your tongue. That way, you don't taste so much."

I'd expected to smell bread, for bread was little more than flour and water. Instead, the firecakes gave off a scorched smell, like damp charcoal. The thinnest of the smears caught fire right atop the rock.

"Must be they're ready," Silvenus said.

Greenlaw wrapped his hand again and chiseled each piece free, then scooped them from the rock and laid them atop his haversack spread on the ground. Smoke rose from the charred edges.

"Who's first?" Silvenus asked.

A few fellows shook their heads and stepped backward.

"I'll take a piece," I said.

"Good lad." Silvenus broke a piece of firecake in two pieces, handed one to me, and bit into the other.

I did the same.

"What's it taste like?" asked Greenlaw.

"Ashes and dirt." I gnawed the hot splinters. "It's hard enough to break rat's teeth."

Silvenus held up another piece. "Are ye real soldiers, or boys who just want to march in the sunshine? Eat this to find out. Who's next?"

"Not me," Burns said. "I'm off to find something better."

After he left, Henry stepped up, then Greenlaw, and one by one, the rest joined in.

CHAPTER XVII

Monday, December 22, 1777

WE HAVE ONE DULL AX TO BUILD A LOGG HUTT.
WHEN IT WILL BE DONE KNOWS NOT.
—SEVENTH CONNECTICUT REGIMENT SURGEON'S
MATE JONATHAN TODD, LETTER
TO HIS FATHER FROM VALLEY FORGE

AFTER WE ATE (IF CHEWING ON BURNT firecake can properly be called eating), the sergeant led us up the long slope to the Outer Line, a mile-long ridge cluttered with thousands of soldiers trying to make a camp out of logs, mud, and air.

"Philadelphia lies eighteen miles that way." The sergeant pointed south. "Now turn around."

We stood with our backs to the distant enemy, looking down the hill we'd just climbed. As far as the eye could see along the slope, and across the level ground at the bottom, soldiers were dragging tree trunks, chopping logs, stripping bark, and trying to form up walls of the wood. It made me think of a swarm of ants hurry-scurrying to build a nest before a storm hits.

"I'll explain the features of the camp, so you don't get lost. This ridge is the long side of a triangle." He stuck his arms out, elbows crooked, fingertips touching. "My left arm is the west border. A few generals have occupied farmhouses at about my elbow. The first hill is Mount Joy. The larger one behind it is called Mount Misery. The creek runs where my hands are. It's a long walk, so you best not waste any water."

He paused while four men harnessed together like horses dragged a massive tree trunk past us.

"My right arm is the Schuylkill River," he continued. "You can get water there, too, but it's a bit farther. The river also protects the house taken over for headquarters, which is"–he studied his arms–"below my right wrist. The Life Guard will camp there to protect His Excellency. Artisan shops are being set up there too."

He dropped his arms with a sigh. "If you get lost, ask for help."

"How many soldiers are here, Uncle?" Ebenezer asked.

"The ensign said ten thousand, the major said twelve thousand. But all that I care about are those of you in my company." He paced out a four-sided figure in the snow. "General Washington's orders are detailed," he said as he walked. "The hut you will build must be sixteen feet on the long sides and fourteen feet on the short. The door must face south, toward the enemy. Put the chimney at the north end."

Greenlaw raised his hand to interrupt. "How deep down do you want us to dig?"

"No digging. Huts are to be aboveground. No windows, either; we need to keep out the cold air, not invite it in. The builders of the first completed hut will win a twelve-dollar reward."

"Twelve dollars!" Burns exclaimed.

"Why can't we dig down, sir?" I asked.

"Because His Excellency General George Washington does not want us to. Greenlaw, you were a joiner before the army, correct?"

"Built cabinets mostly," the big fellow said, "but wood is wood."

"Then you're in charge of building." He pointed to the axe and three shovels lying at his feet. "These are your tools."

"Surely not, sir," Greenlaw said. "We need half a dozen axes, plus adzes and froes, and a small cask of nails."

"Ah." The sergeant took off his cap, a bad portent. "More tools are coming, but orders are to build without nails, for there are none to be had, and the blacksmiths cannot be spared from repairing wagons and guns. You are to groove the logs down the middle and notch the ends to keep them joined."

The enormity of our task hit home. We had to chop down trees and build our own shelter with little equipment and less training. In the snow. Whilst hungry.

"Beg pardon, sir," I said. "We're better armed with shovels than axes. Shouldn't we try to dig the floor down into the earth? That way, we won't have to cut and haul as many trees."

"He's right," Greenlaw said.

The sergeant looked around, worried, perhaps, that other officers would overhear his privates arguing with him. "It's forbidden," he said. "No digging—the orders were clear. You'll only have to fill it back in if caught."

A shout went up at the hut site neighboring ours. A half dozen fellows lifted a sixteen-foot log, their arms shaking, and struggled to place it atop the wall that stood as high as their shoulders. The notches cut in the ends did not fit together and the log could not settle into place. They shouted a second time and leapt back as the log rolled off the wall and near crushed their feet.

Watching this, Sergeant Woodruff winced, then sighed heavily and handed me a shovel. "All right then, dig out the floor. But if I am reprimanded, you'll share the pain of my punishment." He gave the other two shovels to the Janack twins. "You two dig us a privy trench behind the hut. Make it long enough that more than one can use it at a time."

Greenlaw picked up the axe. "Does it matter which trees we take?"

The sergeant pointed to the closest hill. "We've been assigned to cut from the woods at the top of Mount Joy. Take Eben with you; one can rest while the other chops. The rest of you need to gather us a goodly store of firewood. Make up a fire for some heat and get the tents properly raised. And, Burns, run to the regiment headquarters where those flags are and inquire about the use of a grindstone."

John Burns grinned and touched his fingers to the brim of his cap. "Right away, sir."

"Uncle, if I may," Eben said as the sergeant turned to leave.

"What now, Ebenezer?"

"How can we work without food?"

"I don't know, lad." The sergeant's voice went tight, and he paused to clear his throat. "We must try our best."

I figgered it would take a day or so to dig the floor down as deep as my hips. I was wrong. By midday I'd only managed to carve a line in the earth that was the length of one wall, the width of the blade of my shovel, and as deep as my ankle. My thoughts switched back and forth as I dug, planning one moment to secure a position in a forge and the next thinking I ought make myself useful near the officers' tents so one would hire me for the winter and I could live in comfort.

Our midday dinner was more firecake and all the water we could drink.

Greenlaw suggested we try our hands at chopping down a tree, so he could reckon if any of us had a natural inclination for the task. The Janacks were uncommonly strong but had little skill. The rest of the fellows looked more like maids beating a dirty rug than woodsmen felling a tree.

When it came my turn, I stepped up to the trunk with supreme confidence. I was a lad of many talents. I could shoot a musket and drive an oxcart. I could heat up a blacksmith's forge to soften iron and even manufacture nails if given enough time and plenty enough iron to make my share of mistakes. I could shave a gentleman's face, clean his clothes, polish his silver, serve dinner to his guests, and tidy up after a party that lasted until dawn. And I was a better thief than most.

I swung the axe with all of my strength. The blade created a small nick in the thick bark. Eben took the axe from me without a word, swung it, and took a mighty bite out of the trunk.

I reacquainted myself with the shovel after that.

By nightfall the Janacks had finished the privy trench (called a "vault" by some for reasons I never understood) and promised to help with the floor on the morrow. I needed it. I'd only managed to dig a third of the floor to the depth of one hand. The cold had seeped through the soles of my boots and my sweat-soaked shirt froze against my skin.

Supper was again firecake and water.

We ate crowded around a fire that was more smoke than flame and talked about food: platters of roasted chicken, venison stew, bread spread with butter and topped with cheese, flapjacks, puddings, pears, pickles, and pies erupting with berries, swimming in cream. Each description renewed the pangs in our bellies, but we could not stop.

Silvenus did not contribute to the listing of our favorite victuals. He was trying to sew up the rip in Faulkner's shirt with threads he pulled from his blanket, but they were too frayed to hold the stitches together. He finally gave up and announced that we ought sleep.

In the course of the day, we'd taken the time to set up our tents properly and lay pine boughs on the floor of them to help keep out the damp and cold. Edwards had asked to move into our tent and take the place of Peter Brown, who had not come back from the hospital tent. Edwards said he couldn't stand to listen to the witless jabbering of Burns and the foul Barry brothers. We all understood his reasoning.

Silvenus thought it foolish to squeeze the six of us into the small space. He suggested that Eben move out and take Edwards's place in the company's other tent.

"Them Barrys are more your kin than we are," he said.

Eben refused. "Cousin Aaron snores and their tent leaks. I'm staying."

(Our tent leaked rain and starlight and every fellow in it snored. I did not mention this.)

After we lay down, rolled over, lay down again, cussed at one another for taking up too much room, cussed out the King and all his redcoats, and after Edwards said a prayer, the tent fell quiet.

For a moment.

"I'm too hungry to sleep," said Greenlaw.

"Me too," added Faulkner. "And cold."

"Just wait until you're old," said Silvenus. "Then the cold eats away your bones. I wager I won't be able to stand in the morning."

Edwards gave Eben a little shove. "You're flattening me."

I chuckled.

"What's so funny?" Greenlaw asked.

"There is one good thing about not eating," I said.

"What would that be?" Greenlaw asked.

"We've got nothing to fart with."

Anyone walking past our tent must have wondered if we'd all lost our wits, for we laughed so hard, the tent near collapsed.

CHAPTER XVIII

Tuesday, December 23–Wednesday, December 24, 1777

THE ARMY WAS NOT ONLY STARVED BUT NAKED.
THE GREATEST PART WERE NOT ONLY
SHIRTLESS AND BAREFOOT, BUT DESTITUTE OF ALL
OTHER CLOTHING, ESPECIALLY BLANKETS . . .
[SHOELESS SOLDIERS] MIGHT BE TRACKED BY THEIR
BLOOD ALONG THE ROUGH FROZEN GROUND.
—JOURNAL OF JOSEPH PLUMB MARTIN,
SEVENTEEN-YEAR-OLD PRIVATE IN THE FIFTEENTH
MASSACHUSETTS REGIMENT, VALLEY FORGE

TUESDAY'S SUN SHONE BRIGHT AND cold. Breakfast was firecake and water.

Dinner was firecake and water.

The Janack brothers and me shoveled out the entire floor of our future hut halfway to our knees. My weary arms could barely lift my cup of hot water to my mouth.

After the sun dropped, supper was firecake and water.

I did not have anything amusing to say that night.

The snow was crusted with ice next morning, but it was as nice as the finest day in July, for the sergeant received another cloth bag at the roll. We stood around the fire like vultures as he cooked up the rice it contained. Sergeant Woodruff carefully portioned out the feast. We each received one handful, seasoned with vinegar to keep away the scurvy. I thought it likely we would starve or freeze to death before expiring of scurvy, but it tasted better than firecake, so I kept the notion to myself.

"Where's Burns?" he demanded when the rest of us had received our share.

"Squatted over a privy trench, sir," Aaron said. "Farther on down the brigade. His bowels are giving him fits. Didn't want us to see his troubles."

"Fetch him."

For once I did not care a whit about the location or condition of John Burns. I tried to force myself to eat the rice slow. One grain at a time. Three grains at a time. *Too slow.* A pinch, a slurp. *Not fast enough.*

I could not hold back. I shoveled the rest of the rice in my mouth fast as I could, not caring that it burned all the way down.

Aaron returned as we were all licking our fingers.

"Couldn't find him, sir. No one down there has seen him. Can I eat now?"

The sergeant handed a scoop of rice on a piece of bark to Aaron.

"Can we share Burns's portion, sir?" I asked.

"No." The sergeant scraped the last of the rice from the pot. "Half of this goes to Greenlaw, the other half to Ebenezer. Wood-chopping is vastly harder work than shoveling or hauling firewood."

Just because he was right didn't fill up my belly. I drew some comfort, however, when Burns straggled back into camp spouting stories about his afflictions, and then outrage, for he appeared in time to watch the two biggest lads of our company swallow the last of his rice.

That was most satisfying.

That afternoon the Janacks were ordered to help lay the roof beams on the officers' hut, so Benjamin Edwards (who had asked us to call him Benny) and Hugh Faulkner helped me dig the floor. The shovel weighed twice as much as it had the day before. The mud fought against being moved. My hands were too cold and stiff to close around the handle properly and my boots were determined to trip me up.

To distract us from our hunger and fatigue, Benny told us stories about strange creatures: a fifty-headed dog; a horse with wings; and a monster that had the front legs of a lion, the back legs of a goat, and the tail of a serpent.

He leaned against his shovel. "And then there's the one about the fellow who plowed a field of dragon's teeth."

"Where'd you hear of such fantastical things?" I asked.

"In books," he said. "I am a prodigious reader."

"If your family can afford books, why did you sign up to be a private?" Faulkner asked. "Surely your father could have gotten you a commission as an officer or an aide."

Benny picked up the shovel and drove it into the mud. "I was supposed to go to Harvard College this winter, to study law, although I believe my true calling is to be a philosopher. My father changed his mind and was preparing to send me to London instead. He believes the rebellion is a grievous mistake."

"Your father's a Tory?" I asked.

Benny frowned and awkwardly tossed the heavy mud to the side. "If it were up to him, the entire Continental army and Congress would be lined up and shot. He threw me out after an argument about the Declaration of Independence. That's when I enlisted."

His words sounded brave, but his voice cracked with the weight of his feelings and he looked younger than ever, like a boy who should have been in a schoolroom instead of a soldier trying to build a hovel in the snow.

He pushed his hair out of his face and thrust the shovel into the ground overly hard. The shovel skidded on a stone, and Benny stumbled, tripped, then landed on the blade. Faulkner and I hurried over to help him to his feet.

"You hurt bad?" I asked.

"No." He stood slowly and examined the wreckage of his breeches, ripped from just above the knee ties clear up his backside. His skin was cut too, tho' not deep.

"Perdition!" he shouted. "Oh, foul, poxy Devil! By the blasted, sorry dickens!"

I bit my tongue to keep from laughing. The lad's attempts at cussing like a soldier made him sound instead like a mild-mouthed granny.

"You'll be cursing a frozen backside tonight," said Faulkner, pointing to the way Benny's breeches flapped in the wind.

"'Tis a badge of honor," I said quickly. "It makes you look most soldierly. You should say those breeches are veterans of a fierce encounter at Saratoga or the Brandywine."

"Really?" Benny asked.

"Won't help him none if his hindquarters get frostbit," Faulkner said. "Doctors might have to amputate, leaving you rumpless."

"They wouldn't!" Benny covered his bum. "Would they?"

CHAPTER XIX

Thursday, December 25, 1777

To see Men without Cloathes to cover their nakedness, without Blankets to lay on, without Shoes, by which their Marches might be traced by the Blood from their feet . . . and at Christmas taking up their Winter Quarters within a day's March of the enemy, without a House or Hutt to cover them till they could be built . . . , is a mark of patience and obedience which in my opinion can scarce be parallel'd.
—George Washington, letter to John Banister

WE WOKE CHRISTMAS MORNING TO snow as high as my knees, with more falling from the sky. After walking two steps from the tent, what was left of Silvenus's shoes fell apart completely.

"Now what am I supposed to do?" he asked as he fished out the leather scraps.

Before anyone could answer, a rattletrap wagon came along the road, pulled by a horse that was more bone than flesh. The driver climbed down.

"You fellas are the last of the New Hampshire, right?"

"Aye," said Sergeant Woodruff.

"Then this is yours and I can head back to the barn." The driver took two axes and a small cask from his wagon and handed them to Sergeant Woodruff. "Can yer lads give the wagon a push?" he asked. "My horse could use the help."

The sergeant called to us, and we pushed while the poor creature leaned into the harness until finally the wheels moved. We pushed it all the way to the spot where the road sloped downhill, and the driver called out his thanks.

We walked slowly back to our hut site, passing a score of half-built cabins belonging to the Pennsylvania regiment. The others studied the walls and remarked on the few framed chimney stacks. My thoughts were centered on that small cask, wondering what treasures lay inside it. Any addition to our tools would help.

The sergeant was sitting on a stump, prying open the lid of the cask as we arrived.

"Please tell me that's filled with nails, sir," Greenlaw said.

"I hate to disappoint you, lad." The sergeant shook his head woefully. "It's only food."

Our huzzahs shook the snow.

We feasted that morning. We each ate a fist-size piece of pork and enjoyed a soup of dried peas cooked in heavily peppered water. Best of all was the piece of chewy pigskin we had to gnaw on. I knew I could make mine last a full day, at least.

After we ate, the news came down the line that the horse that had pulled the supply wagon had died a short ways down the road. It took half the day to remove the harnesses without ruining either the leather or the nag's body. The wagon was finally pulled away by four fellows from the Eighth Pennsylvania Regiment.

The horse lay where he dropped.

The officers' hut had been finished Christmas Eve, so Sergeant Woodruff could now help fell trees for our use. With three fellows chopping, our pace of work increased. By the end of the day we'd dragged four logs to our hut site, stripped them of their bark, and laid them, one per side, as the ground logs of what would be our walls.

"It'll take till summer to finish the poxy thing," Faulkner said.

'Twas hard to argue that.

We had supper then, the rest of the pea soup, which amounted to a half cup for each one of us. I stuck my piece of pigskin into the bowl for flavor. When I'd licked the bowl clean, the skin went back in my mouth for chewing, but I swallowed it without intending to, and missed it sorely.

No one wanted to turn in early, for it was Christmas. John Burns disappeared into the dark when a few fellows from Pennsylvania started to sing carols. Silvenus, too, though he returned in short order carrying a handful of long strands of horsehair. Some of the fellows protested this abuse of the horse's corpse.

"I just gave the poor beast a haircut of the tail." He sat close to the fire, perched his spectacles at the end of his nose, and set to braiding the horsehair. "Tho' if you was to ask me, I'd say that old horse is waste of good soup meat. Poxy sentimental horse notions of the officers kept us hungry in '58, too."

"You were in the army then?" asked Greenlaw.

Silvenus nodded, his fingers braiding so fast, they were a blur. "I joined up when we went to war against the French. I learned a few things about fighting, so I signed on again when it was time to fight the British, too."

"Did you fight at Breed's Hill?" I asked.

Silvenus snorted. "Wish I had. I was in the troops who marched to Quebec that year. You think you're hungry now? Ha! We were truly starving at one point. Had just the head of a squirrel left to eat."

"What did you do?" I asked.

Silvenus plucked a thread from his cuff and tied off the cord he had braided. "We killed one of the dogs, mixed the meat up with the squirrel's head, added some candle wax, and ate the whole thing."

"I don't believe you," Benny said.

"If you ever get that hungry, you will. You whelps is always caterwauling about your bellies and how you're about to die." He pulled out the two pieces of his shoe from the bag slung over his shoulder and set them on his foot, then wrapped the cord around the shoe to hold it together. "Long as you gets a smidgen of grub, like firecake or squirrel head, every day, you'll last for months."

CHAPTER XX

Thursday, December 25–Friday, December 26, 1777

I AM NOW CONVINCED BEYOND A DOUBT THAT UNLESS SOME GREAT AND CAPITAL CHANGE SUDDENLY TAKES PLACE . . . THE ARMY MUST INEVITABLY BE REDUCED TO ONE OR THE OTHER OF THESE THREE THINGS: STARVE—DISOLVE—OR DISPERSE.
—GEORGE WASHINGTON WRITING FROM VALLEY FORGE TO HENRY LAURENS OF THE CONTINENTAL CONGRESS

I STILL DO NOT KNOW WHAT WOKE ME in the night. A clumsy footstep at the edge of our kindling pile, perhaps. Or a squirrel, for this was before they'd all been hunted. Whatever the cause, my eyes opened and would not shut. I crawled over my grumbling companions and out the tent flap.

I was not due to relieve Eben at guard for another hour or so, but as I was fully awake, it seemed foolish to wait. I loaded up my arms with firewood and made my way down the dark path to the guard post. There was supposed to be a sliver of a moon, but clouds had been thrown across the sky like a heavy quilt. I stepped carefully, for the snow hid tree stumps and rocks.

Halfway there, I slowed, hearing raised voices and the sounds of a struggle.

"Who's there?" I called. "Name yourself!"

Numbskull! The ghost-voice of Isabel in my brain, absent for weeks, scolded me fierce. *What if it's a British patrol? Or a group of desperate banditti? Think, fool!*

Before I could twist my ear, a figure ran toward me, breathing heavy. He veered around me and continued in the direction of camp. It sounded like he stumbled in the snow but then regained his balance and ran on. I waited until the night was again quiet, then walked, cautiously. I had not taken ten steps before I was stopped.

"Halt!" a voice called. "What's the countersign?"

"Eben?" I strained my eyes but could not see anything. "Is that you? What's going on?"

"The sign is Windsor," he said. "Give me the countersign."

I stepped closer to him. "It's me, you ninny. Curzon."

The sound of a hammer being pulled to full cock, preparing a musket to fire, froze me in my boots. "The countersign," he demanded.

"Hartford!" I shouted. "Don't shoot me. Hartford, Hartford, Hartford!"

He sighed and uncocked his gun. "Can't be too sure. Help me up, will you?"

I stepped close enough to see his form sitting in the snow. I shifted the wood to one arm and reached out a hand for him to grasp.

"Were you attacked?" I asked. "Is it the British?"

"No!" He grabbed my sleeve before I could run back to alert the camp. "It's not the British."

"What's the matter, then?"

"We need to build up the fire." He walked in the direction of the guard post without offering any explanation. I waited, then followed several paces behind him, fighting the temptation to push him back into the snow.

By the time I reached the post, he was on his knees, blowing on the coals of the near-dead fire.

"Guards are supposed to guard," I said, "not wander in the night and let the fire go out." I picked through the wood for the driest pieces. "I could well freeze to death, thanks to you."

"'Pologies," he said. "Go back to camp. I'll take your duty."

No fellow in his right mind would say such a thing. I did not know what to reply, so I fussed with the twigs and blew and blew until the flames caught and kindled the wood. We both leaned toward the fire to warm our hands and faces.

I gasped. Eben's left eye was puffy and darkened with blood. His mouth was swollen too, and bleeding, as was his nose and the knuckles on his right hand.

"What happened?" I asked.

"Do you know how to cook a pumpkin?" he asked.

CHAPTER XXI

Thursday, December 25–Friday, December 26, 1777

I LAY HERE TWO NIGHTS AND ONE DAY, AND HAD NOT A MORSEL OF ANYTHING TO EAT ALL THE TIME, SAVE HALF A PUMPKIN, WHICH I COOKED BY PLACING IT UPON A ROCK, THE SKIN SIDE UPPERMOST, AND MAKING A FIRE UPON IT. BY THE TIME IT WAS HEATED THROUGH I DEVOURED IT WITH AS KEEN AN APPETITE AS I SHOULD A PIE MADE OF IT AT SOME OTHER TIME.
—JOURNAL OF JOSEPH PLUMB MARTIN,
SEVENTEEN-YEAR-OLD PRIVATE IN FIFTEENTH MASSACHUSETTS REGIMENT, VALLEY FORGE

HIS STRANGE REQUEST BEFUDDLED me. "Have you gone funny in the head?"

"Mayhaps." Eben opened his sack and pulled out a muddied pumpkin that was just a bit bigger than a cannonball. "I stole this tonight, but I'm not certain how to cook it."

"You fought with the farmer? He caught you in his field?" I packed some snow into a ball and handed it to him. "Put that on your eye, clodpate."

He winced as the snow touched his skin. "It wasn't the farmer who hit me, it was John Burns."

"Burns caught you scavenging?"

"No," Eben groaned. "Burns and me, we went stealing together."

"You cannot be serious."

"Aye," he said with a groan. "My belly was a giant empty pit, Curzon. Tasting those little bites of real food today just made it worse. I was gonna die, no matter what Silvenus said. Burns saw how hungry I was. He was waiting when I came on duty. Told me he'd feed me good after I helped carry some provisions. He's been sneaking off every night to rob fields and root cellars. Never goes hungry. That fit he threw after missing out on the rice was just for show."

"John Burns deserves to be flogged." I cleaned off the pumpkin with another handful of snow.

"It took us four trips to move all the pumpkins and cabbage he'd stolen. I chewed on cabbage leaves the whole time, scared as the dickens that we'd be caught. I thought he was going to share the food with the regiment, but no." He spat and wiped his mouth on his sleeve. "Not him. He sells the food to them for coin."

"He should be flogged to death," I said. "Then brought back to life and flogged all over again."

"Surely so." Eben moved the snow away from his eye. "I told him we had to share with the other fellows, that we had to be honorable. When he laughed at the notion, I hit him."

"And he hit you back, by the looks of it," I said.

"Coward kicked me between the legs. Once I was on the ground, he gave me more kicks, grabbed the bag I was carrying, and ran off."

"How did you get the pumpkin, then?"

"I stole it on the last trip; put it in my own sack when he wasn't looking." Eben put the snow back on his eye. "My aunt Patience would beat the skin off my backside if she knew that I have fallen so low that I steal from a thief."

I poked at the burning twigs and added more wood. "Aunt Patience wouldn't beat you," I ventured. "Stealing from a thief is justice."

"Honest?"

"I swear."

From the fire I pulled a branch that was burning at one end. I told Eben how to prepare the fire and went off in search of the perfect rock. It took a good while, but by the time I returned, he had the fire blazing, with two logs the thickness of my leg lying next to each other, two hands of space between them filled with flame. We laid the rock over the logs, split the pumpkin with the bayonet, and set the pumpkin halves, cut side down, on the rock.

The wet seeds sizzled and smoked.

We stood in silence a good while, both of us swallowing waves of spit conjured by the smell of cooking pumpkin. The temptation to snatch it from the fire and eat it raw was hard to fight.

I ate a handful of snow. "You don't have any more of that cabbage, do you?"

"Sorry."

"It's just as well. Cabbage was never a favorite of mine."

Eben poked at the pumpkin with a stick. "Are you going to tell my uncle about this?"

"Aren't you? He should know about Burns."

He shook his head. "Burns will point the finger back at me. Uncle would never forgive me for breaking the army's rules."

"Then I won't breathe a word of it."

"Thank you." He poked the pumpkin shell again. "Does that mean you're not sore at me anymore?"

Instead of answering, I handed him another snowball. "Your lip."

"I do apologize, Curzon Smith." He put the snow on his lip, winced, and removed it. "I've been pondering the matter ever since we quarreled. You were right. If we're gonna fight a war, it should make everybody free, not just some."

The compass needle inside me whirled. I could not trust him; he was only being nice so I wouldn't get him in trouble. I should trust him; his apology was heartfelt. I dared not be his friend, or the friend of any person. But I wanted to be his friend again.

"I can't accept your apology if you're going to be an associate of John Burns," I finally said.

"That poxy scoundrel can hang himself!" Eben punched my shoulder so hard, I lost my seat on the log. "How much longer until that pumpkin is ready?"

When the pumpkin shell had blackened and cracked, I slid my knife under each half and flipped them into the snow, steaming and hissing. It smelled better than gingercake and honey together.

"We really have to share it with the others, don't we?" Eben asked in a whisper.

I sighed. "We do."

"Plaguey fopdoodles." He tossed his poking stick into the flames. "It might be the death of me, you know. If it is, make sure Uncle buys me a nice headstone. Tell him I want these words carved on it: 'Ebenezer Woodruff died so that others might eat pumpkin.'"

"A noble sacrifice," I said in jest.

"More people should make them," he said, his tone not jesting one bit.

CHAPTER XXII

Friday, December 26–
Wednesday, December 31, 1777

I WAS THERE WHEN THE ARMY FIRST BEGAN TO
BUILD HUTS. THEY APPEARED TO ME LIKE
A FAMILY OF BEAVERS, EVERYONE BUSY; SOME CARRYING
LOGS, OTHERS MUD, AND THE REST PLASTERING
THEM TOGETHER . . . IT IS A CURIOUS COLLECTION
OF BUILDINGS, IN THE TRUE RUSTIC ORDER.
–THOMAS PAINE, LETTER TO BENJAMIN FRANKLIN,
AMERICAN AMBASSADOR IN FRANCE

WE SMUGGLED THE PUMPKIN INTO OUR tent just before dawn and told the fellows to eat their share without asking questions. When they caught a good look at Eben's face, their eyes went wide, but they kept their mouths shut. When they later saw the bloodied lips and a broken tooth of John Burns, a few of them chuckled, but they never said a thing.

As the roll call was breaking up, we heard an artilleryman say that His Excellency General Washington had served his guests veal, mutton, potatoes, and cabbage for Christmas dinner. They had to drink water like us on account of they had no wine.

"Didn't have pumpkin, neither," Eben whispered to me.

"He should have invited us," I said.

We had another wicked snow after Christmas and day after day of cold. General Washington's log city grew in haste, inspired by the weather. A company from North Carolina won the prize for finishing first. I figgered it was on account of they weren't used to the snow the way us from New England were.

We lagged far behind. One of our axe heads fell apart into three pieces and could not be repaired. After that, Greenlaw left the cutting of the trees to the sergeant and Eben, whilst he stayed at the hut site, using an oversized hatchet, adze, and froe to prepare the logs for stacking into walls.

The sergeant said that we'd be building hospital huts as soon as all the troops had decent shelter. Until then, the sick and the injured who could survive the journey would be taken to country churches and barns that had been turned into hospitals. Peter Brown had been taken to the Yellow Springs hospital along with two other fellows suffering from the bloody flux. There was no way of knowing if Peter was on the mend or dead.

By the end of the year, our floor was dug as deep as my hips. It was a mud pit on the bottom, but I promised everyone that the fire would dry it out. (I fervently hoped this was the truth.) Faulkner had taken over the construction of our chimney, and Silvenus appointed himself the dauber of walls, filling in the cracks between the logs with mud, with the assistance of young Benny. The Janack twins were again pulled from our company, this time to go into the countryside with the foraging parties and convince the country people to sell hay, straw, meat, and pretty much anything else to the army. If the folks wouldn't sell it, the foragers were ordered to take it.

The foraging parties soon sent back wagons of victuals into camp. Our rations were small, but they came more or less regular. Most morns, we breakfasted on porridge or hardtack. Dinner and supper both were soup made with whatever meat and bones were to hand, some days with beans thrown in. Once we had a turnip, too. When the meat had green bits on it, we'd roast it in the fire first, to deaden the taste, then put it in the pot. Some fellows called it "carrion meat" and said it was only good enough for vultures. If a vulture tried to take my piece, I'd have roasted him, too.

Snow began to fall from mushroom-colored clouds as I made yet another dreary trip to the woodlot. The walk grew longer every day as the trees required by thousands of huts and fires were felled. Mount Joy would soon be bald, and then we'd have the even longer trudge to Mount Misery. If the ground would have frozen solid, it would have been easier to drag the logs and firewood bundles. But every freeze had been followed by a thaw and the woodlot road was thick with mud that stuck to my boots like cold molasses.

The crows were not at all happy with the destruction of their homes. I stopped at the edge of the woodlot to catch my breath and watch three of them circle over the busy huddle of men who worked with long saws cutting tree trunks down to hut-building lengths. The crows swooped down and landed one at a time on a low branch to scold the men, cawing and screaming loud as I ever heard them.

Only . . .

Someone shouted for the sawing to stop. The men walking out of the woodlot stopped and looked behind them. The birds flew off to the east. The *kchop-kchop* of axes stopped, and for a moment there was silence.

Then the screaming started again; not angry crows, but the sound of a man in agony.

Ebenezer Woodruff burst into the clearing, his hands bright red and dripping.

"Help!" he shouted. "My uncle! The axe!"

I ran.

The sergeant lay screaming a quarter mile into the woodlot. He clutched his ankle, rocking back and forth in the blood-drenched snow, his dripping axe next to him.

"Oh, God. Oh, God," I whispered.

"We can't make the blood stop!" Eben fell to his knees and wrapped his hands around his uncle's ankle, but it made no difference.

A fellow in a hunting shirt and knit cap rushed over, wrapped a length of rope just below the sergeant's knee, and twisted it hard around a stick so that the rope tightened around the leg. The tide of blood slowed. Sergeant Woodruff gritted his teeth and reduced his screams to groans of agony.

"I'll get a doctor!" I ran for the path.

They gave him a half bottle of rum to drink before they placed him on a litter and carried him the bumpy mile to the closest surgeon's tent. The doctor had run ahead of the litter and had his own small saw sharpened by the time we arrived. Uncle Sergeant's anklebone was splintered into too many pieces to heal, and the doctor had to finish the job the axe started. I tried to get Eben to walk away from the doleful sounds made in that tent, but he would not, so I stayed with him.

When it was all over, we sat on upturned logs next to the table where the sergeant lay. The doctor let us keep a candle burning so that Eben could see his uncle's face. The sergeant was overtaken by a violent fever deep in the night.

When the drums sounded the reveille at dawn, he died.

CHAPTER XXIII

Wednesday, December 31, 1777–Thursday, January 1, 1778

IT IS A TRUBLESUM TIMES FOR US ALL,
BUT WORS FOR THE SOLDIERS.
–LETTER OF CONNECTICUT PRIVATE ICHABOD WARD
WRITTEN AT VALLEY FORGE

WE PERFORMED THE LAST DUTY FOR the dead on the last day of the year.

We heated water to wash ourselves. Silvenus, Greenlaw, John Burns, and Aaron Barry shaved the best they could without soap. I used my knife to scrape off the few hairs that grew on my chin and under my nose. The rest were still beardless. We knocked the mud from our clothes and our hair and tried to clean our boots and shoes. We did not have any black cloth to wear around our arms. Faulkner came up with the idea of marking our sleeves halfway between the wrist and elbow with a heavy line of charcoal to show our mourning.

The graveyard was hidden in a small clearing deep in the woods near General Wayne's regiment, tucked out of sight so British spies would not know how many of our army had died. For that reason, too, there were no crosses or headstones to mark the graves. The quiet mounds in the snow would settle by spring. The enemy would never count these dead.

We dug the grave in shifts except for Eben, who did not stop shoveling, sweating, and shivering until the man-size hole was deep enough. He never wiped away the tears that washed his face, nor did he speak a word to any soul. The pines around us bent in the heavy wind.

When the grave was ready, the litter was carried from the hospital tent to the grave by Henry, Greenlaw, Eben, and me; a bleak march across the Grand Parade and past the south-facing cannons of the artillery park down the Baptist Road. The sergeant's face and naked body were covered with a blanket, all except for his one dirty foot. Clothes were too precious to be wasted on the dead. Sergeant Woodruff would go to his eternal reward wearing what he'd been born in.

Every soldier removed his hat when we approached. The women of the camp bowed their heads. As soon as we passed them by, they all went back to work.

We set the litter next to the hole. Eben walked away and stared into the woods while we picked up his uncle, laid him in the ground, and removed the blanket.

When we were done, he came back for the short service. The chaplain read from his Bible in a quiet voice that was hard to hear over the sound of the wind in the trees. There could be no firing of guns in his honor. The ammunition had to be saved for the enemy.

When he closed the book, Captain Stanwell nodded. Silvenus, Greenlaw, and me each picked up a shovelful of dirt to begin the filling in of the grave.

"No, wait!" Eben said.

The captain put his hand on Eben's shoulder. "Mayhaps you should head back to camp."

"Not yet, sir. Give me one moment."

We put the shovels down without waiting for the captain's reply.

Eben unbuttoned his coat—his uncle's coat, now his—and slipped one arm free of it. "Does anyone have a blade?"

We all shook our heads at this unsettling question. Burns whispered something into Aaron's ear. Crows called from the swaying branches above.

"Why do you need a blade, lad?" the chaplain gently asked.

"To keep the dirt from his face."

Eben wiped his eyes on his shirtsleeve, then grabbed the fabric and pulled so hard, the sleeve ripped at the shoulder. He pulled again until all the stitches gave way, and then he peeled off the sleeve, stuck his naked arm back in the coat, and buttoned it. "Can you read that prayer again?"

The chaplain fingered through the pages in search of the right passage. When he began reading, Ebenezer Woodruff folded his sleeve once, knelt, and laid it across the face of his uncle.

He stood and looked at us across the open grave. "Wait till you can't see me before you start."

That night was my turn to stand guard. Halfway through the watch, Eben appeared out of the gloom with an armful of firewood. I took the wood from him, heaped it on the fire, and sat on the log next to him. Eben sniffed in the dark and drew shaky breaths. He did not speak until all the wood blazed and crackled.

"I got in another fight."

"Burns?"

"No. Cousin Aaron. He said I had no right to cry on account of Uncle Caleb wasn't my father. I swung at him and he punched back, and I lost track of myself. Next thing I knew, the fellows were pulling me off him. I'm fair certain I broke his nose."

He sniffed again and made a gulping noise. "Uncle would be disappointed in me for fighting like that."

"Did you live in his house?"

"Aye." Eben cleared his throat. "My father found himself a pretty widow after Mother died. Sent me to Uncle Caleb's."

"How old were you?"

"Five years and seven months. Uncle Caleb and Aunt Patience didn't have any children. They wanted me to be their son. When we enlisted, Aunt Patience made us promise not to get shot and to come home as soon as the war was over."

A log shifted and sparks flew up. I almost told him all my secrets then because he told me his. More sparks flew and I came to my senses.

"Can I punch Aaron too?" I asked.

"Don't. You'll hurt your hand." He pressed his finger against one nostril, blew out the snot, then wiped his nose on his sleeve. "All the Barrys got cast-iron heads."

We sat knee to knee, breathing in cold air and blowing out frost the rest of that night. Above us the sky passed from the Year of Our Lord 1777 to the Year of Our Lord 1778 in darkness. Someone had stolen the moon from the sky.

CHAPTER XXIV

Thursday, January 1–Saturday, January 10, 1778

STEEL: *s.* IRON REFINED BY FIRE; A WEAPON.
—SAMUEL JOHNSON'S DICTIONARY OF THE
ENGLISH LANGUAGE, PUBLISHED 1755

THE NEW YEAR COULD NOT DECIDE if it wanted to snow on us or simply throw ice at our heads. Some days were colder than I'd ever felt as a boy in Boston.

Eben asked me to divide his uncle's clothing amongst us and explained how I should do it. Silvenus got the sergeant's boots and also Eben's shirt with one sleeve for use in patching the holes and tears we all had in our breeches and shirts. One pair of stockings went to Greenlaw, the other to Benny Edwards. Aaron Barry got the sergeant's hat. Henry Barry got his gloves, for his own hands had cracked from the cold and bled every time he picked up a hatchet. I was reluctant to turn over the sergeant's blanket to John Burns, but Eben was unbending. Faulkner was near tears when I handed him the sergeant's worn-down pencil nubs.

When the job was done, I walked with Eben to his uncle's grave. My neck was warmed by the scarf knitted by Aunt Patience for her late husband. Eben himself wore his uncle's shirt and his jacket. To wear the clothes of a good man who was now dead was a sorrowful thing, to be sure, but it kept us warmer.

We removed our hats in respect as we entered the small clearing. Slushy snow covered the grave like a tattered blanket.

"The fellows are grateful," I said after a few quiet moments. "Even the Barry brothers and Burns."

Sleet fell on our bare heads.

"They want to do something," I continued. "In his honor. And to thank you. Only there's nothing to do anything with."

He did not move.

"Eben," I asked, "did you hear me?"

He finally lifted his head. "Tell them the best way to honor Uncle will be to beat the British come spring."

Captain Stanwell resigned his commission, joining the flood of officers who were giving up on the army. Privates were not allowed to quit. We belonged to the army until our enlistments expired, or the war ended, or the army disbanded, which Silvenus wagered would happen before February's end.

Our new captain was named Russell, a small lawyer who kept his chin forward and his shoulders hunched like a turkey. We rarely saw him, for he was muchly involved in the business of the brigade. He ordered us to finish our hut (the most unnecessary order ever given) and promised to find us a new sergeant. He also said that he would write to the leaders of Massachusetts day and night begging for blankets and shoes.

We elected Greenlaw to be in charge of the construction until the new sergeant arrived. Each day we drew straws to see who would have to carry the firewood and who would cook and who had privy duty, if it fell to our company to clean up an overfull piss-trench or dig a new one.

John Burns volunteered to report the roll to the captain each day and run messages or requests to the brigade headquarters. We all gave the matter a hearty "Aye!" His sour humor and idleness made him the most difficult fellow to work with. I was certain he volunteered for the errand duties so he could continue his scavenging, tho' the farms near camp had all been picked clean by then. As long as I didn't have to put up with his noxious presence, I cared not what he did with himself.

The walls of our hut were at half height. Each night we suspended our tent canvas as a roof in the corner. We told ourselves it was a fine hut, but it most resembled a pigsty, floored with cold mud and occupied by the runts of the litter. Each morning we took down the canvas and returned to the business of chopping trees, fitting logs, mudding up the walls, and trying to build a chimney with stones and prayers. Our progress was slow but steady. After a week Greenlaw put Eben to work fashioning shingles with a froe and mallet, and we kept our eyes open for tree trunks straight enough for our roof rafters.

Reveille on the morning of the tenth day of January was extended into a quarter-day's rest so we could all watch the execution of a soldier from the Second Virginia named John Reily. He had freed two of his friends held prisoner in the guardhouse, then the three of them tried to run away.

They'd been caught and court-martialed. The two prisoners got off with two hundred lashes each, delivered on the bare back. Sergeant Reily was not so lucky.

Every soldier with enough clothes to cover himself stood silent on the Grand Parade, all eyes on the gallows. A blue-coated officer helped Reily, his hands tied behind his back, climb upon the stool that stood on the gallows platform. If Reily was crying or cursing, the wind stole the sound of it. I could hear only the fellows around me coughing and scratching.

I opened and closed my hands, though it pained me. The cold had gotten into the bones of my fingers. We'd heard of fellows losing hands and feet to the frostbite. I did not want to join their ranks.

The noose was lowered over Reily's head. The rope was tightened around his neck.

A lone drum played.

Eben had found a small knife in the woodlot and was trying to sharpen it against a smooth stone. Benny Edwards prayed quiet and low. Henry Barry yawned. John Burns did not take his eyes from the gallows. Nor did I.

The stool was kicked away from Reily's feet. His body jerked, then crashed to the platform.

"The rope broke!" came the shout.

We all moved forward a few paces to see what happened, but sergeants and corporals barked at us to step back. Because of the shift in the crowd, the shorter of us—namely, me and Benny—could no longer see the gallows.

"What's going on?" Benny asked.

Greenlaw rose up on his toes, craning for a look. "Didn't kill him," he said. "Fellow's standing again."

"A broken rope at a hanging is a sign of God's mercy,"

Benny said. "He should be spared the hanging and flogged instead."

"Can't have lads running off because they don't approve of the accommodations," Silvenus hawked, then spat in the mud. "We need discipline to beat the British. He needs to hang."

"If we defy God, we'll never win," Benny argued. "He will cause the army to break apart."

"God didn't break that rope," I said. "It was weak from overuse."

"Rotten, like the army," said Aaron Barry.

"Hush," warned his brother.

"Look around you!" Aaron opened his arms wide. "It's a miracle more of us don't run."

"That's treason," said John Burns. "You can't say such things. You shouldn't even think them."

Aaron turned on him. "You said you'd run as soon as we were paid."

Burns scowled. "I've changed my mind. So should you."

We all studied the ground, surely thinking the same thoughts. How much longer could we hold out? What would happen if we couldn't? Soldiers had begun to desert and there was talk of mutiny in some regiments. We woke each morning not knowing if the day would bring food or despair, sunshine or death. Icy doubts were creeping into our bones.

Eben had not been following any of this, so intent was he on sharpening his newfound knife. "Blast!" he murmured.

"Won't hold an edge?" asked Greenlaw.

"Likely why it was abandoned," Eben said.

"There's a fellow up there about to die and you're complaining about a dull blade," said Benny. "You should have more respect."

"I have plenty of respect for him," snapped Eben, turning so that his back was to the gallows. "So much so that I don't want to watch." He looked at me. "If I heated up this blade red-hot, like in a forge, could you pound on it and make it into steel?"

"Doubtful," I said.

"Why not?" Eben asked.

"Some iron has a magical quality that comes out when you work it. If that knife was made from such iron, it would stay sharp. No amount of forging will make a difference."

"Huh." Silvenus spat again. "Sounds like this godforsaken place."

"We can mine iron here?" Eben asked.

"No, blunderhead," Silvenus said. "This camp is a forge for the army; it's testing our mettle. Instead of heat and hammer, our trials are cold and hunger. Question is, what are we made of?"

The gallows drum beat again. The second rope was ready. The wind shifted to the northwest, carrying the stench of rotting horse flesh. The crowd fell quiet.

Reily stepped on the stool, then bowed his head for the noose. Benny Edwards bowed his head, too. The officer kicked the stool away.

This time the rope did not break.

Captain Russell hurried toward us as soon as we were dismissed, walking with unusual vigor with his shoulders pulled down where they belonged.

"Good news, lads!" The captain's smile made him near unrecognizable.

"Yessir." We touched the brims of our hats and caps.

"The brigadier general has approved my recommendation." Captain Russell motioned for Burns to step up alongside him. "Your new sergeant is Mister Burns here, who has recently proved an able assistant to me. I am sure you will all accord him the respect and obedience he deserves."

Burns studied us all gape-mouthed at this news, then focused his attention upon me like a weasel baiting a fox.

"I know these men well, sir," he said. "I will not let you down."

CHAPTER XXV

Sunday, January 11–Monday, January 19, 1778

JETHRO, A NEGRO FROM GUILFORD BELONGING TO CAPT. HALL'S COMPANY, DIED.
—SEVENTH CONNECTICUT SURGEON'S MATE JONATHAN TODD, LETTER TO HIS FATHER

BURNS WAS EVER WATCHFUL OF MY movements, looking for an excuse to report or punish me. I stayed alert to the point of exhaustion, waiting for the blow to fall or disaster to strike. I took care to act the model soldier—never late for duties or shirking my share of the work. John Burns did not speak to me. He just stared.

Eben sensed the threat and roused from his melancholy to become my shadow again. He never let me walk alone, which was as comforting as it was annoying, and cautioned me constantly to guard my temper and my tongue.

But Burns did nothing.

He did not single me out, or spread falsehoods about me, or manufacture an excuse to send me to the guardhouse in shackles. In fact, other than the staring, his actions for the next fortnight were exemplary. He continued our democratic habit of rotating the duties of the company. He secured an extra froe to speed up the shingle-making and delivered a rasp so we could smooth planks of wood. The new tools were certainly stolen. Burns told us to bury them in the snow if anyone came nosing around.

He conjured up food, too, appearing after dark with extra bread, butter, peas, and, once, a piece of meat, still warm from cooking.

"Those Rhode Island bandits are too fat for their own good," he said. "Eat quick and don't ask questions."

First Benny Edwards warmed to the new sergeant, then Faulkner and Greenlaw joined him for a game of cards, and soon old Silvenus started to laugh at his feeble jokes. Eben remained on his guard, thank goodness.

And me? I did not sleep much.

We finished our hut a week after Burns was raised to sergeant. It had no window and the chimney smoked fierce, but it was a palace compared to what we'd been accustomed to.

The first night properly enhutted, we slept sitting up, for there was not enough room for everyone to lie down at once. Next day we constructed sleeping shelves called "bunks." We dug postholes in the floor, then stood poles in them. We lashed more poles crosswise, with Silvenus making sure our knots were tight enough. We laid planks on the poles to create sleeping platforms; one close to the floor, one an arm's length above that, and the third above the second. Six fellows could sleep on the left side of the hut and six could sleep on the right. Burns somehow acquired straw to spread out on our platforms, which made for a softer laydown.

Headquarters had ordered that once a company moved into its hut, all tents had to be returned to the general stores so they could be mended, washed, and packed away for the spring campaign. Burns (in my own mind I never once thought of him as "Sergeant Burns") ordered us to cut up our tents and fashion them into blankets. He bamboozled the brigade clerk into thinking that our tents had been returned right after Sergeant Woodruff died and that the clerk had made an error in his account books.

The fellows in our company all hailed Burns for this; Eben, too. I took my canvas blanket and kept my thoughts on the matter to myself.

We were in high spirits the night we first slept in our bunks. We had a roof over our heads, a door that closed most of the way, and a fire that gave off heat and light as well as smoke. Benny had the itch and Silvenus had lost another tooth, but on the whole, we were in fair health. We were hungry, but not starving, and there is a world of difference between the two conditions.

We were too riled up to settle into sleeping.

"Go ahead and snow, you poxy skies of Pennsylvania!" roared Greenlaw.

"Blow, blow, thou winter wind; freeze, freeze, thou bitter sky," Benny proclaimed. "That does not bite so nigh as benefits forgot. Though thou the waters warp, thy sting is not so sharp as a friend remembered not."

"You said your aim was to be a philosopher, not a poet," Faulkner said.

"I shall be both," Benny said. "But I must not steal credit. Those words are from Mister Shakespeare's pen, not mine."

"Huzzah!" I called. "We've a roof over our heads and theatrical entertainment!"

Eben laughed. "Just like country squires, we are. Taking our ease in a mansion the King would envy."

"Hardly." Henry Barry dipped his mug into the pot of hot water at the edge of the fire. "More like a mess of bear cubs in a den."

"That's it!" shouted Faulkner. He crawled off his bunk and carried his small box of charcoal bits to the fire.

"That's what?" asked Henry.

"I've been trying to figure how I could draw our likenesses." Faulkner tested a piece of charcoal against a chimney stone, frowned, and rummaged in his box again. "To commemorate our momentous feat of construction. But the stones are not smooth enough to draw our faces proper." He tested another charcoal bit by drawing a fat circle on the stone. "Watch this."

He drew a smaller circle atop the first one, then added dashes and dots until the charcoal smear transformed into the image of a bear.

"Huzzah," Henry said.

"That one is Silvenus, for he lacks most of his teeth," Faulkner said. "Next one will be Ebenezer, so tall that he requires two stones!"

Watching him draw our crude likenesses and turn us into a den of bears was like watching a magical show, so much so that when he had drawn the last bear and signed his initials with a flourish, he bowed to his audience and we applauded with vigor.

"What is the date of this day?" he asked, prepared to write it down.

"January the nineteenth," Greenlaw said.

I sat up straight and hit my head on the bunk above. "Can't be."

"Surely is," he countered. "I've been marking it on a stick. I reckon we've got a dozen weeks or so before we march against the British."

"The nineteenth," I said. "Today is the nineteenth day of January?"

"Did you have an appointment?" Eben joked. "A coach arriving? A ship preparing to sail?"

I rubbed the sore spot on my noggin and lied with ease. "No, nothing like that. Just lost track of the days."

Before

One year ago this night, Isabel ran from her owner, stole me out of the Bridewell Prison, and rowed us to freedom. The nineteenth of January would be her birthday ever after, she swore.

Tonight, then, she was fourteen.

When spring had come to Morristown, I made plans for us to journey north, far away from the newspapers that carried runaway notices about a girl with a branded face.

Isabel dug in her heels like a pig being dragged to market. She was going south, with or without me. We argued. I called her a peevish numbskull. She called me a poxy sluggard, a churlish ruffian, and a lazy scoundrel and would not speak to me for two weeks.

I finally begged her forgiveness and promised I'd go with her. I planned on hiding our money the night before we were to leave. I'd act like we'd been robbed. I had already arranged for a job as a cart driver for the army and was due to leave soon for Albany. With no money, she'd have to go with me.

But her mind was just as treacherous as mine, only hers moved faster. She stole the money before I could and left in the middle of the night, taking the small purse of coins, her shawl, and a blanket.

Instead of being afraid for her, I was angry. Instead of setting out after her, I drove that cart to Albany, vowing to keep her out of my thoughts by twisting my ear violently whenever she slipped into my mind.

It never worked.

Everything from that moment on had been plagued with misfortune. The truth of the matter was that I missed her fiercely, and more than anything, I wanted to wish her a happy birthday. Had she found work in Philadelphia? Did she come to her senses near Baltimore or Williamsburg? Had she been captured and returned to the Locktons?

Was she alive?

CHAPTER XXVI

Tuesday, January 20–Friday, February 6, 1778

WE HAVE NEAR NINETY MEN IN THE REGIMENT THAT HAVE NOT A SHOOE TO THEIR FOOT AND NEAR AS MANY WHO HAVE NO FEET TO THEIR STOCKINGS. IT GIVES ME PAIN TO SEE OUR MEN TURNED OUT UPON THE PARADE TO MOUNT GUARD OR TO GO ON FATIGUE WITH THEIR NAKED FEET ON THE SNOW AND ICE. IT WOULD GRIEVE THE HEART EVEN OF THAT CRUEL TYRANT OF BRITAIN TO SEE IT.
—LIEUTENANT COLONEL SAMUEL CARLTON, LETTER TO GENERAL WILLIAM HEATH

I TWISTED MY EAR SO OFTEN IN THE weeks that followed, it swelled like a puffball. Did me no good; I still thought about Isabel. Her face had poisoned my mind the way the cold had taken hold of my bones.

Sore ear and cold bones aside, life had become tolerable on account of our little hut. Sleeping whilst sheltered by walls and a roof is vastly more comfortable than sleeping under the open sky, even if the roof did leak in spots.

Though most huts in camp were completed, thousands of soldiers were unfit for duty because their clothes were falling to pieces. Those without shirts covered their form with blankets or rags when necessity forced them out to use a privy trench. Many suffered from the death of their toes and fingers on account of the frostbite. I cannot bring myself to describe the state of the lads who had no breeches.

Because my company was mostly clothed and shod, we worked more hours than some. We fell into a regular pattern: dawn reveille, work on the fortifications meant to protect us from attack, breakfast, more work, dinner, chop and haul firewood, supper at dark. The middle of the day was tolerable warm, but after dawn and near sunset, the cold ate through my clothes and gnawed on my bones.

The best hours came after the sun dropped behind Mount Misery. We'd retire to our hut, cook up the day's rations of dried peas and meat (with a few cabbage leaves or a potato when Fortune smiled), and eat as slow as we could manage. We devised a rotation to take turns sitting directly in front of the fire, two by two, to play checkers. Greenlaw had fashioned a checkerboard on a plank. Bits of twig stood in for the black checkers and shards of bone for the white.

Silvenus stole extra time where it was warmest by cooking tonics for our health, boiling butternut bark or spruce tips or moss in the kettle. These remedies required constant stirring and tasting. The tailor was near three times as old as us and had grown painfully thin, so there was little protest about his unlawful hearth-sitting.

(Aaron Barry did once whine about Silvenus's habit. Greenlaw lost his temper and offered to remove all of Aaron's teeth with his fist, which caused Aaron to crawl up onto his bunk, gnawing on his toothstick like a discontented beaver.)

When we were not the appointed checker players, Eben

and I worked on our wood carvings. My bird was slowly transforming from the beaked pig into a sheep carrying a knapsack. Eben was much better than I; he could carve the likeness of a horse in two nights' work. He was never satisfied, though, and threw each one into the fire.

The hut filled with boasting, conversating, wagering, and wild tales every night. We'd itch the vermin feasting on our flesh and share the day's many rumors:

The King had declared peace.

No, the King was sending German and Russian mercenaries to destroy us.

A ball of fire as big as a man's head fell from heaven to Hatboro—a good omen. But there'd been an earthquake near York just as a cat gave birth to puppies, which meant the worst.

Congress was fleeing to Spain. No, Congress was coming to Valley Forge.

Smallpox was killing thousands of soldiers. Nay, the variolation against the smallpox had killed them.

Birds flew backward over Philadelphia. A talking cow had been displayed in Georgia.

And always the wild tales that more food, better food, and blankets and clothing were on the way. And we would soon be paid for the first time in months. That made us laugh.

Sooner or later, someone would throw a pebble or twig at Benny and beg a story from him. The lad had read every book ever printed, it seemed, and happily recounted for us the ancient tales of evil kings, beautiful queens, quarreling gods, monsters, and heroes.

At the start of February we enjoyed clear skies and warm days that melted most of the snow and thawed my fingerbones some. Captain Russell armed us with shovels, axes, and hatchets, ordering us to strengthen the Outer Line fortifications. Half a thousand of us dug trenches deep enough for a man to stand in up to his neck. We wove an abatis—a giant tangle of a fence with long, sharp-tipped poles that would gut any British horse that tried to leap the barricades.

I made a point to be friendly with a few of the black soldiers I met on fortification duty: a fellow named Salem from Massachusetts, Shadrack from Virginia, and Windsor from Rhode Island. The vast encampment was home to hundreds of fellows like us, mostly free, tho' some had been enlisted by their masters. We complained about the food and the water and everything else under the sun, the way all the soldiers did, but we were able to do it in full companionship, without worrying about lackbrains like John Burns. It was an uncommon sensation and most pleasant. I asked them to keep a watch out for Isabel, a girl with a scarred face and an irritating manner, after the war, and to show her kindness if they ever met her.

One day it became so warm while we worked on the abatis, we all stripped off our coats and wiped the sweat from our faces. Some lads from Gloucester made a game of hitting at rocks with stout sticks, but officers put a stop to the sport before it caused us to forget our duties. Once they'd gone, the game started up again.

We took care to post sentry guards and took turns batting at the sphere. My company scored the greatest number of hits and claimed the top prize: a freshly killed opossum. We hurried back to the hut to cook it, arm-sore and ravenous.

The provision wagons from Maryland and New Jersey had arrived near empty that week, and the whole camp had been on half rations because of it.

Opossum tastes better than you might think.

CHAPTER XXVII

Friday, February 6, 1778

LIEUTT. ORR, OF 10TH. PENNSYLVANIA REGIMENT, TRIED FOR UNGENTLEMANLIKE BEHAVIOR AND CONNIVING WITH SERJEANT HUGHES IN SECRETING STOLEN GOODS, SECONDLY FOR COUNTENANCING HIM IN CARRYING OFF AND OFFERING FOR SALE A MOLATTO SLAVE BELONGING TO MAJOR SHAW, FOUND GUILTY.
—GENERAL ORDERS OF GENERAL GEORGE WASHINGTON, VALLEY FORGE

MY KIDNEYS WOKE ME LATE IN THE night. I needed to piss.

I tried to ignore the sensation, turning this way and that for relief. The wind had picked up and water no longer dripped onto the floor. This evil portent meant that the roof was again iced over and relieving my kidneys would be a painfully chilly exercise. I shut my eyes tight and resolved to sleep until it was warmer.

My kidney distress increased. I groaned a bit and stood, wrapping my blanket around me and resolving to walk only a few steps from our door before I did the necessary business.

"Don't you dare piss next to the hut," warned Silvenus, above me. "I'll be checking in the morning, I swear. Can't abide lads too lazy to do the proper walking."

"Wouldn't dream of it," I muttered.

I stepped with caution on the dark, frozen path. The cold jabbed my kidneys harder, and I was forced to trot lest I spoil my breeches.

"You there!" called a harsh voice in the shadows. "Negar of the Burns company!"

I ignored this insult and hurried on. The foulmouthed dastard did not follow me.

I took care of the business of the privy trench quick as possible, buttoned my breeches, pulled my collar up and hat down, and headed back to the hut. Snow had started to fall.

I managed only a dozen paces before three figures stepped out of the darkness and blocked my way. I turned on my heel but was grabbed before I could start running. A hard fist drove into my belly. I would have fallen to the ground, but the hands held me fast whilst I coughed and fought to get back my breath.

"That's no way to greet your commanding officer," said John Burns.

I regained my breath and stood. The two men holding me grasped my arms tighter. These new allies of John Burns were larger and more dangerous than the Barry brothers, now snoring in my hut.

"I've come to extract my payment," Burns explained in the tone of a foppish dandy.

"I don't owe you anything," I said.

He chuckled. "I told these gentlemen all about the card games you lost and how you refuse to honor your debts."

"I've never played cards with you!"

"Shut it." The fellow to the right smacked my head so hard, it sent my hat flying.

"I will have your boots now, Private Smith," Burns continued. "It is fair compensation."

"I'll report you to the captain," I threatened.

"Please do," Burns answered. "I've already told him what a troublemaker you are. He is not fond of dark-skinned soldiers, did you know that? He thinks it's against the laws of nature. Anything you say, he'll take for a lie."

"Eben will tell the captain," I said. "And Greenlaw and the others. He'll believe them. You won't get away with this."

"Of course I will, you fool. I'm not going to wear those boots. Your feet have been in them for months. I shall find a home for them far away from here. Any complaints taken to the captain about me will be dismissed as nonsense." His voice hardened. "Take them off."

"Do it yourself, dogmeat."

Burns lunged for me. Both my arms were held fast, but my feet were not bound. As he reached for my throat, I kicked his belly hard as I could with both of my boots. He made a most satisfying sound as he flew through the air.

But then he stood and looked at his companions. "You know what to do."

The two men holding me each had six fists.

When I finally woke up, my boots were gone, my belly hurt wicked, and my skull felt like it had been hit with a hammer. My feet were cold, but not frostbit, so I could not have been lying there overly long.

Burns and his picaroons had vanished, their tracks hidden by the fast-falling snow.

CHAPTER XXVIII

Saturday, February 7–
Wednesday, February 11, 1778

I AM SICK, DISCONTENTED, AND OUT OF HUMOR. POOR FOOD—HARD LODGING—COLD WEATHER—FATIGUE—NASTY CLOATHS—NASTY COOKERY—VOMIT HALF MY TIME—SMOKED OUT OF MY SENSE—THE DEVIL IN'T—I CAN'T ENDURE IT—WHY ARE WE SENT HERE TO STARVE AND FREEZE—WHAT SWEET FELICITIES HAVE I LEFT AT HOME! A CHARMING WIFE—PRETTY CHILDREN—GOOD BEDS—GOOD FOOD—GOOD COOKERY—ALL AGREEABLE—ALL HARMONIOUS. HERE ALL CONFUSION—SMOKE AND COLD—HUNGER AND FILTHINESS—A POX ON MY BAD LUCK.
—DIARY OF DR. ALBIGENCE WALDO, SURGEON,
FIRST CONNECTICUT REGIMENT, VALLEY FORGE

NO, I DID NOT TELL THEM WHO STOLE my boots. Yes, that was a mistake, for it led to evil. But no, I would not go back and change that if I could.

My friends woke to find me sitting in front of the fire trying to warm my toes and dry my stockings. I explained my lack of boots but gave few details of the attack. Claimed I'd been knocked senseless at the start of it. I had hoped they'd be too tired or hungry or cold to pay much heed to my misfortune. Instead, they clustered around me and weighed the matter carefully.

Eben sat on the log seat next to mine. "My stockings are dry," he said, tugging at his boot. "Put them on."

"You need to tell the sergeant," Faulkner said.

"Don't be a half-wit," Eben said. "Sergeant Burns doesn't give a fig for Curzon."

"Then find a lieutenant," Faulkner said. "Tell the new captain, or report it to brigade headquarters. The officers need to know this kind of thievery is afoot." He paused and cleared his throat. "Beg pardon, Curzon, for saying 'afoot.'"

"Ha." I put my left foot on my right knee and rubbed the bottom of it. "There's no point in telling anyone. The officers know we're desperate for boots and blankets—"

"And everything else," interrupted Aaron Barry.

"Their time is best spent finding supplies for all of us," I continued, "not chasing after rogues they will never find."

Greenlaw picked at his teeth with a splinter of wood. "I'll tell the sergeant to mark you 'present but unfit for duty' at the roll call."

"So he can sleep all day whilst we work in the cold?" Aaron's face twisted up with petulance. "That's not fair."

"I agree," I said. "We have seven pair of shoes and boots and eight pair of feet. We should take turns being barefooted. On your day without shoes, you get to stay in the hut."

"We should report as unfit for duty every day until spring," muttered Aaron. "All of us."

"Enough!"

The loud shout came from the meekest of all of us: Benny Edwards. He stepped up to Aaron and stuck his finger in his chest. "Go on! Take your poxy bones down to the redcoats.

You're just the sort they deserve. You are an idler and a traitor, Aaron Barry."

Everyone started shouting then, accusing, a'cussing, and venting their spleens with fury. The winds outside blew fierce, but could not match the storm of discontent in our hut. Benny poked Aaron's chest one more time. Aaron swatted away the lad's hand. We all tensed, expecting Aaron to throw a punch, but he stood still, swallowing over and over, his fists shaking by his side.

Finally, Aaron gave a mighty sniff. To my astonishment, he blinked back tears. "Next time you call me a traitor, you shall regret it, runt," he said. "If the rest of you mangy lot can withstand this encampment, I can too."

Eben pulled a louse from his stocking and pitched it into the fire. "That's what passes for an apology from the Barry side of the family."

The blizzard ambushed all conversation after that.

For the first two days of the storm, we received no rations, but we had to continue building the abatis and other fortifications. I wore Eben's boots the first day and Aaron Barry's shoes on the second. Both gave me blisters that popped and bled.

Toward the end of the second day, snow fell faster than any of us had ever seen and we were sent back to our huts early. Messengers sent to the Congress in York rode only a few miles before turning back, afraid they would die of the bitter cold. Wagons could not pass through the thick snow. Ice choked the rivers and stopped all boats.

The third day began with a heavy knock on the door.

"No roll call today!" shouted Burns. "No work details. Stay in your hut."

We ate firecake for every meal that day and the next, and we were grateful for it. On the fifth day and the sixth, we had only water, flavored with bark, bone chips, and a piece of leather.

We later heard that a fellow in General McIntosh's brigade grew so hungry in that storm, he stole a tallow candle from an officer's hut and ate it. Never heard what happened after they took him to the hospital. There were whispers that some companies had cooked the meat of the dead horses, but no one ever admitted it.

There were also whispers of petitions being written by common soldiers like us begging their officers, General Washington, and most of all, the Congress to ease our suffering. We talked about writing too, but we had no paper to write upon.

CHAPTER XXIX

Thursday, February 12, 1778

OUR FREEDOM DEPENDS ON THE EXERTIONS OF A FEW PATRIOTIC INDIVIDUALS. IT IS WITH GRIEF THAT WE LEARN THAT THE CONGRESS IS MADE UP OF SO FEW OF THEM.
—DIARY OF CHRISTOPHER MARSHALL,
PHILADELPHIA PHARMACIST

THE SKIES CLEARED AFTER SIX DAYS of storming.

Greenlaw came in after the sun rose with an armful of wood. "We're supposed to line up outside for an inspection. Bunch of nobs on horses are making their way down the Outer Line."

"Here? Not on the Parade?" I asked.

"Mebbe they've finally come to their senses," Silvenus said, wrapping his hands in rags. "No point in making us walk all that way."

"Mebbe it's the brigadier general," said Eben. "Come to send us home until spring."

Greenlaw shook his head. "No uniforms on 'em and their horses are fat. Can't be officers."

I wrapped my canvas blanket around my middle and buttoned my jacket over it. "Let's hope they're quick about it."

We waded in the knee-deep snow covered with all the rags and blanket scraps we owned. The wind blew hard, driving the snow into small mountains on the north side of every hut.

John Burns approached. "Two lines, two lines," he shouted to us. "Everybody out. No excuses!"

His cry was echoed by the other sergeants. As far as I could see in both directions along the Outer Line, soldiers stumbled out of their huts into the deep snow. Some leaned on friends because they were weak from fever or frostbitten in the feet. My stockings stayed dry a few heartbeats, then the snow seeped into the wool. From my toenails up to the knee buckles of my breeches soon felt like blocks of ice. I stood on my hat, but it made no difference. The cold knifed through my skin, seared my flesh, and buried deep into my bones. Tears came to my eyes, but I wiped them away before anyone noticed. If I could just stand the pain a few moments more, my feet would go blessedly numb.

A collection of gentlemen in long warm coats atop healthy horses approached from the north. Greenlaw was wrong; there was one officer among them: our brigade commander, Brigadier General Enoch Poor, riding a sickly looking mare. They stopped five huts away to speak to the men there.

When John Burns walked away to confer with another sergeant, Greenlaw dashed over for a quick palaver with the fellows in front of our neighboring hut and came back grinning.

"It's that committee from the Congress."

"Oh, huzzah," Silvenus said. "They've come all the way from York to watch us starve."

"Don't be such a grumbler," said Greenlaw. "You've been shouting that they're ignoring us."

"Tssst," warned Henry Barry. "Burns is coming back."

John Burns took his place in between the fellows from our company and the next hut south, which was also under his command. He wore the boots that he'd worn since Albany, but I was certain his greatcoat was newly acquired, likely the trade he made for my boots.

"Mebbe they'll send us home," Eben whispered to me. "Just until the winter ends."

Silvenus shook his head. "They'll write reports and drink Madeira in front of a blazing fire. Instead of making any decisions, they'll form another committee."

"Shut your boneboxes," Burns ordered.

One day I would toss his greatcoat in the deepest, foulest privy trench in the camp. I would make sure that he was wrapped in it before the tossing.

As the congressmen approached, we put our shoulders back and lifted our chins, even old Silvenus and lazy Aaron. We were American soldiers and there was pride enough in that to make a fellow stand tall.

The wind swirled ropes of snow around our legs.

The four committee members were wrapped in so many layers of warm clothing that they more resembled bolts of cloth than congressmen. Their hats were pulled low and their scarves wrapped high against the wind. The brigadier general was more hardened to the cold and did not require so much padding. A sixth man trailed behind the group. His horse was smaller and he wore an ordinary surtout instead of the comfortable and luxurious greatcoats of the other men. At first I thought he might be a scribe or clerk hired for the writing of notes and reports. But not all men of the Congress were rich; this fellow could be one from a humble background.

The brigadier general waved to Burns to step forward and join them. The two lead riders unwrapped the scarves from their faces and leaned forward, their hands on their saddle pommels, to ask questions of the sergeant. We could not hear what was said; the wind blew their words away from us.

The gentleman on the brown stallion turned in his saddle to speak with the man at the trailing edge of the group. The poorer fellow spurred his horse forward a few steps, bent forward to listen, then unwrapped the cloths from his face so that he could speak.

The sight of his face staggered me as hard as a blow from an axe.

James Bellingham had come to camp.

Before

When I was ten years old, a tailor came to the kitchen of the Bellingham house. I stood on a chair so he could measure me for a velvet waistcoat and breeches with pewter buttons at the knees. The new suit of clothes arrived the day that James Bellingham turned twenty-five years old.

His father, Judge Bellingham, gave young Master James splendid gifts on the occasion of that birthday: a house of his own, a share of the family's ships, and enough money to marry a lady. And me.

My father packed my new clothes in one of the chests that were loaded on the wagon. After much protest, I sat next to it for the short ride to the new house. As soon as Master Bellingham was distracted, I ran down Newbury Street, back to the world I knew. I begged my father to let me stay with him.

Father talked calmly, explaining that we ought be grateful that our masters lived so close to each other. We would be able to pass most Sunday afternoons together.

I hollered and called him a bad name and he paddled my backside.

I ran away a week later, this time to a ship preparing to sail for France. I was unafraid of climbing to the top of the highest mast, so they took me on. The night before we left, the captain set a small gold ring in my right ear—the mark of a real sailor.

The judge's hired men boarded the ship at dawn. They trussed me like a pig and carried me back to Newbury Street.

Judge Bellingham ordered my father to beat me with a leather strap on my naked back. He and Master James watched to make sure Father did a proper job. I tried not to cry, for I knew it would upset my father more. But I could not help myself.

I turned my head to look back at him once, just as the strap cracked in the air. The end of it sliced a line open along my jawbone. Blood fell.

The judge said, "That's enough for now, Cesar."

My father dropped to his knees and wept.

The velvet waistcoat was green.

CHAPTER XXX

Thursday, February 12, 1778

WHEN YOU CONSIDER THAT THE POOR DOGS ARE . . . WITHOUT CLOATHES TO WEAR, VICTUALS TO EAT WOOD TO BURN OR STRAW TO LIE ON THE WONDER IS THAT THEY STAY NOT THAT THEY GO.
—LETTER FROM NEW YORK CONGRESSMAN GOUVERNEUR MORRIS, MEMBER OF THE VALLEY FORGE COMMITTEE AT CAMP

"WHAT'S WRONG?" EBEN WHISPERED. "You look like you're going to puke."

"I'm fine," I lied.

"Tsssst!" hissed the rest of our company.

Bellingham leaned forward, listening to the congressman. His boots were caked with mud and his coat was shabby compared to the coats of his companions. His gloves were split and his neck cloth was stained. Clearly, he was in reduced circumstances.

He said something that made the man on the stallion laugh.

Was Bellingham a congressman, then? A member of the committee? Despite the shoddy gloves and clothes, he was still being treated as a gentleman.

The two men turned and surveyed our company whilst

the brigadier general spoke. For a moment Bellingham stared straight at me. I had thought that if I ever again saw him, I'd be afraid; I'd cower or hide or run.

Instead, I met his gaze.

The north wind howled. Horses stamped their feet.

He owes me.

When he enlisted me, Bellingham had promised two things: that I would be freed at the end of my service to the army and that he'd give me the signing bonus of twenty pounds upon that freedom. I'd earned my freedom and had no worries on that score. But a signed paper that proved my freedom and the twenty pounds would be useful.

Bellingham patted his horse's neck, then looked at me again, his head tilted to one side. He spoke once more to his companion, dismounted, and walked toward me.

"Curzon?" he asked. "Can that truly be you?"

"Is there a problem, sir?" John Burns followed tight on Bellingham's heels. "Has this soldier offended you?"

"Not at all, Sergeant." Bellingham stopped directly in front of me. "It is you!"

Deep lines were carved into his cheeks and above his red-rimmed eyes. Skin hung from his chin; indeed, he appeared shrunken, a smaller man than he once was. My former master had aged ten years in eighteen months. The once proud and powerful now appeared pitiful. Weak. Tho' I stood in rags and upon frozen feet, I felt much more a man than he.

"Good day, sir," I said firmly.

"Good day?" He grabbed my shoulders and grinned. "I should say it's a good day! I thought you were dead."

"Not dead at all, sir," I said.

"This is extraordinary! Extraordinary!" Bellingham released me and stepped back. "You're a head taller since last I saw you."

The brigadier general and the congressman on the brown stallion both rode over to us.

"Is something amiss?" asked the brigadier general.

"I asked the very same thing, sir," Burns said quickly.

"No, no, no." Bellingham shook his head, still grinning. "This lad used to serve me. He was captured at Fort Washington and sent to Bridewell Prison; I thought he died there. He's a sight for sore eyes, I can tell you that."

All eyes, sore or not, were firmly fixed on me, staring as if I'd suddenly sprouted a second head.

Bellingham chuckled. "I have so many questions, I scarce know where to begin."

"James," the congressman called. "A word, please."

"Of course." Bellingham followed the man on the horse far enough away that we could not hear their words.

Eben gave me a shove. "You worked for him? You never said that."

"I didn't work there long," I said.

"Quiet," Burns ordered.

The congressman rejoined the other fellows on horseback. Bellingham walked back toward us and pointed at John Burns. "Are you his sergeant?"

"Yes, sir," Burns said.

"The visiting committee of the Congress requires that Curzon attend us tomorrow at Moore Hall."

"Has he offended you, sir?" Burns asked. "Is he charged with a crime?"

"No," Bellingham laughed. "Nothing like that. The congressmen want to question reliable soldiers about the circumstances here. I have vouched for Curzon's honesty. They want to hear his experiences."

Horror crossed Burns's face. "What time shall I bring him to you?" he asked.

"There's no need to escort him, Sergeant." Bellingham shivered and pulled his collar tighter. "Curzon is quite good at following directions. You know where General Washington's headquarters are?"

"The stone house by the creek, sir," I said, fighting a smile and the desire to dance with glee. I could collect my debt and make sure that John Burns was called to account for his treatment of me.

"Right. Take that road west a bit. Moore Hall is a large house, there will be no mistaking it. I shall expect you at midday."

"I'll be there, sir," I said.

Bellingham nodded, rubbed his gloved hands together briskly, and glanced at my feet. "I have one request, Sergeant."

"Anything, sir," Burns said.

"Make sure that Curzon has something on his feet."

I held my tongue until the gentlemen had ridden off and we were dismissed to return to the warmth of our huts.

"Say there, John," I said to Burns. "Can I wear your boots?"

"This changes nothing," he said, narrowing his eyes like he was sighting down a gun barrel. "Mind how you go."

CHAPTER XXXI

Thursday, February 12–Friday, February 13, 1778

I AM NEITHER AN OFFICER NOR A SOLDIER. THIS, SIR, IS MY UNHAPPY CASE! . . . A THIRST FOR HONOR; THE DEFENCE OF MY OWN PROPERTY & THE COMMON RIGHTS OF MANKIND HAVE, FOR A LONG TIME, WITH UNITED FORCE, INVITED ME TO JOIN THE MARTIAL BAND. . . . IT SHALL EVER BE MY GRATEST PLEASURE . . . FAITHFULLY TO FULFILL THE VARIOUS DUTIES INCUMBENT UPON ME.
—JOHN HOWARD, LETTER TO HENRY KNOX ASKING TO WORK FOR THE ARMY

THE QUESTIONS FIRED AT ME LIKE BLASTS of grapeshot soon as I entered the hut.

"You worked for a congressman?"

"What kind of work?"

"Were you a valet? Did you serve tea?"

"Why didn't you tell us?"

"Is he rich?"

"He's got to be rich, he's a congressman."

"Why would a congressman ride such a sickly nag?"

"Enough!" I shouted. "I can't answer if you keep shouting."

I took my time sitting in front of the fire, trying to sort out what I could and could not tell them.

"When I worked for him, Mister Bellingham was not a congressman. I cannot say for sure that he is one now. He is a man of business." I pulled off my right stocking and wrung the water from it. "His father was a firm supporter of the King, but Mister Bellingham was not. He wrote pamphlets supporting the rebellion and joined the Sons of Liberty, which angered his father so much, the old man disowned him. That's when we moved to New York."

"The two of you moved together?" Eben asked.

I laid the stocking right in front of the fire. "Bellingham and his wife moved. I went with them, of course, because I worked for them." I took off the second stocking and squeezed the water from it, too. "Mister Bellingham opened a trading firm there, both for his livelihood and as a ruse. Part of his true purpose in New York was to operate a hive of spies for General Washington. New York was crawling with two-faced Tories."

"Hold there a moment," Silvenus said. "You worked for a nob who worked for His Excellency General Washington?"

I laid the second stocking next to the first. "I just said that, yes."

"Ever seen the general? Ever serve him wine or light his pipe?"

I dared not admit the truth of the matter. "Only from a distance," I said, "when I was holding Mister Bellingham's horse or delivering a message."

One of my stockings started to smoke. I pulled it away from the hearth before it could burst into flame.

"I'm confused." Henry Barry had wrapped himself in his blankets. "I thought you was apprenticed to a blacksmith."

"That was later. I left Mister Bellingham's service to enlist just before the British invaded New York."

"You must have been young as a pup when you started with him," Greenlaw said.

"Surely was," I answered.

"The past does not matter," Eben said. "Tomorrow does. We should *all* go with Curzon."

"Oh, no," warned Benny Edwards. "We weren't invited."

"What if those ruffians come after him again?" Eben asked. "We'll be his escort of safety. While he talks to the congressmen, we'll wait in the kitchen. Think about it: the kitchen that feeds visitors from Congress. Don't you think there might be a few crumbs there for lads like us?"

"Not to mention a proper floor and chairs to sit upon," Silvenus said.

"No!" I said firmly. "I go alone."

"He's right," Greenlaw said. "There's a reason he was the only fellow invited."

Eben and Silvenus both sighed deeply.

"You want to wear my boots?" Benny asked. "My feet are closest to yours in size."

"Thank you, but no," I said. "I'd rather have Faulkner's."

Faulkner lifted a tattered shoe into the air. "A walk that far will be the death of them."

"If that happens, I shall be sure to shame the congressmen into finding you another pair," I promised. "Your shoes are closest to what most fellows have. I aim to show them the real Valley Forge. Is there any flour left? I want to cook up some firecake for them to eat with their tea."

They roared with laughter, and I finally relaxed, having succeeded in diverting their questions for the moment.

That night the fellows stacked on the bunks above and below me snored and itched through all the hours of darkness. The wind blew through the cracks in the walls; the fire hissed and popped. I watched the light and shadows chase each other across the floor and pondered my course of action.

Bellingham was overly fond of two phrases: "This tea is cold" and "Everything is trade." He always claimed that all of the issues of the world can be boiled down to a bargain sealed between two people. I didn't have much to bargain with, but I had little choice. We'd be stuck in camp for months yet, plenty of time for John Burns to get up to more mischief.

I hit upon my plan just as the *rat-a-tat-tat* of the brigade drummers signaled the new day.

CHAPTER XXXII

Friday, February 13, 1778

First the want of a Waiter, as I shall have to leave the one I now have, & in my Absence from Camp There'l be no one to take care of my tent & Clothes.
—Lieutenant Isaac Guion, Second Continental Artillery, letter to Colonel John Lamb about his need for a servant

THE COLD ONCE AGAIN KEPT EVERYONE indoors. Smoke from a thousand chimneys climbed into the sky and settled there beneath the clouds. The snow had turned the frozen horse carcasses near the artillery camp from frightful skin-covered skeletons into padded humps of wool. The Grand Parade was a white ocean crosshatched by trails. A few fellows dashed here and there, but mostly I was alone with my thoughts and the sound of Faulkner's shoes flapping with every step I took.

I shifted the rock I'd heated for the journey from my left hand to my right and reviewed my plan, sure of its success. A dozen paces later, I moved the rock back to my right hand, confident my plan would fail. My journey continued thus as my feet went cold, then burning hot, then so numb, I had to look at the ground to be certain I was stepping proper.

Beyond the rows of huts of the Life Guard lay the stone house where the general lived and directed the business of the war. There were plenty of soldiers and officers hurrying around headquarters, despite the frost in the air. The artisan workshops on the far side of the Valley Creek bridge were noisy with the sounds of blacksmith hammers, saws cutting, and the *ping-ping* of tinsmith's tools.

I did not see any of the washerwomen or dames who sewed for the army, but their long skirts had left smooth trails in the snow. Some of their children had been recently at play, for I passed a small brigade of snowmen formed by tiny hands. One of the snow figures had suffered a dreadful amputation. I stopped to repair his arm by sticking the twig back into his round body.

I checked to make sure his arm was in the right place and thought suddenly of Ruth, Isabel's little sister, who delighted in play like no other and could see only the good and cheerful side of life. With my finger, I drew a face on the snowman's head and made him smile. My stone had lost its heat, so I volunteered its service as a large button on the snowman's chest.

I walked on.

The noise of the workshops and the bustle of headquarters were soon swallowed by the falling snow. I stepped cautious as I could, but finally, the last bits of cord holding together the left shoe of Hugh Faulkner snapped. After that, I walked one hundred paces with the remaining shoe on my right foot, then one hundred paces wearing it on the left. I carried the pieces of the dead shoe in my pockets. If Silvenus could not find a way to stitch it together again, we might boil the leather in a soup one night.

Then again, if my plan worked, my friends would never dine on shoe soup again.

Moore Hall was three times the size of headquarters, with candlelight flickering in all of the downstairs windows and smoke pouring from two massive chimneys. Chimneys so large signified hearths that were big enough to roast a pig in. I felt warmer just thinking about them.

The steps were flanked by two tall Life Guards, their noses red from the cold.

"What's your business here?" asked one.

"Mister Bellingham requested that I report to the Committee at Camp." I tried for a formal tone of voice, but standing with one foot naked in the snow put me at a disadvantage.

"Use the kitchen door," he said.

I turned, walked five paces, then stopped. I was a soldier summoned by the men of Congress. That was not an errand for the back door.

I spun around and walked back to the guards. "Do all who meet with the committee enter through the back door?"

"No," answered the fellow who had ordered me around back. "Only filthy privates who don't know what's good for them."

The approach of a half dozen men on horseback prevented me from saying something stupid. The snow muffled the sound of the hooves on the road, but the harnesses jingled and the men, deep in conversation, did not stop talking to one another, even as they dismounted and tossed the reins of the horses to the guards. I stood straight and tall, as the committee members and officers stepped past me.

The last to dismount was Bellingham.

"Curzon!" he exclaimed. "Is it that late already? Come in, come in. We've much to discuss."

I followed him up the steps, nodded to the guards, and closed the door behind me.

CHAPTER XXXIII

Friday, February 13, 1778

I WISH MOST SINCERELY THERE WAS NOT A SLAVE IN THE PROVINCE. IT ALLWAYS APPEARD A MOST INIQUITOUS SCHEME TO ME—FIGHT OURSELFS FOR WHAT WE ARE DAILY ROBBING AND PLUNDERING FROM THOSE WHO HAVE AS GOOD A RIGHT TO FREEDOM AS WE HAVE. YOU KNOW MY MIND UPON THIS SUBJECT.
—ABIGAIL ADAMS, WHOSE FATHER OWNED SLAVES, WRITING TO HER HUSBAND, JOHN

THE SMALL ROOM JUST BEYOND THE door was crowded with gentlemen removing their coats, scarves, and hats, then taking turns hanging them from pegs stuck in the wall. Once that was accomplished, they headed down a long hall. One fellow paused, staring at me with curiosity and addressing Bellingham.

"Are you joining us, James?" he asked.

"In a moment," Bellingham said.

I waited for the man to depart, then started in on the speech that had kept me awake all night. "Mister Bellingham, sir, I am greatly relieved to see you alive and in such good health. I pray that your good wife also fares well and that your business has not been too severely damaged by the war."

Bellingham's face was somber. "Thank you for the gracious sentiments, but I fear they are of little use. Lorna died last summer, and there is nothing left of what was my trading enterprise. This war has brought me countless trials." He gestured to my shabby clothing. "It would appear you have suffered as well. I am grateful that Providence has brought us back together."

"Indeed, sir," I answered.

"We can talk more later." He pointed down the hallway. "At the far end there, you'll find the kitchen. The cook's name is Mistress Cook, oddly enough. Can't create a delicacy to save her life, but she's well practiced at feeding hordes of hungry men. She should have a hot meal waiting for you. While you're eating, she'll prepare a bath." He tilted his head to the side in puzzlement. "Is something the matter?"

"I . . . sir . . . ," I stammered.

The front door opened again. More officers crowded in before I could explain. They greeted Bellingham as they shrugged off their greatcoats. The pegs on the wall were all filled, so one of them tossed his coat at me. I caught it without a thought. Before I realized what I had done, the other men had piled their coats and hats in my arms, then they, too, moved down the hall.

"Busy doings here," Bellingham said. "We're trying to repair the Commissary Department and restore the army to strength."

"Bellingham!" shouted a voice down the hall.

"One moment!" he responded.

My shoeless foot stood in a wet puddle on the wood floor. "I'd be happy to eat later, sir, if the congressmen want to question me now." I shifted the wet coats to one arm. "Is there a maid who can take these?"

"I beg your pardon?" Bellingham's brow wrinkled in confusion. "Who wants to question you?"

"The men from the Congress, sir. They want to question me about the conditions for us soldiers."

His eyes lit up and he laughed. "You didn't think I was serious, did you? I spun that story to get you out of there. Didn't want the other fellows to turn on you in their envy."

"But–"

"First things first. Take those coats back to the kitchen, then eat. The cook has found some clothes for you, but you won't have to wear them long. I'll send a note to my tailor in York directing him to sew a suit of clothes for you that is more suitable for serving gentlemen."

He leaned toward me and sniffed. "Exactly how long has it been since you used soap?"

I ignored the rudeness and held steady to my planned course. I would not agree to work for him without a fair wage.

"What shall be my rate of pay, sir?" I asked.

"Pay?" His brow wrinkled again.

"I know that many officers have hired soldiers to be their manservants, but I do not know what they are paid."

"Ah." He grasped his hands behind his back and stared at my bare foot before looking me straight in the eye. "Curzon," he said softly, "I own you."

"Not any longer." I let the officers' coats fall to the ground. "You agreed I'd be free when my first enlistment expired. That was more than a year ago."

"My circumstances have changed," he said.

"That does not concern me."

His eyes widened at my tone. "I will forgive that unfortunate impudence out of respect for the service you've shown our country. But that will be the last of it." He paused and lowered his voice. "I did say that I would one day free you, but that day has not yet come. The war has complicated everything for me."

I thought of all I had endured—battle, prison, starvation, thirst, sickness, and cold—and I chuckled at his complications. I could not help myself.

"Stop that at once," he demanded.

I laughed again, for he had become so small and so small-minded, he could not begin to understand how much had changed between us. "I won't serve you, not for pay, not for anything. However, you still owe me my signing bonus." I stuck out my hand. "Twenty pounds sterling, please. Continental money is worthless."

Bellingham hit me across the face so hard, I flew into the coats that hung from the wall, then tripped over the coats on the floor.

"Never speak to me with that tone!" He stood over me, his fists clenched, a blue vein pulsing by his right eye. "Enough foolishness. You will eat, you will bathe, and you will do as I say."

The ringing in my ears was so loud, I could barely hear him. I had made a grave miscalculation. There was only one thing to do.

I rose up in a fury, shoved all the coats at him, then pushed harder, so that he was driven backward, stumbling, then falling. As soon as he lost his balance, I turned, opened the door, and started running.

"Guards!" Bellingham yelled. "Seize that boy!"

CHAPTER XXXIV

Friday, February 13–Saturday, February 14, 1778

SUCH A PROCEEDING AS THIS, COMMITTED ON A DEFENCELESS STRANGER, ALMOST WORN OUT IN THE HARD SERVICE OF THE WORLD, WITHOUT ANY FOUNDATION IN REASON OR JUSTICE, WHATEVER IT MAY BE CALLED IN A CHRISTIAN LAND, WOULD IN MY NATIVE COUNTRY HAVE BEEN BRANDED AS A CRIME EQUAL TO HIGHWAY ROBBERY. BUT CAPTAIN HART WAS A WHITE GENTLEMAN, AND I A POOR AFRICAN, THEREFORE IT WAS ALL RIGHT, AND GOOD ENOUGH FOR THE BLACK DOG.
—VENTURE SMITH (BROTEER FURRO), WHO WAS KIDNAPPED FROM GUINEA AT AGE EIGHT AND EVENTUALLY BOUGHT HIS OWN FREEDOM (HIS FREE SON, CUFF, FOUGHT FOR THE PATRIOTS FOR THREE YEARS.)

THEY CAUGHT ME.

Everything was done according to the law.

I spent a day and night in the guardhouse, held prisoner alongside soldiers who'd been caught thieving, assaulting an officer, or trying to desert to the enemy. One by one, they were taken to their court-martials. Some were found innocent and didn't return. Others came back in shock, knowing that at week's end they'd be whipped one hundred times, two hundred fifty times, or more to pay for their crimes.

My crime? I enlisted as a free man when I was still owned by Bellingham.

The three court-martial judges sat behind a table in a small room of the bakehouse. I stood in the center of the room, my hands shackled together, Hugh Faulkner's remaining shoe on my left foot. Bellingham sat on a chair behind me. To the side sat Captain Russell and John Burns. A guard stood in front of the door, armed with a cudgel, a thick hickory stick that was rounded and polished at one end.

None of my friends attended.

Bellingham lied, of course. John Burns did too, painting me as a troublemaker and a malcontent who near ruined all the fellows in his company with my evil habits. When it came my turn to speak, I told of Bellingham's promise to free me. The judges—all high-ranking officers—asked me to provide proof of the promise. I had none.

One judge sided with me. I ought be given my freedom, he said, because I chose to enlist a second time when it would have been safer for me to leave the region and go about my life. He said the Congress should pay Bellingham for his loss.

The vote was two against one. Because of my service, neither I nor Bellingham would be required to pay back the enlistment bonus I'd received in Saratoga. When the soldiers of camp finally received their pay, mine would be given to Mister Bellingham, though there was no telling when the money would arrive.

I studied the windows and doors whilst they droned on. There was no point in trying to run. Even if I was fast enough to get by the guard at the door, I would not get far. The time to flee would come, but not today.

Bellingham thanked the court in a high-flown speech that

ended with an invitation to all of them to join him for dinner soon. The judges assembled their papers, pushed back from the table, and said they would soon take him up on the offer. Captain Russell led John Burns over to introduce him to the judges.

Bellingham walked past me. "Come, Curzon."

He reached the door before he realized I was not behind him. He turned, glaring, and retraced his steps until he stood in front of me.

"You have no choice, boy," he said low, not wanting the others in the room to notice my insurrection.

"I am free," I said to him.

He grasped the chain that linked the shackles around my wrists to each other. "Hardly."

I spat in his face.

The guard's cudgel bashed my skull.

CHAPTER XXXV

Saturday, February 14, 1778

COL. JOHN ÉLY WAS ORDERED TO DISMISS A NEGRO SLAVE (OWNED BY JOSEPH CRANDALL) FROM HIS REGIMENT, TO RETURN TO SAID CRANDALL; AND HIS PREMIUM, ARMS, ETC TO BE RETURNED BEFORE HIS DISMISSION.
–ACT OF THE CONNECTICUT GOVERNOR AND COUNCIL OF SAFETY, JULY 7, 1777

BELLINGHAM RODE HIS HORSE ALONGSIDE the wagon that the guard had dumped me in. I sat next to a cask of flour and a small chest of tea.

He spoke.

My ears were stopped up with snow and anger and blood.

And then we were standing in front of the back door to Moore Hall.

And the horse was gone, the wagon gone.

He reached around me. Opened the door.

And then I was sitting in a chair, before a kitchen hearth. An old cook with twisted fingers set a steaming bowl afore me. I picked up the bowl and sipped. My hands were no longer shackled together, but it felt like they were. My feet were dry, but my bones were ice.

I drank all the broth.

My head laid itself on the table and I was no longer master

of my own body, of my head, of my heart, and somewhere my father was angry and I did not know how to explain. My eyes closed themselves.

I will kill Bellingham.

CHAPTER XXXVI

Saturday, February 14, 1778

THE MAN THAT SAYS SLAVES BE QUITE HAPPY IN SLAVERY—THAT THEY DON'T WANT TO BE FREE—THAT MAN IS EITHER IGNORANT OR A LYING PERSON.
—MARY PRINCE, BORN 1778, THE FIRST WOMAN TO WRITE ABOUT HER LIFE IN SLAVERY

WHEN I WOKE, THE CLOUDS WERE scurrying to cover the late-afternoon sun. The food and sleep had drained the befuddlement from my head. It hurt some when I stood up, but I could see and think clear.

A stocky lad carrying a jar and a dirty polishing rag entered the kitchen of Moore Hall. He was taller than me but not too many years older. His eyes were set far apart from each other and bulged a bit, like a frog's. His shoes were polished, both the leather and the fat pewter buckles. Spotless white stockings fit tight to his calves. His breeches were black wool and appeared tailored to his form. He wore a tobacco-colored waistcoat over a linen shirt as white as snow, the sleeves of it rolled up so that he might work without making it dirty. Had his skin been white, I would have figgered him for a manservant, working for one of the congressmen. As his skin was as dark as mine, it was more likely that he was a slave.

"Your master will see you now," he said.

The request was not long enough for me to reckon where he came from: New England, the South, the middle states, or across the ocean.

"My name is Curzon," I said. "You?"

He moved a wooden box on the shelf to the side.

"How did you come to be here?" I asked.

He placed the jar on a high shelf. "I was sent to fetch you, not to stand about jawing."

"Who is your master?"

He folded the rag and set it aside the jar. "You will follow me."

He led me to a dining room converted to be a useful place for the men of the Congress. Mirrors were hung opposite the windows to strengthen the last rays of the sun. Dim portraits glared down from the walls lit by guttering candles in wax-covered sconces. The long table was completely covered with books, half-burnt candlesticks, hills of papers, and an enormous map. I could not read the words at the top of the papers, but I recognized numbers, long columns of numbers that were added up to great sums.

The room was cold, the fire dying.

Bellingham sat at the far end of the table. "Ah," he said, looking up from the papers before him. "Resurrected at last. Fetch some wood for the fire, Gideon; the maid has neglected it again."

Gideon was this fellow's name. He nodded and gave a courteous "Sir" before gliding through the door and closing it behind him without a sound.

Bellingham set down his pen and waved me closer. "Let me see what damage that buffoon did to your pate."

I walked the length of the table, bent at the waist so he could peer at my head, then stood again.

"You'll heal," he said. "It's not deep."

I said nothing.

He sat back in the chair and sighed. "This is for the best. You'll see that in time."

I stared, imagining his wrists in shackles, a noose lowered over his head. Kicking away the stool that he stood upon. The sound the rope would make as it snapped his neck.

"We're crowded here, but it's better than that frozen hovel on the hill. You'll have decent clothes and food."

He waited for a reply, but still, I said nothing. Any words I spoke would surely earn me a fierce beating; I did not yet have control of my mouth or temper.

The silence of the room was broken by Gideon, who entered carrying a scant armload of firewood. He deposited it by the hearth and knelt to revive the fire, but Bellingham waved him away.

"Leave that," Bellingham said. "Remind the cook that the gentlemen will be hungry when they arrive and that she ought heat up some wash water for Curzon. And send the maid in."

Gideon stood and inclined his head. "Yes, sir."

Bellingham waited until Gideon had again disappeared, then he stretched his arms above his head once and yawned.

"The maid takes care of the mending and washing and whatever else is needed."

My mouth remained locked. I would not be goaded into conversating with him, to act as if all was well and natural.

"Gideon is on loan to the committee from one of the congressmen in York. He has struggled to properly serve the five of us. Your help will be most welcome. He'll show you the lay of the house and explain our routines. It will be much like our time in New York, only with more coats to brush and boots to clean."

He speared a cold potato with his fork and bit it. "Where is that blasted girl? Would you attend the fire, Curzon? If we wait for her to do it, we'll surely freeze."

I crossed to the hearth and picked up the fire poker, a length of iron as thick as two fingers and as long as my arm. I could crack his skull with one hard blow. But I was still barefooted and half starved. Even if I outran the guards, I'd perish of the cold. I had to soldier my temper. For now.

I knelt and poked at the dying coals.

"I function as an aide to the committee from Congress," Bellingham said proudly, as if I'd inquired about his position. "It was a stroke of genius to become as close as I did to Morris those last months in New York. You'll remember him: young chap, flirts shamelessly? Rich as Midas. Serve him first, always, then Reed, for he has the ear of General Washington. Then me. The other two fellows are good enough, but they cannot help my plans."

I arranged the wood above the coals in a crisscross fashion.

"Morris has hinted I might be appointed to head up the commissary on account of my mercantile experience. At the very least, I ought to become a person of rank within one of the divisions responsible for supplying the army. I need your ears again, Curzon. Listen in on any and all conversations, particularly when Morris and Reed meet with anyone from headquarters."

I ignored him and blew on the coals to revive them. A few weeks was all I needed. In that time, I'd learn the habits of the gentlemen; who was tidy, who was forgetful. Who carried coin upon his person and who left it in his chamber.

I'd eat everything I could to strengthen myself for the escape. When the right moment presented itself, I'd know who to steal from, how, and in which direction to flee.

The coals glowed red. There was a quiet knock on the door.

"Enter," Bellingham said.

The door opened. "The maid, sir," Gideon announced.

"Perfect," Bellingham said. "That's all, Gideon."

I blew again as the maid stepped softly across the floor. I would not alert Gideon to my plan. There was something about his manner I did not trust. Sparks finally popped.

Bellingham continued conversating with himself. "Morris arranged my position assisting the Congress." He chuckled. "Had two rooms all to myself near the City Tavern—far nicer than this. I bought a sturdy mare for fifteen pounds and this girl for ten."

The coals burst into flame.

"Oh, do stand up, Curzon," Bellingham said. "I can hardly introduce her to your backside, can I?"

I stood, brushing the ashes and wood grit from my hands.

Time stopped. The room was so still, I could hear voices arguing in the kitchen. Heavy footsteps on the floor above. The crackle of fire eating wood. Horses approaching on the camp road.

"I recognized her right away, of course." Bellingham reached for the last potato. The tines of his fork screeched wickedly across the plate. "She tried to help us nab Lockton and his foul nest of traitors, remember?"

No, no, no, no, no, no, no . . .

Candlelight caught the rage in her eyes. Reflected off the scar on her cheek.

'Twas Isabel.

Part III

CHAPTER XXXVII

Saturday, February 14, 1778

I HAD THOUGHT ONLY SLAVERY DREADFUL, BUT THE STATE OF A FREE NEGRO APPEARED TO ME NOW EQUALLY SO AT LEAST, AND IN SOME RESPECTS EVEN WORSE, FOR THEY LIVE IN CONSTANT ALARM FOR THEIR LIBERTY.
—OLAUDAH EQUIANO, MARINER AND FORMER SLAVE

ISABEL STUDIED ME, AND I, HER.
She'd grown tall and didn't much look like a girl anymore. She wore a blue-checked short gown over top of a homespun chemise and had a grimy apron atop her black skirt. She wore the shoes on her feet that she'd worn when we escaped New York, much scuffed now. A length of brown fabric was loosely wrapped below her chin, hiding her neck and covering her shoulders. A kerchief of the same color covered her hair.

Bellingham looked at me, then at Isabel, then back to me. "Do you not remember her?"

How much has she told him?

If I pretended not to know her, he'd be suspicious. But if I admitted the truth, I might expose any lies that she had been forced to spin.

I touched the swollen knot on my head. "My mind is still clouded, sir."

"She was Lockton's girl," Bellingham said. "Lived on Wall Street." He stood up. "Mayhaps that guard hit you harder than I thought."

"Now I recollect," I said. "She is much grown."

"True enough."

The din of stomping boots and loud voices in the front hall drew his attention. "Blast!" Bellingham began gathering up the papers in front of him. "Quick! Curzon, close up all the books with red leather bindings and stack them in the center of the table. Isabel, to the kitchen for wine. The wagon should be ready for you, but prepare the tray first."

Isabel paused at the door that led to the kitchen and looked back at me. I could not tell what she made of any of this.

"Hurry!" ordered Bellingham.

As she slipped out, two gentlemen entered from the hall, brushing snow from their wigs. They were congressmen, but I did not know their names.

"You've returned early!" Bellingham feigned delight with a false smile.

The younger fellow shivered once. "A rider came from Albany with news."

"News about the scheme to unseat General Washington. Disrupted all of the business of the day. Total rot, of course." The older man dropped into a chair with a groan and wiped his nose on a handkerchief. "Is this your boy? He looks a bit worse for the wear."

"There was a misunderstanding after the trial," Bellingham said.

The younger gentleman pointed to the papers in Bellingham's hands. "Did you complete your study of the reports?"

Bellingham set the papers down and straightened the

cuffs of his shirt. I'd seen him do it countless times, always when he was about to shade the truth in his favor.

"I want to go over the numbers again. The situation could be much worse than anyone imagined." He plucked a paper from the center of the table. "These are the reports from Chester County."

The gentleman with the damp nose held up his hands. "Not yet, James, please. Some food first."

"Agreed." The younger congressman sat next to him. "Your boy won't serve table dressed like that, will he?"

"I should say not!" Bellingham said. "He has an appointment with soap and clean clothes right now. You can go, Curzon," he said to me.

I took three steps away from the table before he stopped me.

"One moment," he called. "Have you forgotten how to take proper leave of your master?"

That word—"master"—was a musketball ripping through my guts. I almost bolted for the fireplace and grabbed that poker so I could brain him. They'd catch me, beat me, mebbe kill me, but it would have been worth it.

Except for Isabel.

All three men stared at me, waiting.

I stiffened my back, held my arms tight to my sides, and bowed low, silently cursing every man in the room.

"Thank you, sir," I said as I again stood straight. "Will that be all?"

CHAPTER XXXVIII

Saturday, February 14, 1778

To make a calf's foot pie: First set four calves feet in a sauce-pan in three quarts of water, with three or four blades of mace; let them boil softly till there is about a pint and a half, then take out your feet . . . pick off the flesh from the bones, lay half in the dish, strew half a pound of currants clean washed and picked over and half a pound of raisins softened . . . bake it an hour and a half.
—Hannah Glasse, *The Art of Cookery*, published in 1774

I PASSED GIDEON IN THE HALL. HE WAS carrying a tray of wineglasses and a bottle to the newly arrived gentlemen.

"Pardon me," I started. "Do you know—"

He walked past me without a word.

The kitchen was crowded with so many tables, chairs, crates, and kegs that there was hardly room to turn around. The walls were filled with shelf after shelf of fat ceramic jars, green glass bottles, boxes for cutlery and spices, crockery plates, and wooden bowls. Extra chairs hung from hooks on the beams where wall met ceiling. Four pots bubbled over the flames in the hearth, and the lid covering a massive pan peeked out from the heap of glowing coals.

Most curious of all was the bird sitting in a cage on the table closest to the fire. It was the size of a small crow, but wore brilliantly colored yellow, green, and blue feathers and was possessed of a ferocious beak it was using to open a walnut.

An old white woman came out of the pantry carrying a smoked ham.

I bowed hastily. "Good day, ma'am. Can you tell me where I can find Isabel? Mister Bellingham's maid?"

"That one?" She heaved the ham onto a board and limped to the other side of the room. "What do you want her for?"

"Uh," I stammered. "To become better acquainted with my duties. Here."

The woman grunted, pulled a stool over to the shelves, and climbed up onto it, her limbs shaking.

I rushed over before she fell. "May I please help, ma'am?"

She studied me, her blue eyes clouded with age. "I need that knife box up there."

"Of course."

She put out a hand so I could help her safely find the ground and watched as I took down the box and set it by the ham.

"That Isabel"—she took a large knife from the box—"the wagon just took her back to headquarters. They needed a maid to help with something." She sliced off a bit of the ham and tossed it in the cage. The bird snatched the meat in its beak, then gave a low whistle. "Cheeky devil," she said to the creature.

"Mister Bellingham hired her out?"

"Hires her out every chance he gets. This camp has too

many gentlefolk and not enough servants. Pull down a plate for me, will you? And a bowl."

She piled ham slices on the plate I handed her, then gave it back to me. "Eat." A toothless smile softened her direct manner of speech.

She did not have to say it twice. I sat, grabbed a fork, speared a piece of the meat, and stuffed it into my mouth. The taste was indescribable, but better than that was the satisfying sensation of swallowing, and then the luxury of another and another and another piece waiting on my plate.

"I imagine you'll be hired out too," she said. "After you've had a bath. Are you useful at all? Do you have a trade? The artisans are desperate, I hear. 'Specially the gunsmiths." She filled the bowl with soup from a pot hanging over the fire and set it next to my plate.

Could the key to our escape be so easy; wait until we were hired out to the same house and then run?

"When will Isabel return?" I asked.

She continued slicing and chuckled. "Lads find love in the strangest places."

"No, ma'am," I said, my face suddenly hot. "It's just–"

"Don't you worry none." She reached across the table and patted the back of my hand. "I raised eight sons and a score of grandsons. Know a few things about lads, I do. Your secret's safe with me."

My mouth opened, but for the life of me, I could not think of a lie. The colorful bird gave a tremendous squawk as if laughing at my discomfort.

"Shush, now." Missus Cook tossed more ham in the cage. "Keep up that noise and I'll bake you in a pie, I swear."

I seized upon the interruption to direct the old lady's

attention away from Isabel. "If I may, ma'am, what manner of bird is that?"

"My son William claims it is a parrot. Won it in a card game, he did. Says I ought call it King George, so he can order it about when the war is over." She gave the soup over the fire a stir. "William is a fine cardplayer, Lord forgive him. Have you heard of him? William Farnsworth Cook of the Fifth Pennsylvania Regiment? Blasted fool is too old to be in the army, but he won't listen to his mother. Or his wife."

I wiped my mouth. "Are there many parrots in Pennsylvania?"

She laughed at that. "Goodness, no. The sailor who lost the card game came across it in some heathenish place." She limped back to the table and picked up her knife again. "Ought to be grateful. Imagine if my William had won himself an oliphant. Where would I fit a creature like that in my kitchen?"

CHAPTER XXXIX

Sunday, February 15–Wednesday, February 18, 1778

SHE TOOK DOWN HER HORSE WHIP, AND WHILE SHE WAS GLUTTING HER FURY WITH IT, I REACHED OUT MY GREAT BLACK HAND, RAISED IT UP AND RECEIVED THE BLOWS OF THE WHIP ON IT WHICH WERE DESIGNED FOR MY HEAD. I IMMEDIATELY COMMITTED THE WHIP TO THE DEVOURING FIRE.
—VENTURE SMITH'S (BROTEER FURRO) DESCRIPTION OF STOPPING A BEATING BY HIS LONG ISLAND OWNER

ISABEL WAS A PUZZLEMENT IN THE days that followed. When our paths crossed, she would not look at me. I'd say, "Hello, Country." Or, "Good day, Isabel," but she acted deaf. At first I thought she was being sensible, that there were dangers for us both if we talked freely in front of others. The kitchen always overflowed with people: Missus Cook; Gideon; the Moore family, who owned this house and were reduced to living in one bedchamber; plus any number of messengers and junior officers coming from or headed to the camp. I told myself she was just waiting for the right moment.

By the third day, however, I began to worry that she'd suffered a brain fever. We passed each other in the hall, without another person in earshot, and still she ignored my greeting. I followed her back into the kitchen that time, intent on forcing a conversation, but Gideon was waiting for her, holding the tall rack of bells that he pulled out when readying the wagon to take Isabel for another day of hired-out work.

"I beg your pardon, miss," I said with care, for Gideon stared openly at us. "Do you suffer from an affliction of the ears?"

Isabel tied on a bonnet, pulled on a red cloak and knitted mittens, then walked out the door without answering me. Gideon smirked and gave a little laugh that made me want to punch his face.

Gideon only spoke to me when he was complaining about my work or giving me a new task to do. Tho' we ate most meals together, worked side by side, and slept on the floor of the bake-oven shed, he never conversated with me like a normal fellow. In the daytime, he ignored my questions. At night he'd lay himself down and go straight to sleep. Or at least pretend to.

"A peculiar egg," Missus Cook called him.

Gideon's master, the congressman in York who had loaned him to the committee, was one of the richest men in the South, according to the old woman. He owned four hundred slaves who worked his fields of rice and tobacco. Gideon was as trusted as General Washington's manservant, Billy Lee, but was said to be twice as clever.

"He speaks the French and the Italian," Missus Cook gossiped. "Learned it when he went over the seas with his master."

I did not think this was much of an accomplishment and heartily wished that his master would recall him to York. Or send him to Italy. Anything to keep his sneering face away from me and Isabel. Gideon treated me like a useless piece of furniture, but when it came to Isabel, he was all false kindness and flattery. Because she was so young and unfamiliar with the world, she encouraged his attentions.

These circumstances gave even more urgency to my plans of escape. I pondered how we could run away day and night. When to run. Where to run. How to avoid recapture.

Spring was the most likely time—after the snow had melted, but before the army marched into battle. We ought wait for a confusion-filled day so we could be miles away before our absence was noted. But waiting brought danger, too. Bellingham and the congressmen could soon return to York, where our chances would be much dimmer. He could decide to sell one or both of us, because he was short of coin. My doubts and convictions fought back and forth.

Run now.

Wait for the right moment.

Run while we still can.

Wait to gather information and strength.

But when the gentlemen discussed the birthday ball being thrown for His Excellency General George Washington, the decision was made for me.

I did not sleep the night I heard the news. Gideon snored like a well-fed hog, and the sound of it made me heartily miss all the fellows in my hut. It also helped keep me awake as I waited for Isabel to come outside to use the privy. I prayed that she did not have a chamber pot.

The hinges of the kitchen door squeaked just before the sun rose. I peered out the shed door just in time to see her enter the privy. 'Twas a cold morning; she did not tarry long. I stood at the kitchen door and put a finger to my lips when she returned, then followed her inside.

Isabel walked to the hearth and poked at the fire. "Say your piece," she said bluntly.

"Pardon me?"

She stuck a twist of paper into the flames. "You've been itching to holler at me since you got here. I'll keep working whilst you bluster on. Missus Cook likes everything to be ready when she comes downstairs." She lit two candles with the burning twist and tossed it into the fireplace. "Just don't expect me to apologize."

"I'm not going to bluster or holler and I don't want an apology."

"I don't have time for lies or foolishness," she said.

"Would you please be quiet for one moment?" I walked over to her and whispered, "I can get us out of here."

CHAPTER XL

Wednesday, February 18, 1778

THE YOUNG NEGRO FELLOW WILL SHAG WHO FORMERLY LIVED AT OLD QUARTER AND AS HE WAS ALWAYS RUNAWAY I MOVED HIM DOWN HERE TO SETTLE THIS PLACE . . . BUT HE RUNAWAY SOME TIME IN JUNE WENT TO YORK AND PAST FOR A FREE MAN . . . HE WENT AWAY FOR NO PROVOCATION IN THE WORLD BUT SO LAZY HE WILL NOT WORK AND A GREATER ROGUE IS NOT TO BE FOUND.
—LETTER TO GEORGE WASHINGTON FROM ONE OF HIS OVERSEERS, JOSEPH VALENTINE

ESCAPE?" SHE WHISPERED.

"There's a big celebration at headquarters Sunday night, General Washington's birthday. It will be just like New York," I said. "We'll wait until they are deep in their cups and merrymaking, then run."

Her eyes narrowed. "If you think I'm running away with you, then your wits have indeed been scrambled."

"What?"

She tightened her jaw. "I trusted you in Morristown. You lied to me about where we were headed and went behind my back to lay plans for Albany. One of the other cart drivers told me of the plan when he was looking for you."

I frowned. "Isabel, you lied too, and you stole all our money."

"You lied first. And yes, I took the money, but halfway to Philadelphia, I felt bad about it. So I went back."

"You went back for me?"

"No, not for you. Just to return your half of the money. Only you weren't there. Glad to be quit of me, I figgered."

"I was not glad to be quit of you. What happened then?"

She swung the kettle over the fire. "When I didn't find you, I left again. Found a nice seamstress to work for in Philadelphia. I saved until I could pay for a spot on the coach to Williamsburg. I was waiting for it in front of the State House when I was grabbed."

"By Bellingham?"

She shook her head. "The fellow who sold me to him. He was a violent man." She stopped sudden. "That's all I'm going to say about that."

I was overcome by an unsettling sensation, as if some giant had picked up the whole of the earth and tilted it. She'd been hurt, scarred on the inside of her spirit, and I did not know how to help her.

"I am sorry," I said. "Dreadful, doleful sorry."

The weak words were useless. Since we'd parted in Morristown, she'd been alone and in the worst sort of misery. No wonder she'd treated me ill.

I cleared my throat. "We have to plan for Sunday."

The candlelight jumped and played on the walls, making our shadows as tall as the ceiling. Two tears escaped her eyes. One fell to the floor, the other dropped onto the folds of the cloth wrapped around her shoulders and neck.

"I can't go," she said.

"Of course you can. We'll stay together every step, I swear. We'll head for Baltimore or—"

"Hush." She wiped her eyes and shook her head. "I already tried to run away. Three times." She reached for her neck cloth. "Master Bellingham took me to a blacksmith." She found the loose end of the cloth and began unwrapping it. "And paid the man to forge this."

She let the cloth fall to the ground.

An iron band circled her neck, fastened there by a lock that hung like a hideous jewel. This collar was as good as chains around her ankles; it would alert the world of her circumstance and make escape even harder.

"Bellingham wears the key on a cord around his neck. There is a slot in the back for the bells," she explained. "You've seen Gideon carrying them. He locks them into the collar whenever I leave the house. The ladies I sew for say they give off musical tones when I walk." Her voice choked with anger. "They find the sound delightful."

The ground under my feet tilted farther, and I felt like I was falling down a dank, endless well, stone walls closing in around me, darkness stealing away my breath. Isabel waited in silence.

"It changes nothing," I finally said. "We'll find a way to remove it once we're far away."

"Any blacksmith you approach would have us arrested and pocket the reward. My only hope is to fool him into thinking that I've changed so he'll take this off someday. That's when I'll escape." She picked up the long cloth from the floor. "You'll have to run alone. If you do, mind your mouth. It always makes trouble for you."

Gideon opened the door before I could respond, his bug eyes wider than usual. "Is the tea ready?"

How much did he hear?

"Nearly," Isabel lied.

"Your witless friend here can take it up to the gentlemen," Gideon said smoothly. "I'll prepare the table."

Isabel rewrapped her neck cloth. "Would you fetch some wood for the fire, Curzon?"

CHAPTER XLI

Wednesday, February 18–Sunday, February 22, 1778

RUN AWAY . . . A NEGROE GIRL, NAMED HAGAR, ABOUT 14 YEARS OF AGE, OF A BROWNISH COMPLEXION, HAS REMARKABLE LONG FINGERS AND TOES, AND A SCAR UNDER ONE OF HER BREASTS, SUPPOSED TO BE GOT BY WHIPPING. HAD ON . . . AN OZENBRIGS SHIFT AND PETTICOAT, VERY MUCH PATCHED . . . [AND] AN IRON COLLAR ABOUT HER NECK.
—NEWSPAPER ADVERTISEMENT PLACED IN THE *PENNSYLVANIA GAZETTE* BY WILLIAM PAYNE

BY THE TIME I BROUGHT THE WOOD in, Isabel had loaded the tray with a teapot and three cups and saucers. "For Misters Bellingham, Dana, and Folsom," she said as I picked it up. "Top of the stairs to the right."

My jumbled cogitations of horror and despair left me speechless. All I could do was nod. I carried the tray to the gentlemen's bedchamber and knocked before entering.

The dim light of a single candle left most of the small room in shadows, but I could see that the bed was intended for two bodies and contained three. Valley Forge was so crowded, even congressmen had to bunk together. Mister Dana stood up and made his way to the washstand as I crossed the threshold. Mister Bellingham gave a groan and turned over.

"Careful, lad." Mister Folsom sat up, pulled off his nightcap, and scratched at his short hair that stood up like porcupine quills. "Not much room for stepping."

"Not much, sir." I picked my way through the confusion of boots, trunks, chairs, and discarded clothing on the floor. "May I stack these books?"

"Just leave the tea and begone," Bellingham grumbled into his pillow.

I balanced the tray in one hand and made space on the small table by piling the books scattered there. After I set the tray down, I lit a second and a third candle.

Mister Dana tapped with his knuckles to break the thin layer of ice atop the water of the washing-up basin. "Don't suppose we could get warm water for the washing?"

"Get on with it, you coward," Mister Folsom said. "Ice water builds character, didn't your mother ever tell you that?"

Mister Dana splashed the water on his face and grunted.

"Shall I pour the tea, gentlemen?" I asked.

"No." Bellingham finally sat up. "Go down and make sure that fire is roaring."

I bowed, not trusting myself to speak to him.

"Wait!" Mr. Dana wiped his hands on a rag, crouched at the side of the bed, and drew out the chamber pot. It had been used in the night. "Take care of this, will you?"

I took the chamber pot from him. I wanted to turn it upside down on Bellingham's head, to drag him out of the bed, down the stairs, and into the snow, where I would horsewhip him until he understood what Isabel had suffered.

"Are you ill?" Bellingham asked. "Is your head still muddled?"

"Oh, no, sir," I said. "My head is clear."

I determined then to begin a mutiny. When the gentlemen were breakfasting, I made up their bed, taking care to sprinkle mouse droppings on the mattress first. I emptied the chamber pot, but did not rinse it clean before I replaced it under the bed. I stepped my muddy shoe on a shirt fallen to the floor and kicked it to the corner.

When the gentlemen left for headquarters, I spilled half a cup of tea across their papers, then covered the mess with several ledgers. I closed the fireplace flue to make the dining room smoky, then complained about it to Gideon, who opened the flue and all the windows to air out the room. When the gentlemen returned for their dinner, they had to eat it with their coats and gloves on, for it was as cold inside as out. Gideon received the scolding for this, which was an unexpected bonus for me.

I continued my insurrection for several days, all the while plotting my escape. The iron collar around Isabel's neck meant that I would have to escape first, then find a foolproof way to cast off the collar and take her with me. I ate all of the food I could hold at every meal to strengthen myself for the running. Breakfast was two bowls of porridge and bread topped with molasses and butter. Dinners and suppers always had some sort of roasted or stewed meat and plenty of turnips. Missus Cook took pleasure in my appetite and baked two apple pies for me. I tasted guilt whenever I thought of Ebenezer and the others, but I ate until my belly ached.

I prepared Bellingham's clothes for the general's birthday celebration with great care. I brushed most of the dirt from his jacket, but snipped a few threads from the buttons in the hopes that one or two might pop off in the course of the evening. I polished his shoes, picked off the lint from his black breeches, and inserted a pinch of wood shavings into the toes of his stockings so that his feet would itch all night.

Once I finished dressing him, Bellingham said that he wanted me to lead his horse to headquarters. Mr. Folsom frowned as he heard this, surprised, perhaps, that Bellingham was vain enough to parade his wealth before the general.

I was dismayed. I had not thought he would require me. My plan was to wait a few hours, tell Gideon I had a belly complaint and would be spending the night in the privy, and run as fast and far as I could until dawn.

When the gentlemen were all mounted, Bellingham waved the others ahead. Once they were out of sight, he said, "All right then, Curzon. Walk on."

I took the horse's reins and gently pulled so that she walked alongside me. The falling rain was on the edge of turning into ice. I raised the lantern so I could better see the road.

"How do you find Isabel?" Bellingham asked after a mile of walking.

His voice startled both the horse and me. I slowed until she calmed some, then resumed my pace. "Isabel seems fine enough."

"Gideon tells me that she showed you her collar," he said a half mile later. "Did she?"

"Yes, sir."

"She's quite good with a needle," he said. "Much too valuable to let slip away."

"You are a wise man of business, sir."

"Do not mock me," he snapped. "Stop the horse."

I tugged on the reins. The horse halted and snorted, her breath turning to frosty smoke. We were close enough to the bridge to hear the faint sound of the hammers pounding in the artisans' workshops.

"My patience is at an end, Curzon. Did you think I wouldn't know who ruined the reports on the table, turned the dining room into a smokehouse, and muddied my best shirt? What's next, serving me curdled milk? Poison?"

"No, sir."

"I thought not," he said, "because you're running away. Tonight, correct?"

Gideon.

"Allow me to explain a few things. I purchased Isabel for my wife's use, but then Lorna died. When I realized how much I could earn from the girl's sewing skills, I decided to keep her. Tho' she has that troublesome inclination to run away, she's valuable. As are you, except for the rebellious notions that have infected your mind."

I will kill you slowly, I thought.

He dug his heels into the mare's flanks. "Walk on, Curzon. I do not want to greet the general looking like I just climbed out of the river."

I took the horse's reins again and concentrated on placing one foot in front of the other.

"Everything is trade, you know, even between a master and a servant," Bellingham said. "When you offer me honest labor and dutiful behavior, you earn my kindness. For your recent treatment of me, I should pay you back with a beating. But I suspect pain holds little fear for you after what the army has put you through. I've been pondering this predicament for days and have finally hit upon the perfect solution."

The horse hesitated as we stepped onto the bridge that spanned Valley Creek. Bellingham kicked her again. "Are you listening carefully?"

"Yessir."

"Your punishments shall be given to Isabel."

"Pardon me, sir?"

"Every time you behave improperly, she will suffer. If you deserve a slap, I shall slap her. If you earn a night in the stocks, she will serve out the term. And if you are stupid enough to run away, her pain, Curzon, will never end."

CHAPTER XLII

Sunday, February 22, 1778

CASH PAID THE 22D INST.
TO PROCTOR BAND BY THE G.O. . . . 15S.
—DAILY EXPENSE ACCOUNT OF GEORGE WASHINGTON
SHOWING PAYMENT MADE TO THE FIFE AND
DRUM PLAYERS WHO PLAYED FOR HIM ON
HIS BIRTHDAY AT VALLEY FORGE

"DO YOU UNDERSTAND?"

Bile had risen in my throat. I swallowed it. "I understand, sir."

"Excellent. We will speak no more of it."

Headquarters lay just ahead, ablaze with candle and lantern light. Bellingham dismounted at the bottom of the path that led to the front door of the small stone house. He smoothed his breeches, then removed his gloves and handed them to me.

"Do I look suitable for a dinner with His Excellency and Lady Washington?"

Heavy shadows lay under his eyes. His face was not as whisker-free as it ought be for such an occasion. A stain on his neck cloth was apparent even in the half darkness and his wig was in dire need of pomading.

"If I may, sir," I said, "I should like to adjust . . . there is a stain visible . . ." I pointed.

"Of course."

I tugged at the fabric to loosen the silk cloth that wrapped around his neck. The sounds of the soldiers and officers around us, the noise of the bustling kitchen in the building behind headquarters, the high-pitched laugh of some officer's wife, they all faded, overpowered by the screaming in my head.

My fingers. My hands so close to the cord around his neck that held the key to the iron collar. The cord that deserved to be tightened like a noose. . . .

"Aren't you done?" he asked impatiently.

The voices flooded back, as did the light from the campfires of the general's Life Guard.

"Almost, sir." I refolded the neck cloth to cover the stain and stepped back.

"Better?" he asked.

"Much better, sir. I'll have Isabel clean that tomorrow."

"Splendid. See if you can scare up some oats for this old girl"—he patted the horse—"and there should be victuals for you behind the kitchen. Keep an eye out for that Billy Lee, the general's manservant. It would be good for us if you could establish a friendship with him."

"I shall do my best, sir."

I waited until he disappeared through the door, then I led the horse to the barn and found a handful of oats and bucket of water for her. A servant offered me a mug of hot toddy. I drank it down, declined his offer of a game of cards, and stared into the dark.

One of Benny Edwards's favorite stories was about a fellow who stole fire from the old gods and brought it to the people who were cold. I couldn't remember his name. He was caught, of course. The gods chained him to a rock to punish him. Every day an eagle was sent to peck out the fellow's liver. Every night the liver grew back, so he did not die. The torture started anew each morning. All because he stole something that should have been his to begin with.

When Benny finished his story, Silvenus said if it had been him, he would have bashed his own head into the rock until he was dead. Aaron Barry said he would have grabbed the eagle and eaten it. The rest of the fellows were quiet, including me, because I did not know what I would have done if somebody shackled me to a mountain and sent an eagle to eat my insides, day after day after day.

Now I knew. I would fight the eagle and the chains and that mountain as long as I had breath.

CHAPTER XLIII

Monday, February 23–Tuesday, March 17, 1778

UPON THE WHOLE MY DEAREST FRIEND AND FATHER,
I HOPE MY PLAN FOR SERVING MY COUNTRY AND THE
OPPRESSED NEGRO-RACE WILL NOT APPEAR TO YOU
THE CHIMERA OF A YOUNG MIND DECEIVED BY A FALSE
APPEARANCE OF MORAL BEAUTY, BUT A LAUDABLE SACRIFICE
OF PRIVATE INTEREST TO JUSTICE AND THE PUBLIC GOOD.
–JOHN LAURENS, LETTER TO HIS FATHER, HENRY, PRESIDENT
OF THE CONTINENTAL CONGRESS AND SLAVE TRADER

WE WERE AT WAR IN THE WEEKS that followed, Bellingham and me, a stage play of a war. He acted the part of the kindhearted master but was secretly armed with his ability to hurt Isabel. My role was the slow-witted, dutiful servant. Bellingham did not hire me out even for one day, so the inhabitants of Moore Hall became my weapons.

As Bellingham had requested, I lavished extra attention and care upon Mister Morris and Mister Reed, always making sure that the best pieces of meat were set upon their plates and that their glasses stayed full. I fashioned a stool for Mister Morris to rest his sore ankle upon, after he slipped on the ice. I sharpened Mister Reed's quills, for he never took the time to do it himself.

When Mister Morris asked me to care for his boots, I won a skirmish. When I put all of his clothes to rights, removing stubborn stains and unpleasant odors from his breeches, he expressed his gratitude with a coin and complimented Bellingham on the quality of his servant. That won me a minor battle and earned me the duties of cleaning all of the gentlemen's clothing.

Bellingham was clever enough not to trust my transformation back into obedience. He was shaved each day by Gideon and rarely allowed me in the same room with him if he was alone.

My ears were my valued allies. When the plates and glasses were all filled, and I was required to stand in the corner of the dining room and wait for the next order, I'd fix my eyes upon a spot on the wall and stare as if I were a bit addled. In truth, I was listening close to the conversating, waiting for information that would help us break free from the mountain.

Much of what I heard had more meaning for the soldiers shivering in their huts than for me. The causes of our starving times were many. The men in charge of supplying the army had not prepared for the winter encampment; the army did not have enough wagons to deliver food to camp nor enough money to pay for it; and the local people had already sold their grain and meat to the British, forcing supplies to come from great distances. And to top it all off, there was no salt to be had, which made preserving meat and fish for the journey to camp near impossible.

There were some eleven thousand soldiers at camp, making Valley Forge the third biggest city in America, according to Mister Folsom. To feed them proper required a million pounds of bread and a million pounds of meat every month. I had no notion of what a million was, but I knew it was a vast sum.

The gentlemen agreed that the fellows who had been running the Offices of the Quartermaster and Commissary should all be shot.

Dinner the next night was rabbit pie and more of Missus Cook's turnips, which the gentlemen were fast tiring of. The talk centered on a battalion of black and Indian soldiers being assembled in Rhode Island (news that I could not wait to tell Isabel). The state was largely occupied by the British, and the Patriots could not find enough men to fill the ranks of their Continental brigades. The Rhode Island assembly had passed a law to free slaves if they served for the entire war. They offered to pay the owners of the new soldiers 120 pounds for the loss of their property. This seemed to me such a sensible solution to so many problems, I could not figger why it created discord or why the other states did not follow suit.

Mister Morris then told of a recruitment plan he'd heard that day, a notion put forth by John Laurens, an aide-de-camp to General Washington.

"Laurens claims that if the army does not double or triple in size, the war could drag on for years. He, too, wants to enlist and arm slaves who are willing to fight. He points to the general acceptance of the hundreds of free Negroes here in camp as evidence that it would not cause any problems."

"Ha!" snorted Mister Dana. "What of their masters? How are they to be compensated?"

"Young Mister Laurens has thought this through most carefully," said Mister Morris. "He says the government should compensate the slave owners a fair price for each man who goes into the army, just as they have done in Rhode Island. He thinks it might be a way to stop slaves from escaping and joining the British. A growing number seem determined to back whichever side grants them liberty."

"We have quite enough trouble with the British. To raise the issue of freedom for slaves right now would be setting a spark to gunpowder." Mister Reed lifted his glass. "Cheers."

I fought to keep my face plain and dull as the rest of the men returned the toast. The more I pondered it, the angrier I became. I stole a glance at Gideon. Slaves who were not friends could still share common sentiment about the injustices they suffered. Gideon stood as straight and stiff as a statue. His eyelids did not flicker as the congressmen scorned the ideas of John Laurens. He did not breathe deeper or faster or clench his fists to contain his anger. The gentlemen could have been discussing the age of the turnips on their plates or the chance of snow on the morrow.

His reaction, or rather, the absence of any reaction, made me more curious than ever about Gideon. I resolved to study his actions as carefully as I studied those of my captors.

CHAPTER XLIV

Wednesday, March 18–Sunday, March 22, 1778

This curious Character of a Barber . . . I have a great Inclination to draw for your Amusement. He is a little dapper fellow . . . , a Tongue as fluent and voluble as you please, Wit at Will, and a Memory or an Invention which never leaves him at a Loss for a story to tell you for your Entertainment. . . . He has dressed Hair, and shaved Faces at Bath and at Court. . . . He is a serjeant in one of the Companies of some Battalion or other here. . . . I assure you I am glad to chatt with this Barber while he is shaving and combing me, to divert myself from less agreable Thoughts.
–John Adams, letter to Abigail Adams

I EXAMINED EVERYTHING THAT GIDEON owned the next morning when he drove Isabel to her duties at Missus Shippen's. He possessed three blankets, four fine shirts, two extra pair of breeches with expensive knee buckles, and a blade for shaving his face. I found nothing that gave an indication of his character; no cards or gaming pieces, nothing for praying or for sport or for remembering someone far away.

The only curious thing was a letter folded small and hidden inside his second-best breeches. Missus Cook once asked Gideon to read a page of a newspaper to her when Isabel was busy. Gideon had said then that he could not read. I couldn't either, so I had no idea what the letter contained or who sent it or why he would keep such a thing. I carefully folded it again and hid it back in the breeches.

After that, I kept track of the amount of time Gideon spent on errands to headquarters or the market stalls on Sullivan's Bridge. More than half the time he tarried, sometimes returning much later than he ought. He was never spoken to about this; the gentlemen and Missus Cook all assumed he was doing the wishes of one of the generals or aides to His Excellency. As his real master was a day's ride away, there was no true accounting of his comings and goings.

I suspected he was courting a girl—one of Lady Washington's maids or a girl who worked for one of the regiments because her father or brother served in the company. I hoped it meant he was courting a girl, for Isabel was becoming too familiar with him. She allowed him to stand disrespectfully close when they talked, and laughed when he tried to be funny, tho' he never said a single clever thing. I was beginning to loathe all things about Gideon.

Winter returned with a bitter vengeance on the twenty-second day of March, thirty-seven days after Bellingham stole my life from me. Congressmen Dana and Folsom refused to let the thick ice on the road in front of Moore Hall interfere with their plans to leave for York that morning. Gideon and I wrapped rope around our shoes to give us a better grip on the ground as we carried their trunks and boxes to the wagon. Though normally a strong enough fellow, Gideon struggled with his end. He coughed heavily and shook with chills when I was warm enough from our exertions to be sweating.

"Have you had the smallpox?" I asked him.

"I do not have the smallpox."

"You look sickly to me."

Gideon ignored me. "Go upstairs and turn the mattress in the Greenes' bedchamber. Make sure Isabel has dusted and cleaned the windows." He paused to cough some more. "I'm off with the wagon to collect their belongings. If the room's not ready when I return, the blame is all yours."

General Nathanael Greene and his young wife were moving into the empty bedchamber. General Greene was taking over the quartermaster general's position and would be in charge of purchasing and delivering the food and other requirements for the army. By fetching their belongings, Gideon was wasting no time assuming the role as the general's manservant.

After I turned the mattress, there was wood to be split, manure to be shoveled in the barn, and all manner of chores requested by Missus Cook. A fat-nosed junior officer delivered a message for Bellingham mid-morning and said he was instructed to wait for a reply. I'd been so busy that I'd lost track of Bellingham. I did not think he was at Moore Hall; he was not in the parlor or dining room.

"They said he was here," the lad insisted. "I can't go back without a response. I'll wait in the kitchen."

I took the stairs two at a time, determined to prove the fellow wrong. I opened the door of Bellingham's bedchamber without knocking, so certain was I that the room would be empty.

I was wrong.

Bellingham sat in the chair, a towel tied around his neck and his face well soaped on one side. Isabel stood next to the chair, the lathering brush in her hand.

Bellingham was not pleased. "Since when do you enter my chamber without knocking?"

"Apologies, sir," I said hastily. "A messenger has come from General Varnum. He requires that you write a reply."

"He'll have to wait, then," Bellingham answered. "I am in need of a shave and Gideon won't be back for hours."

"I could have helped you, sir."

"I did not want your help." Bellingham motioned to Isabel. "Finish this side, please."

She dipped the brush in the soapy water, then leaned over to rub it on Bellingham's face.

"Shall I fetch paper and pen so you can write your reply, sir?" I asked.

"General Varnum is getting rather full of himself." Bellingham placed his hand on Isabel's hip. "His messenger can wait until I am finished."

Take your hand off her, you foul whoreson.

"Of course, sir," I said.

Isabel set the lather brush in the bowl, her face hard as stone.

"Since you're here, Curzon, there is mud dried on my good blue coat. Take care of it." He patted Isabel's backside. "Be quick, Isabel. The Greenes will arrive soon."

As Isabel reached for the razor, Bellingham closed his eyes, as was his custom whilst being shaved. He did not see the way she gripped the handle of the blade or the look in her eyes. She was not going to shave his whiskers. She was going to slice open his throat.

Two thoughts collided in my mind like cannonballs: that

I would cheer when the job was done, and that I had to stop her, because our punishment would be swift and merciless. The latter thought carried more force and drove me into action.

"Mister Bellingham, sir, if I may." I quickly crossed the room. "Isabel knows how to pluck chickens and shear sheep, but not how to shave the face of a gentleman. On another occasion it might not matter if your face was nicked or if a patch of whiskers was overlooked, but it will today. Allow me, sir, so that you might look your best."

I put out my hand for the blade.

"I suppose you're right." Bellingham sighed and patted Isabel again. "Give it to him, girl, then ask the cook if she has any of that cobbler left."

Isabel handed me the razor; the horn handle was sweaty and warm. Bellingham studied her backside as she rinsed her hands and dried them on her apron.

I held up the blade so that it flashed in the light from the window. "May I, sir?"

"Of course," he said, closing his eyes again and tilting back his head. "What else is being done to prepare for the Greenes' arrival?"

"I asked the cook to bake up a nutmeg cake," Isabel said. "It is said to be Missus Greene's favorite."

"Excellent notion, Isabel," Bellingham said. "Find out what General Greene prefers on his plate too. Our interests lie with him now, instead of the congressmen. We must do whatever we can to ensure his comfort and keep his wife content."

"I shall learn all that I can, sir," Isabel said.

"Good girl." He pointed at his face. "Make haste, Curzon. The soap is drying and it itches."

CHAPTER XLV

Monday, March 23–Saturday, April 4, 1778

WE ARE TAUGHT FIRST TO MARCH WITHOUT MUSICK BUT THE TIME OF MARCH IS GIVEN US. SLOW TIME IS A MEDIUM BETWEEN WHAT WAS IN OUR SERVICE SLOW AND QUICKE TIME . . . ABOUT AS QUICKE AS A COMMON COUNTRY DANCE."
–CONNECTICUT COLONEL ISAAC SHERMAN,
NOTES ON THE INSTRUCTIONS OF BARON VON STEUBEN

MARCH MELTED INTO APRIL, AND Valley Forge reeked of the foul stench of rotting horseflesh and the thawed privy trenches that had been filled by ten thousand soldiers. The noxious miasma caused birds to fly around the encampment instead of over it.

The filth in the air brought a wave of illness that stretched from camp to Moore Hall and beyond. The soldiers who stood at the front door were recalled back to camp because it was clear the British were not going to invade Moore Hall, and so many Life Guards were ill, the fellows were needed at headquarters. The congressmen had complaints of the belly and bowel. Missus Cook's limp grew so severe, she could walk only with the aid of a stick. Isabel burned her hand on a hot poker and it wept yellow.

My fingerbones ached where the cold had bit into them in February.

Gideon's cough worsened until he collapsed whilst powdering Mister Morris's wig. His master sent a cart from York to fetch him. Isabel had several whispered conversations with him as he lay coughing on his pallet. She was almost tearful when he departed.

I did not pray for his recovery.

Gideon's absence made more work for me, to be sure, but I welcomed it. My day started an hour before sunup and continued long past dark, for General Greene received a constant stream of officers, messengers, reports, and letters. Along with the serving of meals, the ordering of clothes, and the care of the horses, their saddles, and other riding equipment, I took over shaving for Bellingham and the two remaining congressmen, Mister Morris and Mister Reed. General Greene was shaved by his wife each morning, though he occasionally asked me to repair the spots of whiskers that she missed.

Bellingham's eager bootlicking paid off quickly. General Greene appointed him to the post of assistant quartermaster general, with the chance to make profit on goods purchased for the army. Bellingham had hoped that he would be given a commission in the army as well and had already ordered a uniform coat from his tailor and purchased a Maryland colonel's pistol.

When he told me of his favorable change in circumstances, he gave no clue about what it meant for me and Isabel other than to say, "Saddle the general's horse and mine. We're meeting with the brigade commanders on the Outer Line. You will accompany us."

We'd had three days of sun and cold winds, so the road into camp was not too terrible muddy. In truth, I would not have cared if the mud had been up to my waist, for I had not been ten paces away from Moore Hall since the night of General Washington's birthday ball.

The camp was as busy as a city, with soldiers all hurry-scurrying about their business, some wearing coats ill-stitched from blankets, but a few dressed in the recently delivered brown lottery coats. The gentlemen of our company held a brief palaver with General Knox at the artillery camp. From there we continued along the Gulph Road toward the Outer Line in search of a brigade parade ground. General Greene wanted to watch the new drilling techniques of Baron von Steuben, the Prussian gentleman in charge of instruction. I examined the face of every man and boy who passed, hoping he might be a friend, tho' I knew not what I would do or say if he were.

I did not see a familiar soul.

The men of General Poor's brigade were working on their marching techniques when we arrived. I led the horses to a group of officers surveying the confusion of a few hundred fellows in irregular rows on the field. Junior officers walked among them, trying to get the fellows to stand in the proper way and turn their heads to the south.

"It looks more like a dance lesson than field training," General Greene said. "Why aren't they drilling with muskets?"

"The baron feels it is more important to get the men to move as one before they learn the new firing orders," explained a nervous-looking lieutenant.

"How long will it take to train them?" General Greene asked.

"If you speak French or German, you can ask the baron

himself." General Poor pointed at the small group of riders coming down from the ridge.

Baron von Steuben was a stout man who rode an enormous horse and was accompanied by a large dog and a group of gentlemen who translated his every word. The baron loved America, they said, but he did not speak English yet.

The baron bowed in the saddle to General Greene, then dismounted to chat with the junior officers, one hand on his walking stick and the other petting the dog's head. He wore a woolen blue cloak over his blue coat, but he had arranged it so that his medals–one pinned to his coat, the other worn on a ribbon around his neck–could be seen. He wore his own gray hair pulled back into a long queue instead of a wig and a black beaver hat that I was quite sure Bellingham was coveting.

The baron raised his hand and the drums started beating. The soldiers struggled to straighten their ragged lines. The drum cadence changed and the soldiers stepped. Some stepped to the left. Some stepped to the right. One company at the back of the field spun halfway around.

Baron von Steuben shouted and the drumming stopped. A group of young men huddled around him.

"He gives his orders in French mixed with a heavy dose of German. Those chaps turn it into English," explained General Poor.

The orders were shouted and the companies re-formed their lines. The drums beat the cadence.

"Common step!" called out an officer. "Step! Step! Step! Step!"

The baron beat the rhythm with his walking stick. The lines moved as one body as the soldiers moved forward with the exact same strides.

"Step! Step! Step! Step!"

"That's better," murmured General Poor.

"Right wheel!" called the officer.

Disaster. The soldiers again forgot which way to turn and the field turned into a confuddled mess.

The baron snatched his hat from his head, threw it on the ground, and stomped on it with both of his boots, shouting loud enough to be heard in Philadelphia. The translators tried as best they could to keep up with him, repeating his words in full-voiced English, blushing and fighting laughter, for the baron was cursing. Not just the ordinary kind of cursing that can get your ears boxed if a lady is close enough to hear. This was a barrage of curses like I'd never heard before. His face grew redder and redder and his hat grew flatter and flatter until he stopped jumping and shouted, "Gottam, gottam, gottam!" which we could all figure out for ourselves.

He put his hands on his knees and bent over to catch his breath. The entire field was silent. He stood straight, removed his cloak and his coat, handed them to an aide, then rolled his right sleeve up above his elbow and thrust his half-naked arm straight up in the air, his fingers open wide. He shouted some German words. When they came out in English, they sounded like this:

"Soldiers who do not march together make an army of baby birds."

The baron ran along the front line of soldiers, brushing their faces with his fingertips like a bird's wing might. A few of the men laughed, and the baron laughed too, seeming happy that they understood his point.

He ran back to the front and thrust his arm in the air again, folding his thumb and each finger into a meaty fist and shouting again.

"Soldiers who march together make an army of steel!"

He ran at the front line, waving his fist. The fellows closed their eyes as he approached, knowing that one of them would be punched and he'd best take the blow without flinching.

The baron stopped with his fist a whisper away from the first fellow's nose and spoke.

"You, my friends, are almost an army of steel. Your hearts know how to march together. Now you must convince your feet. Agreed?"

He gently patted the face of the man in front of him, and they both broke into laughter that spread across the field as the baron walked back to the drummers. He picked up his hat and knocked it against his leg to shake off the dust.

"Wieder!" he shouted. *"Encore!"*

"Do it again, lads," repeated the translators. "One, two, three, four! Step, step, step, step!"

It took the better part of an hour, but in the final drill four hundred men moved as one, stepping, turning, wheeling, returning to position. My heart beat to the sounds of their boots on the ground. For a moment I forgot Isabel and forgot about running. I wanted to be on the field learning how to be a fist of steel.

The drill ended and the baron clapped his hands and shouted, "Bravo! Bravo!" stopping to pat the backs of every fellow in his reach. As the companies left the field, they did so in good cheer, with laughter and boasting.

"'Tis unexpected," General Poor said, "but they do love him, almost as much as they love His Excellency."

Bellingham said something then, but it slipped past me, for I was staring at the form hurtling toward us from the back of the parade ground. Ebenezer Woodruff was galloping like a three-legged cow and grinning so hard, I thought certain his jaw would break.

CHAPTER XLVI

Saturday, April 4, 1778

THE GENIUS OF THIS NATION IS NOT
TO BE COMPARED . . . WITH THAT OF THE PRUSSIANS,
AUSTRIANS, OR FRENCH. YOU SAY TO YOUR
SOLDIER, "DO THIS," AND HE DOES IT; BUT I AM OBLIGED
TO SAY, "THIS IS THE REASON WHY YOU OUGHT
DO THAT," AND THEN HE DOES IT.
—BARON VON STEUBEN, WRITING ABOUT
AMERICAN SOLDIERS TO PRUSSIAN BARON DE GAUDY

I SHALL GO TO MY GRAVE BLESSING the name of Quartermaster General Nathanael Greene of Rhode Island. Bellingham raised his voice and said he'd report Eben for insolence for running at us like that, and General Greene stepped in the middle of the fray.

"I fail to see any insolence, James," said the general mildly. He inclined his large head toward Eben. "What is your concern here, Private?"

Ebenezer held his hat in front of him, nervously twisting it round as he spoke. "Curzon here, this gentleman's . . . servant, him and me fought together at Saratoga. Didn't mean any harm, sir. Just wanted to visit with him a bit."

General Greene regarded me. "You were a soldier? Where?"

"I fought in the Battle of Brooklyn, sir, and at Fort

Washington, as well as Saratoga. I lived here in camp with my company until Mister Bellingham again . . . required my service."

"No need to bore the general." Bellingham's polite words carried a note of warning. "I'll explain the circumstances later, sir."

"Sounds like he's earned the chance to visit with friends," General Greene said. "We have no need of him for a bit. Give him leave to go."

The officers rode off to General Glover's brigade headquarters, and Eben and me walked in the opposite direction at top speed.

"The other fellows called me a jack-eyed liar when I pointed you out to them. Then they all saw that it was you, and we wanted to wave our hats and holler, but that Baron, he gets riled up at that sort of thing. Did you feel us all staring at you? We couldn't help ourselves; look at you! That is a fine coat you're wearing there, Master Thrower of the Stones. Seems like you're eating well enough. Don't get much firecake, I wager."

His voice was so loud, I wondered if the winter air had broken his hearing. Many of the soldiers we passed stopped their work—repairing a hut roof, cleaning rusty muskets, digging a new privy trench—to watch the gap-toothed plowboy shouting like he was calling his goats in from the field.

I turned west on the shortcut that led to our hut, but Eben shook his head and said in a low voice, "Not that way. I'll explain later." Then he resumed talking loud as a trumpet, telling me about the death of his old breeches and the miraculous appearance of the new ones.

"They showed up on Saint Patrick's Day. Did you hear how the Irish fellows from Virginia celebrated that night? Fun lads, but can't play base to save their lives. We played base against some lads from Chester. All the artillery camp plays wicket. What was I talking about?"

We were moving uphill so fast, I was panting like an overworked horse. "Breeches," I gasped.

"Right. Our lads in Delaware captured a ship filled with cloth and British uniforms. That's where these breeches come from. The sergeant finally got himself a proper officer's coat, though the sleeves are too short. And we dyed it with walnuts on account of no self-respecting Patriot wants to wear a red coat."

I stopped to catch my breath. "Burns isn't a big fellow—how could the sleeves be too short?"

"You don't know!" Eben smacked his forehead. "Of course you don't know, how could you know? Big news around here, but it must have been a mouse fart to the generals and congressmen. John Burns is dead. Smallpox."

"You're joking."

"Serious as the grave, my friend. He took ill right after you left and died at the Yellow Springs hospital. Haven't missed him one bit. We do miss Silvenus, tho'. He died a few days after Burns. He went to sleep one night, same as the rest of us, and didn't wake up the next morning." He kicked at a clot of dirt and it crumbled. "We buried him near Uncle Caleb. Figured the two could keep each other company complaining about the state of the world."

"Anyone else?"

"Dead? Nope, that's it. We had one lad come back from the dead. Remember Peter Brown, who could run so fast in Albany—took sick when we first arrived? He strolled in last week, fat, happy, and married to a girl from Yellow Springs. A more content lad you never saw, except mebbe for Greenlaw. Captain made him sergeant; he's the one who needs the longer sleeves in his coat."

"How fare the others?"

"Faulkner got himself some paper to draw on. Benny Edwards is teaching Aaron Barry his letters. Waste of time, if you ask me. The Barrys have very small brains. Henry spends every minute he can at the creek trying to catch frogs. Swears he's going to cook up a mess of frog's legs fried in grease with spring onions and potatoes." Eben shook his head. "I am still hungry all the time. Soon as I get home, I'm planting my backside at Aunt Patience's table and eating for a month."

"Wish I could join you there," I said.

"You can." Eben glanced around us before dropping the pretense of his act and lowering his voice again. "We have a plan."

CHAPTER XLVII

Saturday, April 4, 1778

HIS EXCELLENCY TODAY APPEALED TO THE OFFICERS OF THIS ARMY TO CONSIDER THEMSELVES AS A BAND OF BROTHERS CEMENTED BY THE JUSTICE OF A COMMON CAUSE.
–GENERAL ORDERS OF GEORGE WASHINGTON, VALLEY FORGE

IT BEING WARM OUTSIDE, THERE WAS no fire in the hearth of our hut. Thin fingers of sunlight poked through the spaces between the logs where the mud chinking had fallen out. It smelled heavily of lads unfamiliar with soap.

"Sit and listen." Eben pushed on my shoulders, forcing me onto one of the bunks, then closed the door.

He quickly explained what had happened after I left back in February. Burns had announced I'd been arrested and returned to my rightful owner. Benny had written up a petition to Captain Russell, asking the army to free me on account of my service. Every man in the company signed it, except Burns, of course. The captain threw it in the fire and said the matter was not to be discussed again.

"That didn't sit well with any of us. We knew you'd try to run one of these days. We talked about it and decided we'd help, if we could. Here." He pulled a haversack out from under the bunk. "This is yours."

I untied the cords. Inside was the compass box, along with my knife, my sorry-looking carving, and all my other belongings in the world. The lump in my throat would not allow me to speak.

"Benny should be here soon," Eben said. "You need to strip off those fancy breeches and lose the coat, I'm sorry to say."

I swallowed the lump. "What do you mean?"

"It was the only thing we could think of in such a short time. Benny is going to dress in your clothes and pull your hat down low. You're about the same size. I talked extra loud on purpose when we walked up here—that was Faulkner's idea—so I'd be noticed. Me and Benny will walk back down the Outer Ridge Road, down to Wayne's regiment. The trees are heavier there. When we're out of sight, he'll change back into his own clothes. You'll need a place to hide. Greenlaw and Aaron are working on that."

I finally figgered his aim. "This is all to get me away from here?"

"Of course, you chucklehead! Greenlaw will walk you over Sullivan's Bridge after dark. He'll say the two of you are going after a deserter. Once far enough away from camp, he'll turn back and you're free to keep going . . . to Aunt Patience's house outside Leominster, if you'd like. What say you?"

His homely face looked just as it had when we stood in the ravine and heard the approaching sounds of the Battle of Saratoga, eager and scared at the same time.

"You would do this for me?" I asked.

"Surely," he answered. "As you would for me."

The lump reappeared in my throat and required several sharp coughs to move it.

"I can't let you," I finally said. "Anyone who helps me will earn at least fifty lashes, mebbe more."

He peeled some bark off the bunk pole. "Mebbe it's not the soundest plan, but we didn't have much time. We could devise a better one, if you wish."

I shook my head. "Even if you made the best of plans, I couldn't go. Bellingham has a maid, a friend of mine. I have not yet convinced her to run away. I can't leave her behind, and if I run, she'll be mistreated."

"A girl?" He punched my shoulder hard enough to knock me over. "Ten thousand fellows in this camp and you're the one who meets a girl."

"It's not like that." I shoved him back.

"Is she pretty? Uncle Caleb always said to stay away from the pretty ones. Smart girls are better, he said."

"She's pretty and smart. Sharp-tongued, too, and stubborn."

"Sounds like a good match. Why won't she run away?"

I stood up and walked to the hearth. "She tried to escape several times before." Anger flashed over me. "She was . . . sorely abused with each capture. She desires freedom as much as me or you, but she won't run unless the plan is guaranteed and secure."

"Shhh!" Eben lifted his hand to quiet me.

Heavy footsteps approached the hut, then the door was thrown open by Henry Barry.

"It won't work," he gasped. "Not today. The gentleman on the horse is already looking for him. Sergeant says to hurry back."

He dashed off, leaving the door open and the light pouring in.

I walked toward the door, but Eben stood and grabbed my arm before I could step outside. "Wait. What should we do? How can we help you get out of there?"

"There's no point trying to liberate us from Moore Hall; the place is crawling with soldiers." I hesitated. There was one avenue of escape, but it carried risk. "Our best chance will be when the troops march out of camp."

"Against the British?"

"Aye. We could try to blend in with you, somehow, and walk with the army out of camp." I stepped over the threshold and saw Bellingham trotting up the road. I had only a few moments left. "But you don't have to do this, Ebenezer. I don't want any of you to come to harm on account of me."

"You're still a soldier, Curzon. You signed up till the end of the war, remember?" Eben looked me square in the eye. "What's the point of being a soldier if you can't count on your mates?"

CHAPTER XLVIII

Sunday, April 5, 1778

IT HAS EVER BEEN MY STUDY AND EVER SHALL BE, TO RENDER YOU AS HAPPY [AS] POSSIBLE. BUT I HAVE BEEN OBLIGED IN MANY INSTANCES TO SACRIFICE THE PRESENT PLEASURES TO OUR FUTURE HOPES. THIS I AM SENSIBLE HAS DONE VIOLENCE TO YOUR FEELINGS.
—GENERAL NATHANAEL GREENE,
LETTER TO HIS WIFE, CATHARINE

AFTER WE RETURNED, THE GENTLEMEN held another long meeting that required hours of my presence to fill their plates, their glasses, keep the candles blazing and the fire fed, for the night turned cool and damp. I had just laid my head down to sleep when Isabel knocked on my door and loudly announced that breakfast was ready. I served the meal and saddled the horses so the gentlemen could attend a church service held outside headquarters.

Missus Greene kept Isabel hopping all day. A militia captain named Peale, whose grubby cuffs were stiff with every color of paint, had come to work on his portrait of the general's pretty wife. To keep her amused while she was required to sit still, Lord Stirling's plain-faced wife and her flirtatious daughter came with the gossip of which junior officers were courting which ladies. Then one of Baron von Steuben's French translators and Mister Duporteil, the long-haired fellow who drew maps for General Washington, joined them.

The company grew so large that Missus Greene sent a note to Bellingham asking if I might be spared to assist Isabel. As General Greene was at that moment sitting directly across the table from him, Bellingham could hardly refuse. And so I crowded into the parlor too. The air filled with French words punctuated by loud giggles, for Lord Stirling's daughter spoke French atrociously.

French gave me a sharp headache.

When the light faded from the south window, Mister Peale packed up his paints and bid the company farewell. Shortly after that, the rest of them rose, for they were all to dine at the Shippens' that night. I had their driver bring the wagon around and assisted with the delivery of the various greatcoats, hats, gloves, muffs, and scarves.

Missus Greene pulled on a pair of gloves in the front hall. "Isabel, please remind the general that he is expected to join us this evening."

Isabel handed her a bright blue shawl. "Yes, ma'am."

"I shall have to teach you French." Missus Greene arranged the shawl around her tiny shoulders as I opened the front door. "You will enjoy Paris much more if you can speak to the other servants, Isabel. *Au revoir!*"

"Paris?" I asked as soon as the door closed.

"Hush!" Isabel pointed at the dining room door that separated us from General Greene's meeting.

I followed her back into the parlor. "What was she talking about?"

"Don't you have work to do?" Isabel asked.

"I'm supposed to be helping you."

"Then air out the room and don't fuss at me." She sat heavily on a cushioned chair and rested her feet on a stool while I fought to open the first of the three windows.

"Is she buying you?" I asked.

"Soon as she convinces General Greene."

The first window opened easily. I moved to the second one, keeping my face from her. "I thought the Greenes lived in Rhode Island. Why was she talking about Paris?"

"Missus Caty hopes her husband will be appointed the French ambassador after the war."

The window stuck a bit, then flew up, rattling the glass in its panes. Cold air flooded in. "You won't find Ruth in France."

"You won't find me there either." Isabel stood and began assembling the glasses and small plates on the tray. "Gideon said it will be easier to escape from Missus Greene than Bellingham."

"Gideon?" I tugged at the third window sash. "Why would you listen to him?"

She quickly crossed the room and tossed dried bits of cake and bread from the serving platter into the flames of the hearth. "He has sworn to help me find Ruth."

"He's a lying conniver, Country."

She put her fists on her hips. "Just because you were too cowardly to help me does not make Gideon a conniver."

I checked the window lock. "I wasn't cowardly. I was sensible." I banged at the window sash with my fist. "He says what you want to hear so that you'll trust him. He has improper ideas about you."

"You have an evil mind, Curse-on." She opened the door, peered into the empty hall, then closed the door and joined me by the window. "Missus Greene has promised to remove this collar. When she leaves camp, it will be just me and her traveling alone. I'll slip away after we leave Peekskill. Gideon will meet me there."

"Did you see how sick he was when he left here? He could be dead by now."

"He wasn't really that sick."

"He wasn't?"

"It was a ruse to return him to his master in York. He needed to attend to things there before we could flee."

She did not sound as if she entirely believed that. I took advantage of her doubt.

"I have a better idea," I said.

She sat on the windowsill as I told her of my conversation with Ebenezer and my thoughts on our safest path out of camp. When I finished, she crossed her arms over her chest and frowned.

"What if they change their minds? What if they notify Bellingham in hopes of a reward? Gideon's plan is better." She yawned and leaned her head against the wall. "That breeze feels good, doesn't it?"

Despite the fresh air, the room suddenly seemed hot as an oven, causing my head to swim and my brain to boil. The most ridiculous notion occurred to me: I wanted to kiss Isabel.

No!

I couldn't kiss Isabel. It would be improper and disrespectful, and besides, Father had a rule about things like that. I could only kiss a girl after I told her the story behind my name. If I didn't want to tell the story, I shouldn't kiss her. (Even from his grave, Father could be an annoying fellow.)

I banged on the third window as hard as I could.

"That's painted shut." Isabel hopped off the windowsill and moved back to the center of the room. She took two books from a small table and placed them back on a shelf. "What will you do if your friends let you down?"

"They won't."

She picked up a cushion from the settee and beat it so violently that dust filled the air. "So you're just counting on them to deliver you? You don't have another plan? And you think I'm the foolish one?"

"What of this, then?" I lowered my voice further. "Let's go tonight, out that window. We'll just run and run. Or steal a horse. Flee."

"You know better than that." She replaced the cushion. "Running without thinking is foolish. You must be prepared, like Gideon is. You could learn a lot from him." She picked up the tray and left the room.

I followed her down the hall. "I have nothing to learn from that cad."

The parrot squawked as the two of us entered the kitchen, causing Missus Cook to awake from her nap by the fire with a start.

"You haven't changed a bit," Isabel said. "You think you know everything and you don't."

Her sharp tone kindled an angry response in me. "And you're still stubborn and vexatious."

"Being stubborn is my finest quality." Isabel set the tray on the table with a bang.

"You're not merely stubborn, Isabel. You're pigheaded."

"Better pigheaded than chickenhearted!" Isabel slammed the back door so hard that every plate and bowl on the shelves jumped.

Missus Cook, King George, and I watched through the window as she stormed to the half-turned garden armed with a hoe and flailed at the dirt in the last light of day.

"Well, then." Missus Cook scratched behind her ear with a spoon. "Doesn't know you're sweet on her yet, does she? Throwing vinegar and names at her won't help your cause, lad. Try honey."

CHAPTER XLIX

Monday, April 6–Wednesday, April 29, 1778

MELANCHOLY . . . WILL FORCE THE BLOOD INTO THE BRAIN, AND PRODUCE ALL THE SYMPTOMS OF MADNESS. IT MAY LIKEWISE PROCEED FROM THE USE OF ALIMENT THAT IS HARD OF DIGESTION, OR WHICH CANNOT BE EASILY ASSIMILATED; FROM A CALLOUS STATE OF THE INTEGUMENTS OF THE BRAIN, OR DRYNESS OF THE BRAIN ITSELF. TO ALL WHICH WE MAY ADD GLOOMY OR MISTAKEN NOTIONS OF RELIGION.
—DR. BUCHAN, *DOMESTIC MEDICINE*, PUBLISHED 1785

I EMBARKED ON A CAMPAIGN OF honey and kindness, which, if you've never tried it, is very hard to do with someone who thinks you are chickenhearted and has in the past called you a poxy sluggard. It is especially hard if every day you are plagued with fear about what might happen next.

I had no chance to further talk with Ebenezer. A white soldier named Timothy Hubbard who hailed from General Greene's hometown became both wagon driver and errand runner for the inhabitants of Moore Hall. Timothy also led the horses when the gentlemen inspected troops or visited headquarters. I was every bit as caged as the kitchen parrot.

The business of the army moved at a faster pace than ever. New recruits arrived daily and needed huts, food, and weapons. A load of muskets smuggled in from France arrived, but there were not enough wagons to transport them safely from the port to camp, which made General Greene almost have an attack of the apoplexy. Late at night, after the junior clerks had been sent back to their huts and the gentlemen lit their pipes and rested their feet upon the table, talk always turned to the upcoming campaign and the different battle plans Washington had to choose from.

When the gentlemen finally retired to their bedchambers, I opened the windows to let out the smoke and sweat of a long day and considered the possibilities for my own spring campaign. I had to come up with a proper plan, one that would suit Isabel. The fastest way to a town big enough to hide in was to cross Sullivan's Bridge in the middle of the camp and head east. But the bridge was guarded, as was the road that led south. The road north from Moore Hall offered no place to hide and led deeper into the countryside, where strangers would be quickly noticed. I knew nothing of the land west beyond Mount Misery so I dared not venture in that direction.

As the month drew on and the days warmed, my humors fell out of balance and I became tetchy and sour-minded. My efforts to appear the perfect servant to Bellingham, and to be patient and kind with Isabel (whose own humors were severely out of balance), all seemed fruitless.

Isabel laughed at a few of my jokes, but she was just as likely to tell me that I wasn't funny at all and that I had a spot on my forehead. Bellingham snarled whenever I entered a room. I polished the boots wrong. I was clumsy. His tea was cold. I moved too fast. I moved too slow. My hair needed to be trimmed. My whiskers needed shaving.

Once he lost his temper when Isabel and I were clearing the table and I dropped a plate that shattered on the floor. He snatched Isabel's wrist and gave it a hard turn, causing her to cry out. The other gentlemen froze, Mister Morris with his wineglass halfway to his lips.

"Do you remember our conversation about these things?" Bellingham asked me.

"Humble apologies, sir." I bowed deeply. "It shall not happen again."

He released Isabel. "It had better not. Repair your manners and do your job. And for God's sake, Curzon, shave your face."

The rapid beard growth and the bumps on my forehead were more evidence of the imbalance of my humors. The bumps multiplied no matter how much vinegar I rubbed on them. I tried to shave myself with a razor Missus Cook found for me, but it is near impossible to shave your own face, even for men who have been doing it a score of years. I must have cut myself forty times and had to resort to slicing up a rag and sticking the bits of cloth all over my face, for the cuts would not stop bleeding. When I stepped in the kitchen to ask Missus Cook if she had a salve to take away the stinging, Isabel laughed so hard that the milk she'd been drinking came out of her nose.

That night I ate my supper alone on the back porch. The wind brought the sound of the drums beating at camp, which made me melancholy and angry all rolled into one.

CHAPTER L

Thursday, April 30, 1778

WHEN LOVE ONCE PLEADS ADMISSION TO OUR HEARTS,
(IN SPITE OF ALL THE VIRTUE WE CAN BOAST,)
THE WOMAN THAT DELIBERATES IS LOST.
– JOSEPH ADDISON, *CATO*, ACT IV, SCENE 1,
PERFORMED AT VALLEY FORGE

BELLINGHAM AND GENERAL GREENE and the congressmen rode off to headquarters that morning, led by Timothy Hubbard. I was left behind to clean the barn. Shoveling horse manure smelled worse than the waiting on gentlemen, to be sure, but it was worth being free of Bellingham's sly gaze and the endless recounting of the numbers of tent poles, shot pouches, and water buckets the army required. I hung my coat from a peg, rolled up my sleeves, and surveyed the barn.

Benny Edwards had told us the story about a fellow named Hercules who moved an entire river to clean out a stable that had one hundred years of muck in it. I did not know how to move a river, so I set to the task with a wheelbarrow and a large shovel. I shoveled horse manure, pushed the barrow to the dung heap, and returned for more over and over again.

My progress was observed by a pair of swallows busy

building a nest from bits of straw and long strands of horsehair. I tried to imitate their whistle but failed. Instead, I sang—quietly, for my voice was known to make dogs howl. By midday I felt more like myself than I had in months. Missus Cook teased me about the smell when I went in for dinner, but she gave me three helpings of dumplings and gravy.

By dusk I was too tired to give any thought to Isabel or our plight. My hands were so sore I could barely move my fingers, and my back so stiff, I walked like an old man as I returned the barrow to the shed. But the job was done; each stall was laid with fresh straw and the center of the barn swept clean.

"Sure hope the horses appreciate this," I said to the nesting swallows. They did not reply.

I hung up the broom and headed for the well. I was halfway there when I noticed Isabel talking to someone standing next to a horse in the shadows just beyond the east wall of Moore Hall, away from open windows and curious cooks.

Gideon was back.

I walked faster, the pains in my arms and back forgotten. He was standing much too close to her.

"What are you doing?" I asked as I approached them.

Isabel stepped away from Gideon, startled. "I was just—"

The import of the scene hit me. Gideon was dressed like a country boy, not a congressman's manservant. The horse's saddle was poorly made, and the harness was old rope, not leather. Canvas saddlebags hung heavily behind the saddle.

He's running.

"Begone," I said.

Gideon shifted nervously from foot to foot. "I've come to speak with Isabel, not you."

Isabel had gathered the edge of her apron in her hand and was worrying it with her thumb. Her eyes darted this way and that, her entire form tense as a cat preparing to pounce.

"Go inside, Country," I said.

"Would you enslave her too?" Gideon asked. "Stay if you wish, Isabel."

"Leave her alone, you lying frog."

"She's made her decision," Gideon said.

"What decision?"

"I'm leaving tonight," Isabel whispered.

The barn swallows swooped past, not paying any mind to the three of us huddled together.

"Tonight?" My voice cracked. "Why tonight?"

"A fortuitous circumstance arose," Gideon said. "My master sent me here from York with letters for the general's staff and a note to Congressman Morris, stating that I had recovered and was to again serve at Moore Hall. I burned it. I've been preparing for months, waiting for the right moment. It's here."

"Come with us," Isabel said to me.

"He can't," Gideon said. "It will ruin everything."

Isabel frowned.

"Don't trust him," I said.

"She can and she should trust me," Gideon said. "I have friends who will keep us safe. I know a blacksmith who will remove that collar."

I was sorely tempted to punch him in the nose, but if I did, Isabel could be gone forever. I needed to attack his flank. "She says you've agreed to find Ruth. Are you going to head for Charleston along the coast or go over the mountains?"

Gideon hesitated. "Neither. We cannot head there right away–"

"Because you have no intention of going there. Ever." I tapped the side of my head with my finger. "Think, Isabel. He's not going to take you to Charleston any more than I would, only he's lying about it and I am telling the truth. Do you really think the folks in Carolina are going to let you walk in, grab Ruth–if she's alive, if she's there–and then allow you to steal her away from them?"

Isabel lifted her chin. "Gideon knows people who will help us."

"Balderdash. He knows how to twist your mind."

"You're a jealous boy," Gideon said.

"Not jealous," I said. "Afraid. You'll be the death of her."

Isabel put her hand on my elbow. The cool touch of her fingers rooted me to the ground, and I was certain that I would never be able to leave that spot of ground on the east side of Moore Hall. Even if my feet moved, my heart would be forever chained to that place, to that moment, because I looked in her eyes and knew that she was leaving with him.

She dropped her hand.

"Enough talk." Gideon put on his hat, a large black felt farmer's hat that made it hard to see his face. "The moon will set around midnight," he said to Isabel. "Leave when it sits just above the treetops."

CHAPTER LI

Thursday, April 30–Friday, May 1, 1778

In Memory of JENNY
Servant to the Rev. Enoch Huntington,
and Wife Of Mark Winthrop,
Who died April 28, 1784.
The day of her death
she was Mr. Huntington's Property.
—Epitaph on a gravestone in a cemetery
in Middletown, Connecticut

ISABEL AVOIDED ME THE REST OF THE evening. She didn't have to. I could not think of any words or deed that would change her mind.

The hours disappeared like a puff of smoke in a hurricane.

Missus Cook thought certain I'd been taken ill from the stench of the dung heap. She made me drink a potion of horseradish root and mustard seeds cooked in gin. I did not taste it. She told me to wash in icy water straight from the well. I did not feel it.

I served the supper for the gentlemen. Cleaned the dining room. Laid the fire to be lit in the morning. Blew out the candles. Checked the window latches. A mug of the horseradish potion was awaiting me, set on the kitchen table by Missus Cook. I poured it on the ground outside.

I moved my pallet in the shed so that I could see out the small window that faced west, then sat down cross-legged and waited. The crescent moon, which had crossed the middle of the sky about the time I spoke with Gideon, fell into the west like a fast-moving comet. Clouds hurried across its path, scattering rain on the roof, then dashing away.

The moon sat half a hand above the treetops, then a finger's width above them, waiting for Isabel. Horses slept in the barn. Highborn and lowborn people slept in the house. The road was empty. The wind that blew earlier in the day had died. Owls called to the night and–

A ratcheting sound; the hook being pulled from the latch of the kitchen door.

Hinges squeaked.

I scrambled to my feet, mouth dry, heart pounding.

The sound of shoes on the kitchen steps. *One, two, three.* They stopped. I put my ear to the crack of the door and thought I could hear her breathing.

I gripped the door handle.

She walked to the bottom of the steps–*four, five . . . six, seven*–then started for the door that I stood behind. She stopped.

I put my eye to the crack. She stood with her back to me, studying the sickle of the moon sinking below the leaves.

The owls called again and Isabel ran into the night.

CHAPTER LII

Friday, May 1, 1778

She was indeed the object of my first love,
a love which can only be extinguished with my
existence; and never at any period previous was the
yoke of bondage more goading, or did I feel
so sensibly the want of that freedom . . . which was
now the only barrier to my much wished for union
with one I so sincerely and tenderly loved.
–Robert Voorhis, born a slave in New Jersey in 1769

I CLOSED MY EYES AND LEANED MY forehead against the door.

On the back of Gideon's horse, she'd make it to Whitemarsh by dawn, Bucks County by midday, if they were headed east.

Bellingham would be angry, but his duties would keep him too busy to mount much of a search. He'd likely advertise in the newspaper, but it would take days to arrange that. Mayhaps he'd beat or sell me. I could rouse neither fear nor anger at the thought.

They'd likely hide in the daylight, try to sleep. They should head to the Watchung Mountains in Jersey, then go north. I could not think further than that.

My ribs crushed in around my heart until it burst.

CHAPTER LIII

Friday, May 1, 1778

May poles were Erected in every Regt in the Camp and at the Reveille I was awoke by three cheers in honor of King Tammany. The day was spent in mirth and Jollity the soldiers parading marching with fife & Drum and Huzzaing as they passed the poles their hats adorned with white blossoms.
—Journal of Private George Ewing,
Second New Jersey Regiment, Valley Forge

A WOODPECKER THUDDING THE planks of the shed woke me. The sky was still dark, but the robins were awake and calling to one another. I sat up, befuddled, then lay back down with a groan.

She's gone.

We had been together at Moore Hall for scarce two months and spent most of that time fighting like a dog and a cat confined in a barrel. How was it, then, that I was so melancholy? I ought be happy she'd found a route to liberty. If I could not be joyful about her release, I should at least be content to be free of her scorn and sour face.

My heart was too sore to beat, my head felt flattened by a hammer, and my limbs so heavy that sitting up required an effort worthy of Hercules.

The woodpecker stirred again. *Tap-tap-tap.*

I slapped the board above my head and came away with a sliver in my palm, which I cursed mightily.

Tap-tap-tap-tap-tap-tap.

The poxy creature had flown to the doorway.

I stood, shouting to scare off the woodpecker: "I'll see you baked in a pie!"

I snatched open the door, hoping to frighten it off.

Isabel stood there, her eyes swollen from crying, holding a candle that she sheltered from the breeze with her hand. "I got the water hot in the kitchen for you."

"What did you say?" I was not certain if I was awake or dreaming.

"Come in the kitchen so I can shave your whiskers. They are a disgrace."

She turned and walked away, pausing at the kitchen door. "If you leave your mouth open like that, a bird is gonna fly in it."

She sat me on a chair in front of the fire. A basin of hot water steamed on the table next to me. She lit three candles to give her light to work by, then sat on the chair in front of me, picked up the lathering cup, and brushed the soap foam onto my face.

I did not move, afraid that if I did, the dream would end.

Isabel set the cup on the table and picked up the razor. She dipped it in the hot water, shook the blade once, then gently pushed my chin with her fingertips so my right cheek faced her. She applied the edge of the razor to the soap on my stray whiskers and pulled it down in short, rasping strokes. "Does that hurt?"

"No," I whispered.

She rinsed the blade in the water. "I imagine you want to know what happened."

She unfolded her story as she shaved my whiskers with great care. The guards on Sullivan's Bridge had been playing cards and did not notice her crossing. Gideon had been waiting just beyond the bridge, south of the road, behind the remains of a broken-down barn. He gave her a bundle of boy's clothes he'd collected for her, and after she said she'd changed her mind, he told her to keep them.

"You were wrong, you know," she said as she paused to sharpen the razor. "He wasn't sneaking off to visit girls. He was delivering messages to the British."

"What?" I almost leapt out of my chair. "Gideon was spying?"

"He said they paid him well."

My mind raced. It explained much: Gideon's absences, his odd behavior, his desire to be of service when the gentlemen were discussing matters of the army and the war. But it raised new questions.

"Do you know how much he told them?" I asked.

"Why do you care?"

"I don't want the British to win."

"Don't see what difference it makes," she said. "Gideon said all kinds of folks take news about the camp to the British. The rebels have plenty of spies in Philadelphia as well. Let them have their war, I say. We have our own battle to fight. Turn your head."

Isabel's fingers were gentle on my face. *Scrape, scrape, scrape,* the blade sang. I tried to put Gideon out of my mind and prayed that the sun would rise late. But by the time she was finished, the night sky had paled and the robins sang in full chorus, with a steady beat of woodpeckers in the distance.

Isabel wiped my face and stood up. "Almost as easy as shearing a sheep," she said.

"Thank you." I felt my cheek—cold and smooth—as she poured the water into the washing-up tub. I had to ask her—right now, or lose the chance. "Why did you come back? Was it because he was a spy?"

"Not at all!" She laughed. "I don't care about the rebellion or the King, you know that." She strode to the larder. "I have to start the tea."

"But why, then?"

She stopped and came back to stand directly in front of me. "If I tell you, you have to swear not to tease me about it."

"I promise."

"The ghosts didn't come with me."

To laugh then would have meant certain death. "What ghosts?"

"I never told you this before. Never told a soul." She took a deep breath. "That night we left New York, when you lay insensible and I rowed, ghosts helped us cross the river. They stayed with us the whole time in New Jersey and then they disappeared."

"You can see ghosts?"

"It's not a seeing, it's a knowing, sensing they're near. When you and me were talking to Gideon yesterday, the ghosts returned. It was a sign that I should go with him, I thought. But they went away again when I left last night. They want me to stay with you. If I'm ever to find Ruth, somehow, you're going to be a part of it."

She picked up the towel on the table. "You must think my brainpan's cracked." She handed the towel to me, pointing to a spot below my ear. "You're bleeding a little."

"There is nothing wrong with your brainpan or your ghosts." The new sun brightened the kitchen, and I saw my way clear to do something I'd been wanting to do for a long time. "I have a ghost, too," I confessed.

Her eyes widened. "Really? Do you know who it is?"

"My father." I tossed the towel on the table. "His ghost is this instant demanding that I tell you a story. May I?"

She nodded, puzzled. We sat down facing each other, so close that her skirt brushed against my knees.

"Once upon a time," I started, "a girl named Marguerite was born a slave in Brazil. When she was ten years old, she was taken on a ship to Boston and bought by a preacher whose wife needed help caring for her many children."

Isabel frowned and pointed again at my ear. "That blood will stain your shirt."

I sighed, picked up the towel, and held it against the cut.

"Who was this Marguerite?" she asked.

"Let me tell the story."

She sat back and crossed her arms over her chest. "It was a harmless question."

"Shhh." I folded the towel. "Marguerite hated Boston because it was cold and she didn't understand English, on account of she grew up speaking Portugee. One day she met a handsome fellow named Cesar and they fell in love and they got married, even though it caused all kinds of trouble. Marguerite gave birth to a son and then she died."

"Why would your father's ghost want you to tell such a sad story?"

"Can you please let me finish it?" I asked.

She shrugged. "I'm not stopping you."

"Thank you." I swallowed hard. "Cesar was so filled with sorrow, he might have destroyed himself except for the baby. He decided to choose a name for his boy that would keep Marguerite alive."

I wiped my sweaty hands on my breeches. If my father had been wrong about this, I didn't know what I was going to do. "Cesar loved it when Marguerite would whisper to him, *'Você é meu coração.'* He took out the most important word, *coração*." I stretched the sound of it. "Core-a-sao. Cesar turned it into a word that sounded more like a name, the name of his son: Curzon."

"Those are your parents!" A smile broke across Isabel's face. "That is a good story. But what does it mean, what your mother said?"

"It means, 'You are my heart.'" I leaned forward, took her hands in mine, and whispered into her ear. "You have always been my heart, Country."

Before I could kiss her, Isabel kissed me.

CHAPTER LIV

Friday, May 1, 1778

This evening we had the agreeable news that the Courts of France and Spain had declared these United States free and Independent.
—Journal of Private George Ewing,
Second New Jersey Regiment, Valley Forge

THE KISS ENDED MUCH TOO SOON because a heavy fist pounded the front door with such violence that my first thought was that the British were attacking. I hurried down the hall and threw open the door just as General Greene and Bellingham appeared at the top of the stairs, both wearing their nightshirts, the general carrying his sword.

Mister John Laurens swept by me. "France!" he shouted. *"Vive la France!"*

"What is this?" asked General Greene.

"A rider just arrived from York with the official news from the Congress. Louis the Sixteenth of France has formally recognized our United States as an independent nation. The French have joined in alliance. They will fight the British alongside us!"

Laurens broke off from his story and danced a jig in the middle of the hall. Congressman Reed joined the commotion and all three men ran down the stairs, cheering and thumping one another on the back.

"This changes everything!" exclaimed Reed.

"The King must have pissed his drawers when he heard," said Bellingham.

General Greene laughed and tried to dance his own clumsy jig.

"There's more," Laurens said. "Our spies have brought the news that the King's replacement for Howe has landed."

"Who is it?" asked General Greene.

"Henry Clinton. There's no telling what orders he brings. His Excellency would like all of you to join him at headquarters as soon as possible. He has summoned a Council of War; a few more congressmen are riding to join us today."

Bellingham seized the moment. "Curzon, ready the horses. Isabel, help the cook prepare something we can eat in the saddle."

War was heading for us at a gallop. This was almost as important as the fact that Isabel came back. And she kissed me.

CHAPTER LV

Friday, May 1–Wednesday, May 6, 1778

THE WELFARE OF AMERICA IS INTIMATELY BOUND UP WITH THE HAPPINESS OF HUMANITY. SHE IS GOING TO BECOME A CHERISHED AND SAFE REFUGE OF VIRTUE, OF GOOD CHARACTER, OF TOLERANCE, OF EQUALITY, AND OF A PEACEFUL LIBERTY.
—MARQUIS DE LAFAYETTE, LETTER TO HIS WIFE, ADRIENNE

THE HOURS AND DAYS FLEW AFTER we learned that France had joined our side in the war. Even more men crowded into Moore Hall to conduct the business of the Quartermaster's Office and the Commissary Department. Before General Washington could lead the army against the British, General Greene had to make sure all the soldiers had shoes. General Biddle took over the parlor for his sleeping quarters and duties as forage master. Two more assistants to General Greene moved in, and the Moore family was displaced so their chamber could be turned into an accessory office.

The daily presence of so many junior commissary officers and ink-stained clerks kept Missus Cook and Isabel busy to distraction. The overwork led to a lowering of standards. One night Mister Bellingham instructed me to complain to Missus Cook about his less-than-clean plate and soggy bread.

When I reported this to the kitchen, the old woman grew very red in the face and told Isabel to fetch her a clean apron. Once the apron was properly pinned, she smoothed her hair and walked into the dining room without knocking.

"The girl and the boy and me are doing the work of ten folk and cannot do the work of eleven. Any gentleman not satisfied with the condition of the crockery or the taste of his grub is welcome to pitch in and help. Are there any complaints about the pudding?"

The gentlemen all spooned up their marrow pudding, tasted it, and pronounced it wonderful.

"That's as it should be," Missus Cook said.

His Excellency General Washington decreed that the camp should celebrate the French alliance in high style, with a banquet for the officers and a demonstration of marching and day of leisure for the soldiers. Isabel thought we should plan to flee during the celebration, but I knew we'd have to serve at the banquet.

"But when, Curzon?" she asked.

When, indeed. When should we run? Would Ebenezer still help? How to get word to him? Which direction should we take? And every time I looked at Isabel: How would we remove that horror from her neck? She had already tried every key she could find and a broken fork to no avail. If I had access to a forge and a short bit of iron rod, I could try to hammer out the proper key shape, but only after days of work and a generous helping of good luck.

The only comfort I took that week was that Bellingham was as fatigued and overworked as we were. The dark circles under his eyes made him look as if he'd been thrashed in a tavern fight. It seemed no matter how many papers he read and letters he wrote and columns of figures he added, there was more work to be done.

It was a delight to behold.

The night before the grand festivity, Bellingham worked late into the night, and I with him. He'd given me leave to polish General Greene's sword and the uniform buttons in the dining room so he would not have to shout and wake the household to get coffee or more cake.

He opened another letter from the pile on the table and leaned closer to the candle to read it. "When was the last time you saw Gideon?"

I did not look up. "The day he left, when he was so sick." I could feel his eyes on me, but I kept to my task. "Did he die?"

"He's run away from York. The congressman is rather stunned that Gideon would betray his trust and is seeking news of his whereabouts. Did you know of this?"

I rubbed the sword's blade clean. To tell of Gideon's spying would put Isabel and me in danger. "No, sir," I said. "Gideon didn't much like me. We never talked."

The grandfather clock struck two of the morning before Bellingham could answer. The lateness of the hour caught him unawares.

"Is that time correct?" he asked.

"Yes, sir."

He rubbed his eyes and then stretched his neck to both sides.

"I was going to wash up before bed. Wanted to look my best form tomorrow–rather, today. Will you tell Isabel to start heating water for me as soon as she wakes?"

"If I may, sir," said I, ever the perfect manservant, "I have bathing water ready now. The kitchen is quiet and private at this hour. If you can bear a few more minutes of wakefulness, you'll be fresh and clean on the morrow."

"That is a brilliant notion, Curzon."

"Thank you, sir."

I'll spare you the details of Bellingham's disrobing. Assisting with a bath has long been serving folk's least favorite duty, after chamber-pot cleaning. Once he'd removed every stitch of clothing and the cord around his neck that held the key to Isabel's collar, and folded himself into the soaking tub in front of the fire, I handed him a block of soap and a cloth for scrubbing, and I laid his clothing neatly on the back of a chair.

"Shall I set up the screen, sir, in case anyone wanders through to use the privy?"

"Thank you, Curzon. I'm so tired, I would not have thought of it until too late."

I murmured a polite noise while I set up the wooden screen. Bellingham rubbed the soap on his hands, rubbed his hands together, then squeezed his eyes shut and scrubbed his face.

A cool breeze came through the open window, causing the candles to sputter. I shut the window before he could tell me to do so. The candles on the kitchen table had burned down to guttering islands of soft wax lakes and did not have much more light to give. "If I may, sir, I need to fetch new candles from the pantry. These stubs won't last long."

Bellingham soaped his neck. "Do what you must."

I stepped to the other side of the privacy screen and picked up one of the candles. A thin stream of wax spilled over the base and puddled on the table. When I was little I used to amuse myself by sticking buttons and forks into soft wax and then showing the impressions they made to my father.

A chill shook me, as if I'd not closed that window. I was standing an arm's length away from key to Isabel's collar.

I glanced cautiously around the screen. Bellingham had lifted a foot out of the water to wash it. I quietly stole the key from the top of his folded clothes and pressed it into the wax, then said a prayer and lifted it carefully and checked to make sure that no wax was stuck to the metal. As Bellingham splashed water on his face to rinse away the soap, I returned the key to where he'd last seen it. By the time he called for a towel, the plate that contained the wax impression had been hidden in the larder and I was putting out new candles so that he did not trip in the darkness.

CHAPTER LVI

Wednesday, May 6, 1778

GREATEST DAY EVER YET EXPERIENCED IN OUR INDEPENDENT WORLD OF LIBERTY.
—COLONEL PHILIP VAN CORTLANDT,
LETTER TO HIS BROTHER PIERRE ABOUT THE FRENCH ALLIANCE CELEBRATION

EACH REGIMENT HELD ITS OWN service of thanksgiving after breakfast the next day. Most officers and their ladies had attended with the New Jersey troops. Whilst they were worshipping, their servants, including Isabel and me, finished the preparations on the pavilion set up along the Grand Parade and unloaded the tables, chairs, benches, and crates that held dishes, glasses, food, and wine.

The officers and ladies arrived just after we had set the benches in the best location for watching the Grand Review of the troops. They took their places, with General and Lady Washington in the center. His Excellency was one of the tallest men I'd ever seen, with a calm face not much marred by the smallpox scars on his nose. Lady Washington was so tiny, the top of her head did not even reach his shoulder. They sat close to each other, and sometimes he gazed at her with tenderness and she at him in the same manner.

"Here they come!" shouted a voice.

All eyes looked to the top of the ridge. At the far end of the Grand Parade a matross touched a flame to the fire hole of a nine-pound cannon. It roared. All of those seated rose to their feet, clapping and calling.

Billy Lee, General Washington's manservant, motioned for us serving folk to move away a bit. I knew the names of only a few of the slaves: Malvina, Lord Stirling's cook, with her bright yellow turban; Shrewsberry, John Laurens's valet, who had been back and forth to York all winter; and Hannah, Isaac, and Jenny, owned by the Washingtons. We nodded politely to one another and turned our attention to the army.

Eleven thousand soldiers in five columns marched down the slope and onto the Grand Parade for the review as the fifes and drums played. A distant voice shouted a command, and the men shifted from column formation to line. Another shout and they wheeled in their platoons until they had formed into two long lines of more than five thousand soldiers each.

They halted.

The Continental army that had starved and froze and survived the winter stood perfectly still–shoulder to shoulder–on the field of honor in front of their commanding officer. A few companies had been outfitted with buff-and-blue uniform coats. Most fellows were in rifle dress–long hunting shirts worn over breeches that buckled at the knee, stockings under boots or shoes. They all wore hats, folded up in three places, and every man (and every boy) was whisker-free, with hair pulled back in a queue. Nearly everyone wore a new or well-repaired cartridge box hung from a leather strap, and they carried muskets that had been freshly oiled. All of the muskets had bayonets secured in place under the muzzles.

I thought to myself, *Huzzah, General Greene. Well done, good sir,* for he had indeed pulled the matter of supplying the army out of the fires of disaster.

Someone shouted a command at the far end of the field. The entire line of thirteen cannons fired at once. All of the ladies and most of the serving folk covered their ears at the sound, but before there was even a moment for them to shriek or laugh, a running fire of shots started. This was the *feu de joie* I'd heard mentioned whilst serving–French words that seemed to mean, "Make a loud ruckus in a coordinated and impressive manner."

The first man standing closest to the cannons lifted his musket and shot, and half a heartbeat after him, the fellow to his left shot, and then the next and the next, one by one, five thousand fellows lifting their muskets and firing and reloading all the way to the last man in the front line. After he shot, the fellow behind him fired, and one by one, in perfect order, the five thousand soldiers in the back executed their task; musket to shoulder, barrel raised, trigger pulled, and the shots roared along the rear line, left to right.

When the last gun was fired, the soldiers shouted in one voice, "Huzzah! Long live the King of France!"

The cannons fired another thirteen-gun salute. The army responded with a second round of running fire. Right to left along the first line, left to right along the second. When the last gun was fired, the soldiers again shouted in one voice, "Long live the Friendly European Powers!"

And to my astonishment, the thirteen cannons roared a third time, and a third wave of running fire unfolded with proud precision. The field was clouded in thick smoke. None of the guns had been loaded with musketball or grapeshot, but every man had used his full complement of gunpowder. As each man shot this third time, he did not reload his weapon, but stood at parade rest.

After the last gun fired, there came the loudest shout of all: "Huzzah for the American States!"

We all clapped until our hands were sore.

The rest of the serving folk walked to the pavilion, but Isabel and I lingered. The soldiers stayed on the field long after they were excused from duty, laughing from the delight of a perfectly performed ceremony. Sergeants passed among them, sharing the extra rum rations that had been ordered. I rose up on my toes and shaded my eyes to better see the fellows.

Isabel tugged on my sleeve. "Are you looking for your friends?"

"They've probably already gone back to the hut."

"You really liked being a soldier, didn't you?"

"I'm still a soldier," I said. "I enlisted until the end of the war."

"But they don't want you."

"You're wrong." I pointed to the officers and congressmen making their way to the pavilion for the feast. "Those are the folks who don't want me."

"What about those fellows?"

A raucous group of lads loped out of the smoke shouting, "Huzzah, Huzzah!" at the top of their lungs. The three fellows in the front–Ebenezer, Benny, and Faulkner–caught sight of us first and stopped in their tracks, ten paces away from Isabel and me.

Greenlaw stepped forward and yelled, "Fourth New

Hampshire, Russell's Special Detachment, men of Luke Greenlaw, stand in line!"

The company of eleven fellows formed two lines with five standing in the front and six in the back. Several of the faces were new recruits I'd never met.

"Formation!" shouted Greenlaw. "One missing soldier!"

"Sir!" shouted the company. The two fellows on the right-hand side of the front line–Ebenezer and one of the new lads–stepped sideways, leaving a gap in the line big enough for another fellow. "Sir," they screamed again.

Greenlaw spun on his heel so that he faced us. He touched the brim of his hat. "This company will always hold a space for you, Private Smith."

I bowed.

"Wheel right!" Greenlaw shouted. The company turned to the right and marched off, keeping open the place that was mine.

For once I did not mind pouring wine, carrying plates of half-eaten food, and standing by while the gentry ate and laughed and made merry. It did not bother me to see Isabel ferrying dishes of strawberries and cream cakes from the wagon to the pavilion, not even when she wiped the sweat off her brow with her apron.

Our army was ready to go to war. When the Continental army marched out of Valley Forge, we would be hidden in the middle of it.

CHAPTER LVII

Thursday, May 7–Wednesday, May 13, 1778

RUN AWAY FROM BIRDSBOROUGH FORGE, IN BERKS COUNTY, PENNSYLVANIA . . . CUFF DIX; HE IS AN ACTIVE, WELL MADE FELLOW, AND A MOST EXCELLENT HAMMERMAN . . . THERE IS A RING OF IRON IN ONE OF HIS EARS . . . HE HAS OFTEN RUN AWAY. AS NEGROES IN GENERAL THINK THAT LORD DUNMORE IS CONTENDING FOR THEIR LIBERTY, IT IS NOT IMPROBABLE THAT SAID NEGROE IS ON HIS MARCH TO JOIN HIS LORDSHIP'S OWN BLACK REGIMENT.
—NEWSPAPER ADVERTISEMENT PLACED IN THE *PENNSYLVANIA GAZETTE* BY MARK BIRD, FORGE OWNER AND DEPUTY QUARTERMASTER OF THE CONTINENTAL ARMY

WE LOST OUR FAVORITE ALLY AT Moore Hall the next day.

Missus Cook had received news that the wife of one of her grandsons was carrying a babe and was not having an easy time of it. General Greene arranged for a pass for the old lady so that she could travel into Philadelphia to help. Her son in the Fifth Pennsylvania had hired a farmer to transport his mother and his parrot into the city.

Isabel and I watched as William Cook helped his mother into the wagon and secured the birdcage at her feet.

"I hope she feels better soon," Isabel said.

"Soon as she's holding the little one, she'll feel fine," Missus Cook said. "She's a strong one. Isn't that right, William?"

"Yes, Mother, Lucille is a sturdy lass," her son said as he threw the cloth over the cage of King George. "Mayhaps she'll name that babe after you, if it's a girl. What the world needs to set it to rights is another Matilda Cook."

"I should say not!" scolded Missus Cook.

Isabel handed up the old woman's shawl. "What should they call her, ma'am?"

"They ought call her 'Mattie.'" She wrapped the shawl around her shoulders. "'Matilda' sounds like an old hen. 'Mattie' is a name with some gumption. I'll make sure Lucille agrees." She grabbed the wagon seat as the farmer climbed up next to her and picked up the reins. "Farewell! Good luck!"

Cooking was not a natural occupation for Isabel. Her pudding hardened into stone. Her stews tasted of the river. She served vegetables raw or charcoaled and did not pick out a slug from the salat greens, which caused Missus Greene to scream when she found it wiggling on her fork. Mister Bellingham came to the kitchen to shout after that, and General Greene wrote letters inquiring about a replacement cook.

I knew even less about cooking than Isabel and could not help her. But I did not much fret. She only had to tolerate this life for a few more weeks. General Washington had held a Council of War and determined to stay in camp awhile longer, possibly until the middle of June, before striking at the British. That gave us all the time we needed to prepare.

I helped Isabel weed the garden so that I could explain my

plan and tell her about the impression of the key that I had made in the wax.

"I need some kind of substance that will fill the form and harden," I said. "I think we can make a mold in a box of hard-pressed sand, but I need something that will take the exact shape of the key to press into the mold. I thought of manure."

She carefully plucked weeds from the base of the pea plants. "What do the men who make things like bells use?"

"I have no idea. I've never seen it done, just heard the blacksmith talking about it in Morristown."

"So how do you know it's going to work?"

"I don't."

She threw the weeds into the pile at the end of the row. "Do you remember that misbegotten custard I made? The one that had no eggs? Hard enough to drive nails, you said. I wager that would pour and harden good. But what are you going to fashion the key from?"

"For that, I need to steal a musketball."

"Aren't you in luck." She grinned. "There are plenty of soldiers hereabouts."

It took a few more days, but eventually, we assembled everything we needed: a pail with wet sand that Isabel had pounded tight; two musketballs removed from a pouch in General Greene's bedchamber; a ladle that would not be missed; and a fire in the kitchen hearth that blazed much higher than it needed to be.

We waited an hour past the time that the last of the upstairs folk had gone to sleep, then Isabel wrapped my hands in thick cloth so I would not be burned. I set the musketballs in the cup of the ladle and hung it from a chain over the hottest part of the fire. We sat silent while the lead softened, then turned runny.

"Ready?" Isabel asked.

I nodded. She moved the sand pail next to the fire. Her pudding-dough key had turned out as fine as we could hope and was planted firmly in the sand. She now lifted the key out. I took the ladle off the chain and—holding my breath—tried to pour a steady stream into the rough mold. It splattered some, but it quickly filled the key shape. Isabel poured more sand on top to cover the mold and then carefully set upon that a brick.

"How long until it is hard enough?" she asked.

"We have weeks, mebbe a month before the army leaves. It will be ready by then." I sat back on my heels and let out my breath. "Can you feel it, Country? We're almost gone."

CHAPTER LVIII

Thursday, May 14–Sunday, May 17, 1778

We don't know what will happen, but we are determined to lay our bones in the American cause.
–Adionghhonras (Deacon Thomas) responding to Washington's request for Oneida warriors

Two days after we poured the key, a group of Oneida warriors arrived at camp, there at the request of General Washington. They brought with them bushels of corn, for they had heard how hungry our soldiers were. An Oneida woman came too, name of Polly Cooper, to show how to make a good soup from the corn in the manner of her people.

His Excellency and General Knox were grateful for the corn, but they were most excited by the weapons. The warriors had brought their bows and arrows in addition to their muskets. In the time it took to load and shoot a musket once, a warrior could shoot four arrows or more. When I heard this discussed in the dining room, I thought to myself that it would be smarter to teach the entire army in the ways of bow and arrows.

General Greene left for the Fishkill fort that same day. Bellingham had tried his best to convince the general he should accompany him, but he was foiled, to my relief. If he'd gone, he would have taken me and left Isabel behind to serve the ladies. Any separation now would be disastrous.

In her husband's absence, Missus Greene arranged for a supper to keep her amused. Lady Washington loaned her Hannah, His Excellency's cook, for the occasion, which freed Isabel to put on her good blue short gown and clean skirt and serve the table with me.

All of the windows in the dining room were open, as the May evening air was warm. Instead of smelling of sour soldiers and wood smoke, the room was filled with odors of roasted beef, pickled beets, baked onions, the rose water worn by Missus Greene, and the freshly powdered wigs of the gentlemen. Missus Greene had requested extra candles to light the table and fresh flowers in a bowl at the center of it.

Despite the setting, Bellingham's mood was foul. Whilst the others laughed and conversated, he mostly drank wine and scowled. His nature was keenly sensitive to slights, and he took being left behind by General Greene as a bad omen. I avoided his gaze.

We served the meal, which was much grander than anything ever prepared by Missus Cook. The ladies tried to steer the talk away from the war, but the gentlemen, most of them wearing officers' uniforms, always brought it back. New recruits were pouring into camp and needed time to learn the fighting drills of Baron von Steuben, which provoked a series of funny stories about the baron's teaching techniques.

A young fellow who was an aide to General Washington waved Isabel to the table to serve him more biscuits. He took two from the plate she held.

"Did your girl bake these?" he asked Bellingham.

"I should say not," answered Bellingham. "Isabel can't cook to save her life."

Missus Greene rapped the back of Bellingham's hand with her folded fan. "Do not disparage the talents of young Isabel. Her understanding of her needle is far superior to any I've met."

Isabel backed up, set the platter of biscuits on the sideboard, and stood with her hands folded in front of her, her face empty.

"Knowing how much you appreciate her skill," said Bellingham, "makes it more the pity that she will not join your household."

Missus Shippen laid down her fork. "You're not buying her, Catharine?"

"Sadly, no." Missus Greene sighed dramatically. "Nathanael says it would be imprudent with the war still on."

"Well, then," Missus Shippen said, "I have a friend in Virginia who could use a seamstress."

Bellingham nodded. "Your concern is touching, madam," he said as I removed his plate of bones and gristle. "But I've already concluded the matter. Colonel Gilpin of Maryland has purchased Isabel as a wedding gift for his new bride."

Missus Greene pouted. "Please tell me she won't be leaving until I do."

Isabel placed a dish of gooseberry tart in front of Bellingham.

"I am afraid she must," Bellingham said. "The colonel has arranged to send a wagon of his belongings home this week. Isabel shall be going with it."

There was a knocking on the front door, but I was too stunned by Bellingham's words to respond. Isabel did a better job at concealing her thoughts than I did. She collected the dirty plates from the other gentlemen. After she stacked them on the tray by the door to the kitchen, with her back to the table, she quickly wiped her eyes on the loose neck cloth. She sniffed once and took a sharp breath before turning around, her features again a mask of indifference.

There was a second knock at the door.

"Attend that," Bellingham ordered.

"Bonsoir!" the Marquis de Lafayette said as I opened the door.

Though only twenty years of age, the marquis was said to be one of the richest men in France. He'd volunteered to help the American cause and had become a favorite of General Washington's, as well as Missus Greene's, for he was handsome, charming, and a wee bit devilish, which made for good gossip, as all the ladies in camp were fond of him.

"Good evening, sir," I said.

"It is indeed!" He handed me his hat and gloves and hurried past me into the dining room, where he was greeted with cheers from the assembled company.

I set his hat on the shelf by the door and laid his gloves flat next to it, then followed him, taking up the wine bottle from the side table as I passed it.

Isabel had disappeared into the kitchen with the tray of dishes to be washed. I poured the marquis a glass of wine, which he lifted up.

"*Mon Dieu*, you must hear my news," he said. "His Excellency has appointed me to lead a battalion and hunt the British."

Bellingham lifted his glass. "Huzzah! May you thrash them soundly!"

The entire company toasted the sentiment, and I was kept busy refilling their glasses.

"Which companies are you leading?" asked the fellow who so loved the biscuits.

"All of Poor's brigade, McLane's men, and the Oneidas; some two thousand fellows in all." He could not help but grin. "I can tell you I am most honored by His Excellency's faith in me."

Missus Greene said something quickly in French that made the marquis blush.

"No, *madame*," he answered. "It is not the same as leading the entire army. That is the privilege of General Washington alone. My forces tomorrow will provide only a prelude of what is to come."

"Tomorrow!" Missus Greene fluttered her fan.

"Oui." He sipped his wine. "That is why I come so late to your lovely dinner and why I must leave so soon."

I took my place by the door, hoping that no one could see that I was shaking.

Tomorrow is our last chance to run. Our only chance.

CHAPTER LIX

Sunday, May 17–Monday, May 18, 1778

Oh! think what anxious moments pass between
The birth of plots, and their last fatal periods,
Oh! 'tis a dreadful interval of time,
Filled up with horror all, and big with death!
—Joseph Addison, *Cato*, Act I, Scene 3,
performed at Valley Forge

The Marquis de Lafayette left early along with the officers' wives, but more fellows arrived to continue the party long after Missus Greene had retired. Hannah's husband, Isaac, came from headquarters with the wagon to take her home. She was a kind soul and had prepared much more food than required for the dinner party when she realized how Isabel had been struggling in the kitchen.

I moved back and forth between kitchen and dining room, helping Isabel with the washing up and tending to the needs of the gentlemen deep in conversation about the best way to unseat the British from Philadelphia. Just when I was on the brink of screaming at them, a contagion of yawning passed from one fellow to the next. The visitors asked me to bring their horses around to the front door.

Once they'd departed and the gentlemen of Moore Hall had gone up the stairs, I finally had a chance to speak with Isabel and plan our escape. But I did not even get the first word out of my mouth before Bellingham walked in.

I jumped to my feet. "Sir? Is something the matter? Do you require me?"

He yawned. "Not me and not you. Missus Greene is restless in her sleep and says she feels ill. I think she just misses her husband. She would like Isabel to sit with her."

"Now?" Isabel asked.

"For the night," Bellingham added. "You may move your pallet to her chamber. Make her up a pot of tea with whatever herbs one uses for calming."

"Yes, sir." Isabel swung the kettle over the fire.

"Thank you, sir," I said, tho' there was nothing to thank him for.

He gave an absent nod but did not leave, preferring to watch Isabel take down a clean teapot from the shelf and walk to the larder for the tea. "Fetch her pallet, will you?"

I did not want to leave her alone in a room with him, but I had little choice. I ran up the two flights of stairs, not worrying about the sound of my heavy footsteps disturbing the sleep of anyone. If he had ill intent in mind, I might prevent it by causing a ruckus. I grabbed her pallet and blankets and thudded back down the stairs. Isabel must have been working as fast as me, for as I came down the attic steps, she and Bellingham were coming down the hall.

I took it upon myself to knock loudly on Missus Greene's door. "Isabel is here, ma'am."

I followed Isabel into the chamber, laid out the pallet as slow as I could, then bowed and departed. Bellingham had gone into his chamber by then, to my relief.

I waited a bit in the dark kitchen, hoping that Isabel would be able to sneak out and we could escape in the night. We could make our way close to camp and hide in the woods near the bridge, then work our way into the crowd that was sure to gather to see off Lafayette's troops.

When she did not creep down the stairs, I realized I had to prepare for the both of us. My first task was to examine the key we'd cast. I took a candle out to my sleeping shed and uncovered the pail from its hiding place behind the woodpile. After removing the brick and the top layer of sand, I held the lead piece in the light. For that was all it was—a thin puddle of lead with sand stuck to it. In no way did it resemble a key.

CHAPTER LX

Monday, May 18, 1778

WE FLEW, WE SEPARATED, BUT A YOUNG MAN, WHOM I HAD BECOME ATTACHED TO, SAID HE WOULD NOT LEAVE ME, LET THE CONSEQUENCE BE WHAT IT WOULD. . . . WE HAD GOT WITHIN ABOUT TWO MILES OF HOME, THINKING OURSELVES OUT OF DANGER, BEGAN TO TALK, WHEN IN AN INSTANT WE FOUND OURSELVES SURROUNDED.
—STORY OF A KIDNAPPED AFRICAN GIRL TOLD TO BOYREREAU BRINCH (JEFFERY BRACE), WHO WAS KIDNAPPED FROM MALI AT AGE SIXTEEN AND ENLISTED BY HIS MASTER TO SERVE AS A PATRIOT SOLDIER FOR FIVE YEARS

I WORKED THROUGH THE NIGHT TO clean the dining room, prepare for breakfast, and steal the food we'd need for our journey. When I couldn't keep my eyes open any longer, I laid my head on the kitchen table and slept for a few hours. Isabel was taken aback to find me there in the morning.

"What—"

I put my finger to my lips and pulled her into the larder with me. Even there, behind a closed door, I whispered.

"We don't have much time," I said.

"What about the key?" she asked.

"It's, uh . . ."

Her face fell. "It didn't work, did it?"

I grasped her arm tighter. "We have no choice. We have to leave."

"But how?"

"You have to write two notes. Make the first one look like it came from headquarters requesting the presence of Bellingham and the other gentlemen. Tell them to arrive before eight o'clock."

"But I've not written anything in ages; he's sure to notice my script."

"I'll spill tea so that it is difficult to read. I'll say that the messenger told me what it contained."

"What's the second note for?"

"To tell them about Gideon. That he gave news of the army and Congress to the British."

"Why do you care?" she asked. "It doesn't matter who wins the war."

"I think it does. Write the note, please. We'll leave it out so they can find it after we're gone. We should wait a bit after they depart; they are forever forgetting things."

She nodded. "Then what?"

"Then we follow the river toward camp and wait for our luck to turn."

Many girls (and lads) would have been overcome by fear at that moment and blubbered or backed out of the plan. Not Isabel. The reverse side of her pigheaded stubbornness was unshakable courage that was worthy of a general.

"If our luck does not turn for the good on its own," she said, "we'll make it turn."

The early part of my scheme unfolded better than I had hoped. Bellingham and the others had already been inclined to join in the farewell to Lafayette's troops, so the note Isabel penned—dripping with tea and suitably smudged—was well received. But Missus Greene declined to join them, for she was still feeling poorly. She asked if Isabel might stay with her and Bellingham agreed. We had gotten rid of one obstacle, and it was replaced with another.

I brought the horses to the front of Moore Hall and handed Mister Bellingham his gloves.

"Would you care to accompany us?" he asked me. "To witness the troops leaving."

No instant falsehood appeared in my mind. I covered my hesitation by petting the horse's nose. "If it's all the same, sir," I finally said, "I've had my fill of watching soldiers."

Bellingham stopped in the middle of putting on his gloves. "I find that hard to believe."

I dropped my gaze to the ground. "In truth, sir, I have been neglectful of mucking out the barn. I wouldn't want General Greene to find it in its current state."

He looked for a moment as if he was going to question me further. If he did, I'd lead him on a tour of the rather odiferous stalls.

"Very well." He gave the glove a tug, gathered the reins in his hands, and mounted the horse. "You must become more diligent about your chores, Curzon. Caring for the horses is every bit as important as caring for the gentlemen who ride them."

"Yes, sir." I bowed as he rode off with his companions.

We went about our regular duties for an agonizing half hour, Isabel washing up and me making a halfhearted effort in the barn. When I could stand it no longer, I hung up the shovel and went into the house. Isabel had just finished preparing a breakfast tray for Missus Greene—a full teapot and a delicate cup and saucer, the leftover biscuits, a wedge of sharp cheese, and a pot of blackberry preserves. It also held a dusty bottle of cordial and a large wineglass.

"I'll try to get her to drink the whole thing," Isabel said. "Then mebbe she'll sleep."

I did not think it likely, but it didn't matter either way. Even if Missus Greene noticed we had fled, there was no horse for her to ride to camp upon, and it was unlikely she'd walk that distance.

When Isabel went in to care for Missus Greene, I entered Bellingham's bedchamber and stole the paper money from his traveling chest and the two gold coins hidden in a folio of old letters. He called the coins his "emergency treasure trove." If any situation was an emergency, this was it. I was tempted to rummage through his belongings and steal more clothes, but the thought of wearing something that had been on his form was sickening. I dropped the note about Gideon's betrayal on the center of the bed, closed the door behind me, and hurried down to my sleeping shed.

It took only a few moments to remove the clothing that had been tailored for me in York. Bellingham would describe my waistcoat, coat, and breeches in the runaway advertisement. We would carry them with us and burn them the first chance we had. The stockings and shirt were less remarkable, so these I placed in an old potato sack, along with my blanket. I dressed myself in the tattered shirt, breeches, and the coat that I'd been wearing the day I walked into Moore Hall for the first time.

Into the kitchen I went. My mind raced down the list of actions I'd thought about all night, ticking them off one after the next like they were drill commands. Clothes changed. Money secured. House in good order (this was necessary because it might help delay the search for us). Gentlemen departed. Food–

My thoughts were cut short as Isabel hurried into the kitchen and closed the door that led to the hall.

"Laudanum!" She grinned.

I could not speak.

"Don't worry," she said. "I didn't force a sleeping potion on her. She had already taken it, quite a big dose, to relieve her headache. She'll sleep the day away! What's wrong? Why are you looking at me like that?"

I pointed, still speechless. Isabel wore breeches. I'd never before seen how breeches allowed one to gaze upon the entire length of leg of the wearer, as well as a good eyeful of that person's rump. When boys or men wore breeches, I'd not taken notice of this. But with the breeches upon Isabel, it was all I could think of.

She looked down on her legs. "My mother would thrash me if she ever saw me like this. Truth be told, it is an odd sensation. But I like this jacket."

"You should be more covered than that."

"I don't want to be. It's nice to walk like this. Odd, but nice."

"I think you should put your skirt back on and–"

"Shhh!" Isabel froze. "Did you hear that?"

I listened, but there was nothing. "The sun is warming up the house, that's all," I said. "If not your skirt, then a long greatcoat."

"No," Isabel said, relaxing from her fright. "Wearing a coat on a day as warm as this will draw more attention to me."

I sighed. "We don't have time to argue. Let's just go."

Another loud creak came from the hall, but it was not the wooden sigh of the house. The door to the hall swung open. Bellingham stood there.

He pointed his pistol at Isabel.

"You're not going anywhere," he said.

CHAPTER LXI

Monday, May 18, 1778

THAT WE ARE THE CREATURES OF THAT GOD, WHO MADE OF ONE BLOOD, AND KINDRED, ALL THE NATIONS OF THE EARTH . . . WE CAN NEVER BE CONVINCED THAT WE WERE MADE TO BE SLAVES. . . . IS IT CONSISTENT WITH THE PRESENT CLAIMS OF THE UNITED STATES TO HOLD SO MANY THOUSANDS . . . IN PERPETUAL SLAVERY? CAN HUMAN NATURE ENDURE THE SHOCKING IDEA?

—PETITION OF PRINCE AND PRIME, SLAVES WHO REQUESTED CONNECTICUT TO OUTLAW SLAVERY IN 1779

IT IS TRUE WHAT THEY SAY: WHEN YOU find yourself in circumstances that are too horrible to behold, like on a battlefield or in a kitchen with a man holding a gun, time changes and you notice the strangest of things. His boots were muddy. He was breathing hard. He must have tied up his horse down the road, then run the rest of the way so we would not be alerted. Bellingham was not at all accustomed to running.

"I knew you'd try this," he said. "I saw how you reacted when you heard she was sold. And this morning?" Sweat trickled down the side of his face. His eyes burned like those of a hungry wolf. "You turned down the chance to go to headquarters and watch the troops. That was very unlike you, Curzon."

His hands shook a bit from the weight of the barrel.

Bellingham was not at all accustomed to guns, either.

"Isabel, you are going to find me some rope and then you are going to sit in a chair with your hands folded in your lap," he ordered.

"No, she's not." I stepped toward him.

"Stay right there," Bellingham warned.

I took another step. "I don't want to." A third step and I was only four paces away from him, close enough to make him nervous. He pointed the pistol at my belly, as I had hoped.

"Run, Isabel," I said. "Ride his horse until it drops."

She fled out the kitchen door without a word.

"How noble," sneered Bellingham. "Stupid, but noble. Do you think I won't be able to track her down? I did before, several times. She's not very good at hiding herself."

His hand shook even more. It had a pinkish hue, like the rest of his skin, hands that had never seen the sun. Had never chopped wood or manned a bellows or loaded a wagon.

I stepped closer.

"That's far enough," he said. "Put your hands above your head."

I did. Slowly. Everything was slow, but loud: the sound of my heartbeat in my ears, Bellingham's ragged breathing, the clock in the parlor ticking away the minutes. Was she far enough away yet? Could I risk it?

"Mister Bellingham, sir," I said, slowly. "If I may."

"Are you coming to your senses? Ready to beg my forgiveness?" He chuckled and smiled broadly, showing all of his teeth.

I stared; there were no black specks on his lips or between his teeth. His tobacco-colored breeches were spotless too, except for a few drops of mud near the knee, likely from when he dismounted in a hurry. The sleeves of his coat were still as clean as when I'd brushed them, and the cuffs of his shirt were bright.

"Actually, no. I wondered what you thought of the taste but realized you didn't have the chance, did you?"

"What taste?" He frowned. "Have you lost your wits, boy?"

I took one more step and tapped on my front tooth. "Your teeth are very clean."

"I said that's far enough!" he roared, not making any sense of my words. "I will shoot you, Curzon, I swear."

The pinkness of his hands and the cleanliness of his breeches and his cuffs and his teeth all bespoke one thing to me: He had not ripped open a gunpowder cartridge. He had not loaded the pistol. But I could have been wrong, which is why I prayed Isabel was on that horse and galloping away. I took one more step and reached for the gun.

He pulled the trigger. The flint hit the empty firing pan.

Click.

Time sped up to normal and then ran ahead of itself. I grabbed at the gun. He pulled it backward and we were both off balance, crashing against the door frame and then spinning across the kitchen floor and onto the table. I released the gun and punched his head, which hurt more than I imagined it would. He cursed and tried to hit me with the gun, but I leaned away just in time, and instead the heavy pistol gouged the table. I shoved him at the same time that he pulled, and we regained our feet, grappling with each other. We staggered and crashed against the shelves, sending crockery and boxes to the floor.

Something hit me square on the head. The room tilted and the air burned and I had the sudden urge to puke. My legs gave out and I fell.

Bellingham stood over me, breathing hard. "That was a mistake, boy."

The gun had disappeared. In his right hand he held a knife.

Somebody gave a shout, and a door slammed against a wall. Bellingham didn't have time to turn around before the broad side of a shovel blade cracked against his head. His eyes rolled up and he fell to the ground with a grunt.

Isabel stood over him, holding the shovel like an axe. "Did I–"

I crouched by the still form. "He's still breathing."

"Want me to hit him again?"

I tugged at Bellingham's neck cloth. "I have a better idea." I fished out the cord that Bellingham wore around his neck, used the knife on the floor to slice it, and stood up, holding the key.

"Hurry," Isabel said.

The key fit perfectly. I twisted it and the lock opened. I took it out, then, gently, opened the iron collar and freed Isabel.

CHAPTER LXII

Monday, May 18, 1778

THIS LAND WHICH WE HAVE WATERED WITH OUR TEARS AND OUR BLOOD IS NOW OUR MOTHER COUNTRY.
—RICHARD ALLEN, BORN A SLAVE, WHO FREED HIMSELF AND DROVE WAGONS DURING THE AMERICAN REVOLUTION

IT WAS TEMPTING TO LEAVE BELLINGHAM on the floor and run, but we needed to make sure we'd have enough time to escape. First we carried him out to the barn, where we trussed him up good, tying his hands and feet with rope. We ran a leather strap through the ring at the back of the iron collar before we locked it around his neck. This strap I fastened to an overhead beam, leaving enough length that Bellingham could sit or lay on the ground, but keeping him tethered inside the barn.

We used his own neck cloth to wrap around his mouth so his shouts would not carry far and took the key with us.

The confusion and crowd started at headquarters: soldiers shouting, soldiers laughing, soldiers ready for war. The fellows had forged themselves into an army that was ready to march and take its country back. A part of my heart was gladdened, but most of me was desperate. Every moment we stayed gave Bellingham another chance to escape.

I asked a few questions of the fellows milling about. There had been some disagreements between the junior officers of Lafayette's force and that was why the troops had not yet left. I explained this to Isabel as we made our way toward Sullivan's Bridge, keeping to the edges of the crowd, hats pulled low on our heads. We wormed our way until we were on the south side of the gathering, putting several thousand bodies between us and anyone who might come riding down from Moore Hall.

All at once the drums started rattling and commands were being shouted. The crowd quickly thinned as the fellows who were staying in camp backed away from those who were leaving.

"What are we going to do?" asked Isabel.

"Greenlaw's company is in here somewhere," I said. "Keep looking."

Another order was shouted. "Forward!" The captains and sergeants echoed it down the ranks, and four thousand boots moved toward the bridge, with Lafayette at the head, followed by the Oneidas, and then the first company of Continentals. The men were not forced to march with the precision of Baron von Steuben's drills; those were reserved for the battlefield. But the companies walked together. We could not just walk alongside them. We needed to belong somewhere to have safe passage.

I scanned the lines of men, not bothering to hide my face any longer.

"Master Stone Thrower!" shouted a familiar voice.

I looked at the mass of moving soldiers, but they all had their backs to us. Suddenly, a long arm shot up from the center of the crowd, the hand waving a hat like a signal flag.

"Follow me," I told Isabel, "and don't say a word."

We fought past hundreds of fellows, with me loudly muttering things like, "Pardon me . . . beg pardon . . . Sarge is gonna kill us . . . shoes fell apart . . . beg pardon," as we bumped and squeezed our way up to the section where Sergeant Greenlaw's company was walking.

"A bad day to be late, Private," Luke Greenlaw scolded. "Privates."

Isabel opened her mouth and I kicked her ankle.

"Shhh," I reminded her. The breeches, coat, and large-brimmed hat would not shield her at all if she were to open her mouth. Isabel's voice would never be mistaken for a boy's. If she was overheard by an officer from a different company, our goose would be cooked.

"All right, lads," said Greenlaw. "You know what to do."

The company rearranged itself, one fellow lagging behind for a moment, another stepping to the side, until they had formed a box around us that shielded us from sight. Faulkner and Edwards leaned forward to give me a wave and went wide-eyed at the sight of Isabel and her remarkable breeches, which made me laugh.

We marched onto the bridge. Looking back, I know it could not have been longer than thirty or forty paces. It felt like forty miles. With every step, I wanted to turn around and see if there were men on horseback searching for us. But to do so would give them a look at my face. I glanced once at Isabel. Her eyes were forward, her jaw set firm. She did not look back.

"Here." I slipped her the key.

She grinned and threw it over the heads of the lads and into the river.

I laughed then, walking out of Valley Forge the way I walked into it—with my friends.

RUNAWAYS

NOTICE TO READERS!!!
One & All, Be Hereby Advised
that the Account of Runaways

ISABEL BELLINGHAM
who likes to go by the name
Isabel Gardener

& Companion
CURZON BELLINGHAM
known to call himself
Curzon Smith

WILL BE CONTINUED
in the Forthcoming Volume

ASHES.

APPENDIX

Was Curzon a real person?

Like *Chains* and *Fever 1793*, *Forge* is a fictional story based, in part, on historical events. The most important characters in the book–Curzon, Isabel, Ebenezer, John Burns, Gideon, Bellingham, and Missus Cook–are fictional, though I borrowed bits and pieces from the lives of real people as I was creating them. Some elements of Curzon's character are based on the lives of Prince Estabrook, Peter Nelson, Peter Salem, Austin Dabney, Jude Hall, John Peterson, and Jehu Grant. The Sixteenth Massachusetts Regiment and the Fourth New Hampshire Regiment are fictional as well.

Read More:

Sidney Kaplan and Emma Nogrady Kaplan, *The Black Presence in the Era of the American Revolution.*
Janet Lee Malcolm, *Peter's War: A New England Slave Boy and the American Revolution.*
William D. Piersen, *Black Yankees: The Development of an Afro-American Subculture in Eighteenth-Century New England.*

Are *any* characters in the book real?

Many real-life historical figures appear on the pages of this story. The blue-coated, sword-waving officer who led the charge in Chapter 5 was Benedict Arnold. At Saratoga, Arnold was an impatient, brave officer who defied the orders of General Horatio Gates. Historians say that Arnold's leadership was critical to the

American victory there. He later betrayed his country to the British and is today known as the most vile traitor in United States history.

Agrippa Hull, mentioned in Chapter 7–a tall, free African American from Stockbridge, Massachusetts–was a soldier in Paterson's brigade for the entire war. After his service at Saratoga, he served as an orderly for General Tadeusz Kościuszko. In Chapter 26, Curzon mentions Salem Poor from Massachusetts, Shadrack Battles from Virginia, and Windsor Fry from Rhode Island, all free men of color who served at Valley Forge.

Baumfree and Bett, seen in Chapter 12, were real people owned first by Colonel Johannes Hardenburgh of Esopus, New York, and later by his son, Charles. Baumfree and Bett had thirteen children; most of them were sold away from their parents at a very young age. Their next-to-youngest, Isabella, was born in 1797, twenty years after the events in *Forge*. Isabella was sold at age nine, along with some sheep. After escaping to freedom, she changed her name to Sojourner Truth and became one of the most important voices of the abolition movement in the nineteenth century.

Details about the washerwoman from Virginia (Sarah Van Kirk) who was drummed out of camp in Chapter 15 and John Reily, who was hanged in Chapter 24, came from letters written from the encampment and the daily General Orders issued by George Washington.

The congressmen of the Committee at Camp–Gouverneur Morris, Joseph Reed, Francis Dana, and Nathaniel Folsom–took over much of Moore Hall for the winter while they studied the conditions of camp and consulted Washington and his staff about ways to save the army.

Nathanael Greene was one of the most important generals of the American Revolution. After rescuing the army from disaster at Valley Forge, he went on to lead the American troops in the South, ultimately defeating the British there. In gratitude for his actions, several southern states gave Greene land and money. After the war Nathanael and Catharine settled in Georgia with their five children and used slave labor to work their plantation.

After Nathanael's death in 1786, Catharine befriended a tutor from Connecticut named Eli Whitney. Some historians believe that Catharine Greene had a hand in the development of Whitney's famous cotton gin, the machine that led to the explosive expansion of slavery in the South.

Charles Willson Peale was the most popular portrait painter of the American Revolution. He was also a captain in the Pennsylvania militia. He painted forty miniatures during the Valley Forge encampment, including portraits of General Greene and his wife, as seen in Chapter 48. (If you read *Fever 1793*, you might remember that Nathanial Benson in that story was an apprentice of Charles Peale. The parrot, King George, is found in that book too.)

Other real-life people who appear on the pages of *Forge* include the Oneida warriors and Polly Cooper, Hannah and Isaac Till, Billy Lee, Malvina, Shrewsberry, George and Martha Washington, John Laurens, the Marquis de Lafayette, Missus Shippen, Lord Stirling's wife and daughter, and Mister Duporteil, the Frenchman.

Oh, and Baron von Steuben and his dog, Azor. Can't forget those two!

Read More:

Thomas Fleming, *Washington's Secret War: The Hidden History of Valley Forge.*

Sidney Kaplan and Emma Nogrady Kaplan, *The Black Presence in the Era of the American Revolution.*

Janet A. Stegeman and John F. Stegeman, *Caty: A Biography of Catharine Littlefield Greene.*

Sojourner Truth, *Narrative of Sojourner Truth: A Northern Slave Emancipated from Bodily Servitude by the State of New York in 1828.*

How could Isabel have been kidnapped in Philadelphia and sold like that?

In Pennsylvania and many other states during the Revolution, any black person suspected of being a runaway could be arrested and imprisoned for months or sold, even if there was no proof of the accusation.

> ***Read More:***
> Billy G. Smith and Richard Wojtowicz,
> "The Precarious Freedom of Blacks in the Mid-Atlantic Region." *PA Magazine of History and Biography*, Vol. CXIII, No. 2 (April 1989).

Which events in Forge are real?

Weaving the fictional stories of Curzon and Isabel through real historical events was one of the most exciting challenges of writing this book. Here are the story elements that are based on reality:

- The Second Battle of Saratoga
- The surrender of the British army after that battle
- Burning of Kingston, New York
- Troop movement from Albany south to New Jersey and Pennsylvania to join the main body of the army for the winter encampment
- The conditions of Valley Forge:
  - The starving times
  - The lack of shelter, clothes, shoes, blankets, and tools
  - Eating firecake, squirrel, and opossum
  - The occasional flares of mutiny
  - The scavenging and desertion
  - The way that the huts were built

- The pumpkin cooking
- The fierce determination of most of the soldiers to endure the winter to keep the army together
- The training conducted by Baron von Steuben
- The defensive fortifications
- The medical treatment of sick and injured soldiers
- The bodies of dead horses lying about
- The spying done by both Patriots and the British
- The presence and responsibilities of the Committee at Camp
- The use of Moore Hall by both the committee and General Greene
- The arrival of the Oneidas and their generous gift of corn
- The celebration of the French alliance, including the three rounds of running fire (the *feu de joie*) performed by ten thousand soldiers
- The troops led by the Marquis de Lafayette to Barren Hill

Read More:

Wayne Bodle, *The Valley Forge Winter: Civilians and Soldiers at War*.
Richard M. Ketchum, *Saratoga: Turning Point of America's Revolutionary War*.
George F. Scheer, ed., *Private Yankee Doodle*.

Did African Americans really fight for the Patriots?

Absolutely, they did! Historians have used muster rolls, pension applications, letters, regimental histories, census data, church records, eulogies, and tombstones to come up with the estimate that at least five thousand African Americans—some free, some enslaved—fought for the Continental army. Another thousand served on privateer ships and in the navy.

The rules about the military service of African Americans

changed many times over the course of the war. Black soldiers fought in northern militias from the beginning of the American Revolution. About 5 percent of the men who fought the Battle of Bunker Hill (also called Breed's Hill) were African American.

At first George Washington and Congress did not want African Americans in the Continental army. Washington soon realized this was a mistake and allowed free blacks to enlist in January 1777. Even before he made it official, though, recruiting officers had enlisted hundreds of men of color. Eventually, some states allowed enslaved African Americans to serve too. Some slaves were enlisted to serve in place of their owners. Others were enlisted with the promise of freedom when their service was over. I found several instances in which a master promised freedom to a slave who served in the war, then refused to honor that promise.

By the end of 1777, African Americans, both free and enslaved, were serving in integrated regiments. In his book *The Forgotten Fifth*, historian Gary Nash says that throughout the war, black soldiers from the northern states "responded to the call to arms more readily than white men" (p. 8). A census of most of the Continental army compiled by Adjutant General Alexander Scammell the summer after the Valley Forge encampment showed 755 black soldiers serving at a time when the entire army totaled only 7,600 soldiers.

The American Revolution was the last war in which black and white Americans served in integrated units until the Korean War in 1950.

Read More:

Christopher Leslie Brown and Philip D. Morgan, eds., *Arming Slaves: From Classical Times to the Modern Age.*
Douglas R. Egerton, *Death or Liberty: African Americans and Revolutionary America.*

Lt. Col. Michael Lee Lanning, *Defenders of Liberty: African Americans in the Revolutionary War.*
Gary B. Nash, *The Forgotten Fifth: African Americans in the Age of Revolution.*
Benjamin Quarles, *The Negro in the American Revolution.*

Did African Americans really fight for the British?

Absolutely! Just like Americans of European descent and Native Americans, African Americans had different opinions about which army—Patriot or British—they wanted to support. But there was one important difference. The Patriot declaration that "all men are created equal" did not extend to people of color when it was written in 1776.

At the time of the American Revolution, slavery was legal in all thirteen colonies and all of the British colonies in the Caribbean. Slavery was also accepted and practiced in French and British Canada. American slaves did not have a place of freedom they could escape to. Slaves had to choose between the side that liked to talk about freedom and the side that actually offered it to them. The British said that any slave who fled a Patriot master to join them would be instantly freed. This offer of real freedom motivated 80,000-100,000 enslaved people, about one third of them women, to run to the British. Most of them worked as laborers, but some served as soldiers. Many were abandoned to recapture or death after the British fled America.

Read More:
Christopher Leslie Brown and Philip D. Morgan, eds., *Arming Slaves: From Classical Times to the Modern Age.*
Douglas R. Egerton, *Death or Liberty: African Americans and Revolutionary America.*

Why did they have such a hard time feeding the soldiers at Valley Forge?

A combination of bad decisions and poor planning made the Valley Forge encampment unnecessarily harsh. Part of this was because the United States was a young country (not even two years old) and was still learning how to govern itself. In addition, people were realizing that getting rid of the British was going to be harder than they thought. Politicians argued constantly about how to win the war and how to pay for it.

To make matters worse, the men in charge of preparing for the army's winter encampment were overwhelmed by the huge challenges. The supply chain that was supposed to bring food, clothing, and other necessities to Valley Forge was broken.

And then? There was a salt shortage. That made it almost impossible to preserve meat so it could be shipped to camp without spoiling. That meant that cattle and pigs had to be herded to Valley Forge, often over long distances in the middle of winter, when there was little hope of finding food for the animals along the way, and the roads were often impassable because of bad weather.

As if all of that wasn't enough, the British army was camped eighteen miles away in Philadelphia, and they could pay higher prices for everything.

Read More:

Wayne Bodle and Jacqueline Thibaut, *The Vortex of Small Fortunes: The Continental Army at Valley Forge, 1777–1778.*

Jacqueline Thibaut, *The Fatal Crisis: Logistics and the Continental Army at Valley Forge, 1777–1778.*

Are you sure that there were women and children at Valley Forge?

Historians say that between three hundred and four hundred women lived and worked alongside the soldiers at Valley Forge, taking care of cooking, washing, and mending for soldiers. This is in addition to the officers' wives at the camp. We do not have solid numbers for how many of them had their children with them, but children are mentioned in several letters from the camp.

Read More:
Nancy K. Loane, *Following the Drum: Women and the Valley Forge Encampment.*
Holly A. Mayer, *Belonging to the Army: Camp Followers and Community During the American Revolution.*

How many soldiers died at Valley Forge?

Historians estimate two thousand or more soldiers died during the Valley Forge encampment, most of them from disease.

Read More:
Wayne Bodle, *The Valley Forge Winter: Civilians and Soldiers at War.*
National Park Service website: www.nps.gov/vafo/historyculture/index.htm.

Was Valley Forge the coldest winter of the American Revolution?

Not at all. The Continental army was encamped at Morristown, New Jersey, during the worst winter of the eighteenth century: 1779–1780. They endured twenty-eight snowstorms and much colder temperatures than they had faced at Valley Forge. But by

1780 the army was much better prepared; only one hundred men or so died at Morristown.

Read More:
Ray Raphael, *Founding Myths: Stories That Hide Our Patriotic Past*.

So why do we talk about Valley Forge so much?

Valley Forge was a turning point for the Continental army and for the United States. The boys and men who gutted out the months of cold and hunger turned into a professional fighting force there. The officers and politicians had their commitment to the cause of freedom tested. Those who weren't up to the challenge stepped aside—or were pushed aside—so that stronger and more dedicated men could take their place.

Anyone can talk about freedom. The soldiers at Valley Forge and their families acted upon it. Their example has inspired generations of Americans ever since.

How did you learn all this stuff?

I read a lot. You can find a list of sources I used on my website, www.writerlady.com, as well as the sources of all the primary source quotes that open each chapter.

VOCABULARY WORDS

addlepated: foolish or silly
bamboozled: tricked
banditti: robbers
bayonet: a blade that attaches to the end of a musket barrel so the gun can be used as a spear or sword
befuddlement: confusion
bonebox: mouth
breeches: Colonial-era pants that ended just below the knee, where they were fastened with a string, buttons, or buckles
cartridge box: a leather box that contains paper gunpowder cartridges, usually worn on the belt or slung over the shoulder
caterwauling: complaining
chemise: shirt
churlish: mean and nasty
clodpate: dummy
confuddled: confused
dandy: a wealthy guy who doesn't need to work
firing pan: part of a musket that holds gunpowder
foppish: in the style of a spoiled, rich person
grapeshot: small pellets of iron shot instead of one large musketball
hullabaloo: a loud commotion
idler: a lazy person
lackbrain: a fool
Madeira: a kind of wine popular during the Revolution
melancholy: sadness
miasma: an unhealthy vapor, often smelly
militiamen: soldiers who fought for their state's militia instead

of the Continental army; they usually fought only for a few months or less

molatto: a person whose parents come from different ethnic groups, spelled "mulatto" sometimes

musket: a long-barreled gun, similar to a rifle

nob: a wealthy person

noggin: head

noxious: obnoxious

palaver: chat

pate: skull, head

peevish: cranky

picaroons: scoundrels

plaguey: a mild curse, like "darn"

portent: an omen or sign

powder horn: a carved-out cow horn used to store gunpowder

poxy: a mild curse, like "darn"

queue: a short ponytail worn by many boys and men during the Revolution

reveille: the sounding of military drums in the morning to wake up the troops

ruffian: a crook

ruse: a trick

score: unit of measurement that means twenty

sluggard: a lazy person

swoon, fell into a: passed out

tatterdemalion: a person dressed in ragged clothes

toothstick: a primitive toothbrush

trencher: a plate

variolation: a method of smallpox inoculation

vexing, vexatious: irritating

victuals: food

whelp: an insulting term for a boy

ACKNOWLEDGMENTS

While an author writes a story in solitude, it is not transformed into a book without the help of a veritable army of support. I shall try my best to salute all of those whom helped make *Forge* into the novel you are holding in your hands.

Four history professionals combed the manuscript in search of errors and I am grateful for their time and expertise. Thanks go to Dr. Holly Mayer, Chair of the History Department of Duquesne University and author of *Belonging to the Army: Camp Followers and Community during the American Revolution* (University of South Carolina Press, 1999); Dr. Douglas Egerton, an expert on slavery and race in Early America, history professor at Le Moyne College, and the author of *Death or Liberty: African Americans and Revolutionary America* (Oxford University Press, 2009); and Dr. Wayne Bodle, who teaches at Indiana University of Pennsylvania, is a specialist on early America, particularly colonial Pennsylvania and the middle colonies, and is author of *The Valley Forge Winter: Civilians and Soldiers in War* (Penn State University Press, 2002). Special thanks go to historian, author, and educator Christopher Paul Moore, the curator and research historian for the New York Public Library's Schomburg Center for Research in Black Culture, who reviewed both *Forge* and *Chains* for me.

My splendiferous editor, Caitlyn Dlouhy, offered cheery "Huzzahs!" and soothing murmurs of support as I struggled against the cold winds of the writing process. I am most grateful for her keen eye and attention to both detail and nuance. Further, I am blessed to call her my friend. Gratitude also goes to Caitlyn's assistant and able sergeant, Kylie Frank, and to Christopher Silas Neal, for another great cover. Book designer Lizzy Bromley deserves her own *feu de joie* for creating a book with both Colonial texture and Patriotic verve. Her artistic vision enhances my words and for that I am in her debt. Cartographic gratitude to Drew Willis for the excellent map. Thanks to the rest of the Simon & Schuster family, particularly Jon Anderson, Justin Chanda, Anne Zafian, Michelle Fadlalla, Catharine Sotzing, Laura Antonacci, Alison Velea, and, last but not least, Paul Crichton, for rounding up the troops and leading the charge. And to Deborah Sloan of Deborah Sloan and Company for arranging such fabulous book tours!

Thanks to the librarians at the Mexico Public Library, the Oswego Public Library, the North Country Library System of New York State, Penfield Library at SUNY Oswego, and Bird Library at Syracuse University. Thanks also to the rangers at the Saratoga National Historic Park and Valley Forge National Park; Dona McDermott, archivist at Valley Forge; and Norm Bollen of the Ft. Plain Museum. Thanks to all of the reenactors of the American Revolution who shared their expertise and experience with me, particularly the units and camp followers who attend the annual Redcoats & Rebels reenactment at Old Sturbridge Village in Sturbridge, Massachusetts, and the members of the Revlist community on yahoo.com who cheerfully dug through their own collection of primary sources to help me in my search for the history of this story.

Deep appreciation goes to Tobias Huisman, for again helping with Dutch translations, and Maria Bomfim for her gracious help in sorting out the proper eighteenth-century Brazilian Portuguese.

Several key chapters in this book were written in a creative fervor sparked by the Kindling Words writing retreat in Vermont, and the first pages were written in the special writing chair at the River's End Bookstore in Oswego, New York. Big hugs and thanks to the owners, Mindy Ostrow and Bill Reilly. My friends Deborah Heiligman and Tanya Lee Stone both offered much-appreciated feedback, as did Maria Nikki Grammer, Steven Cheryba, and my daughters Stephanie and Meredith. Our other kids, Jessica and Christian, supplied much-needed encouragement and shooed me back to my writing cottage whenever I lingered by the coffeepot. Will Hoiseth, citizen of the world, offered valuable comments on an early draft of this book. My parents, Frank and Joyce Halse, remained ever ready to remind me to get more sleep and not fuss so much about the primary sources—advice that I respectfully ignored. Profound and humble gratitude goes to my assistant, Queen Louise (known in the real world as Lori Stolp Costo), for taking care of so much of the business side of being an author, I actually have time to write. All hail Queen Louise!

The most important acknowledgment—again and always—goes to my husband, Scot Larrabee. He walked the battlefields of Saratoga and hills of Valley Forge with me, helped me find gold in the archives, and listened to a chapter each night by the fire. He also built me the writing cottage in which I wrote this book, complete with a magic window and a woodstove. Yes, I am the luckiest author in the world.

FORGE

by Laurie Halse Anderson

READING GROUP GUIDE

"We have it in our power to begin the world over again. . . .
The birthday of a new world is at hand."
–from *Common Sense* by Thomas Paine

1. Explain what Curzon means when he says that "the freedom could kill us." (p. 5) How does freedom separate Isabel and Curzon? Curzon makes references to Isabel throughout the novel. When does he miss her the most?

2. Valley Forge wasn't a battlefield. Instead it was a winter encampment for Washington's army. What types of personal battles did the soldiers endure at Valley Forge? Why is Valley Forge considered the turning point in the American Revolution? Discuss the symbolism of Valley Forge.

3. Eben is a mere boy when he enlists in the Continental Army. How is his inexperience obvious when he kills the British soldier? Curzon saves Eben's life by throwing a rock at the British soldier. Discuss why Curzon allows Eben to think that he is a soldier. Why does Curzon feel guilty about lying to Eben?

4. Do you think Curzon is justified in stealing from Turnbull? What about from Bellingham, at the end of the novel?

5. Explain why Curzon is especially sensitive to Turnbull's insults in front of Eben and his uncle Caleb.

6. Curzon enlists in the Sixteenth Massachusetts Regiment, Second Brigade of the Fourth Division of the Northern Continental Army. Why does joining the army seem to be the best decision and protection for Curzon at the time?

7. When British General Burgoyne surrenders to the Continental Army at Saratoga, Curzon is surprised that no one in the Continental Army shames the British soldiers with insults. Why does Eben's uncle say that the British troops should be honored? How does this reasoning confuse Curzon about the point of war? Discuss how Curzon comes to realize that silence is powerful.

8. Curzon is the victim of prejudice. He deals with it by remembering something that his father once told him: ". . . a lot of white people have twisted hearts. It prevents them from seeing the world properly and turns them into tools of the Devil." (p. 54) Who has the most twisted heart

in Curzon's company? How does he spread "poison" about Curzon? At what point does Curzon begin doubting Eben's loyalty?

9. At the beginning of the novel, Curzon saves Eben's life. How does Eben help Curzon at the end of the novel?

10. Bellingham comes to Valley Forge and recognizes Curzon. What does Curzon mean when he says, "Tho' I stood in rags and upon frozen feet, I felt much more a man than he?" (p. 149)

11. Curzon is brutalized by Bellingham. He deals with it by remembering a mythology story that Benny Edwards told about a guy who stole fire from the gods. He was chained to a rock and an eagle was sent in to peck away at his liver. Curzon says, "Now I knew. I would fight the eagle and the chains and that mountain as long as I had breath." (p. 199) Who is the eagle? What are the chains? What is the mountain that he must fight?

12. Describe Curzon and Isabel's reunion. How do they have to learn to trust one another again? How does Gideon interfere with this trust? Explain the role of ghosts in Isabel and Curzon's final reunion. How does the search for Ruth become a symbol of hope at the end of the novel?

Turn the page to see the conclusion to

ISABEL, CURZON,

and

RUTH's

remarkable story.

Monday, June 25, 1781

IN SHORT, MONARCHY AND SUCCESSION HAVE LAID . . . THE WORLD IN BLOOD AND ASHES. 'TIS A FORM OF GOVERNMENT WHICH THE WORD OF GOD BEARS TESTIMONY AGAINST, AND BLOOD WILL ATTEND IT.
–THOMAS PAINE, *COMMON SENSE*

"VEXATION, BOTHER, AND BLAST," I muttered, trying to blink away the sweat that stung my eyes.

Curzon dug his elbow sharply into my side, scowling, then tapped his finger on his lips. He wanted me to be silent as the grave, even though the British patrol we were hiding from was much too far away to hear us.

"A little closer," I whispered low, "maybe I could read it then."

"Any closer and you'll be gutted by bayonets." He turned his head so his lips touched my ear. "Patience."

That foul word again. "Pox on your patience."

I shifted my gaze to the lobsterbacks gathered at the edge of the woods. If they weren't a patrol, then they were a foraging party sent to plunder farms. Whatever their purpose, they looked about to expire of the heat. The cool shade of the enormous live oak had so delighted them that they'd quickly stripped off their sweat-soaked coats and waistcoats and hung them from branches to dry. Two had even removed their shirts and rinsed them in the stream, showing a shock of white skin paler than any ghost would ever dream of being. 'Twas a frightful sight, but their desire to cool themselves had allowed Curzon and me to crawl safely to a hollow that was sheltered by tall ferns and overhanging magnolia and bayberry branches.

We'd had several encounters with patrolling soldiers in the previous weeks. Our course of action had always been to retreat slow and careful, and then circle wide to avoid them. This time we could not. A milestone stood at the crossroads a few paces from their fire. Hidden under their collection of bloodred coats and dingy haversacks was the carving of letters and numbers that showed travelers the direction and distance to Charleston, South Carolina.

After walking more than a thousand miles, after months spent laboring first in Lancaster, then Baltimore, then Richmond, and at whatever mountain farm would have us . . . After having been cheated, lied to, near captured twice . . . After months lost in worry, waiting to see if Curzon would recover from the wounds inflicted by a falling hemlock, then another half a year wasted as I fought an intermittent fever that gripped my lungs so tight I could barely walk . . . After dodging two armies, wild packs of banditti, and armed Loyalists deep in liquor . . . After sleepless nights haunted by ghosts and endless days of empty bellies . . . After all that, I was close to finding my baby sister, Ruth.

The thought of it made my heart pound.

All I needed was the information on that milestone.

We stayed hidden under the ferns in the hollow so long that the sun swung from the east to the west, and the damp ground soaked through both my skirt and the chemise under it. The smell of the rabbits roasting over the British cook fire pained me. We'd eaten our last meal—a small, hideous fish boiled with bitter greens plucked from the edges of the swamp—more than a day and night previous. We were out of salt and hadn't tasted bread nor porridge for weeks.

A mosquito bit my neck. I pinched it dead between my fingertips. In our years of journeying I'd grown accustomed to being bone tired, starving, and filthy, but I could not abide the bloodsucking demons.

"I'm going to move a wee bit closer," I said.

Thunder rumbled in the distance. "Too dangerous," Curzon said.

I killed another mosquito. "Not knowing where we are is the real danger. What if they decide to camp here for the night?"

A broad-shouldered, pink-faced soldier placed his damp coat at the end of a long stick, which he held above the fire in an attempt to dry it. Not a moment later the stick broke, the coat fell onto the rabbits roasting on the spit, and the whole lot tumbled into the flames. The soldiers roared with laughter, save the one who owned the coat. He snatched it out and stomped on the smoldering cloth, cursing vile and loud, while his companions rescued their supper.

"They're barely keeping watch." I pointed to a fallen tree trunk halfway between our position and the road. 'Twas alarmingly close, true, but several young pines sheltered it from view, the tips of their branches touching the ground like a drapery. "If I hide behind that log, I'll hear every word they say."

"The sun has fried your wits." Curzon used his sleeve to wipe away the sweat trickling down my cheek, the scarred one. The unexpected kindness of his gesture startled me.

As we lay silent, my tired mind drifted into the past, to the day I'd first met Curzon back in '76. I'd been a terrified maid of twelve, still in shock from the circumstances that had landed Ruth and me in New York. He'd been a cheerful lad, two years older than me and foolish enough to be eager for war.

Thunder rumbled again and a cool breeze stirred the moss that hung from the branches above.

I snuck a look at Curzon. He now stood a head taller than me and had the forged-steel strength of a man. He was still capable of mischief on occasion, but his smile was rare. He'd long ago traded the red hat he affected for a dark blue cap that did not draw attention. Likewise, the piratical earring he used to wear was now hidden in the lining of his filthy jacket.

There was no way of figgering what he saw when he looked at me, for he'd grown skilled at hiding the truth from his eyes. Time and hard travel had much changed us both.

Our friendship lay in ashes, another victim of the unending War of Independence. Months earlier we'd argued terribly, as fierce as two armies, when he declared that he needed to enlist again with the Patriots. We'd called each other ugly names and exchanged cruel words that cut deep. By the end of the battle he'd agreed to stay with me only until we found Ruth, but the damage was done.

The thunder rumbled again, dragging me from my remembering.

"I'll backtrack," Curzon whispered, "circle around and come down the road from the north, act as if I'm fleeing a rebel master. I'll ask for their protection."

I snorted. "So they can drag you to Charleston and put you to work with a shovel?"

"I'll invent a tale of some Continentals I saw up the road. That will shift them away from here."

"Blast your eyes!" I muttered. "You just want to play soldier."

"Play? I'll gather information and . . ." Curzon broke off speaking. His gaze shifted left, tracking a group of swallows as they flew betwixt the trees. Something shuffled in the distance behind us.

"Did you hear that?"

"A squirrel," I said. "Nothing more."

He rolled onto his back and lifted his head so he could better study the heavily wooded forest behind us. Our recent time lost in the swampy wilderness had revealed Curzon to be mortally afraid of alligators. In truth, I suspected half of his excuses for dawdling in the last few days were due to his unnatural fixation on the beasts.

'Twas not charitable to prey on his fears, but I knew my plan was the wiser one.

I gave a start, as if I'd heard something else. "Over there!"

"What?" He tensed. "Where?"

"I heard something."

"You said 'twas a squirrel."

"Nay, this was a different sound, low and slithersome. As if a heavy tail was dragging through the brush."

"A tail-slither sound?"

"A long and heavy tail." I feigned deep concern. "Reminded me of that big fellow, the one we saw with the fawn in his jaws."

He swallowed hard and squinted, trying to see the alligator that did not exist.

"Or it could be nothing," I added. "The wind, mayhaps. I can go back and scout for it, if you'd like."

"'Tis likely nothing." He swallowed hard. "But I'll go."

"You swear you won't circle round to meet the soldiers on the road?" I asked.

He nodded curtly. "I swear. But don't move from this spot."

I waited until he'd slipped out of sight, then rose up on my elbows to study the soldier standing guard, musket resting on his crossed arms. When he turned away to say something to his companions, I crawled forward one pace, keeping low to the ground. I'd become rather clever at moving without attracting notice. Months of dirt had erased the colors of my clothes, so I blended into the landscape. My few belongings fit in a small haversack, and my hatchet was secured to the leather belt I'd fashioned from reins taken off the skeleton of a horse. I was as skilled at moving without being seen or heard as an army scout.

After another check of the guard I crept forward two more paces. Just then he stepped onto the road. I pressed myself against the dirt as he gave a quick glance north and south, then returned to the comfort of the shade.

I studied the ground ahead, eyes keen to spot poison ivy, which I never wanted to touch again. I crept ahead a third time, only to be stopped by another noise in the woods behind me, this time off to the left. I slowly turned my face that direction. Shadows danced as the strange moss that hung from the trees swayed like tattered laundry in the breeze.

A branch snapped.

I flinched. Curzon was too wily to make any such noise this close to danger. The Carolina woods were filled with treacherous creatures: bear, wolf, and panther. Was one stalking me for its next meal?

I forced the thought aside and trained all of my senses on the enemy ahead. The minutes ripened slow and fat, caught in the sweltering heat. When the guard put down his musket and knelt to fiddle with his boot, I crawled four full paces, moving silent and steady, until I ducked under the low branches of the pines and reached the advantage of the log. I breathed slow as bits of the soldiers' conversation drifted over me: "bloody rebels," "consarned heat," and "affliction of my great toe on both feet." Grumbling complaints were the common language of all armies.

The sound of a sharp *cr-rack*, like a branch trod upon by a heavy boot, echoed through the woods. The guard stood up, alert now, staring in my direction. He said something over his shoulder that I could not hear, and one of his companions got to his feet and joined him, musket at the ready. The two men raised their guns, aimed at the log, just above my head.

That's when the rattlesnake appeared.